BREAKING MEREDITH

DISCIPLES 4

IZZY SWEET
SEAN MORIARTY

Copyright © 2018 by Izzy Sweet and Sean Moriarty

All rights reserved. This book or any portion thereof may not be reproduced or used in any manner whatsoever without the express written permission of the publisher except for the use of brief quotations in a book review.

Published by Izzy Sweet and Sean Moriarty

This is a work of fiction. Names, characters, businesses, places, events, and incidents are either the products of the author's imagination or used in a fictitious manner. Any resemblance to actual persons, living or dead, or actual events is purely coincidental.

Copyright © 2018 Izzy Sweet & Sean Moriarty

 Created with Vellum

ABOUT THIS BOOK

For five years - one thousand, nine hundred and twenty-two nights to be exact - I've watched her from afar...

Protecting her. Keeping her safe from the world.

And stalking her every move.

What started as a favor for her brother has grown into something so much more.

A full-blown obsession.

I can't sleep, I can't eat, unless I get my Meredith fix.

Claiming her could start a war, and might very well result in my death.

But she's mine, she's always been mine.

She just doesn't know it yet.

PROLOGUE

Meredith

One week before Christmas

The cool Mediterranean breeze pulls at my hair, causing my curls to slap at my shoulders and lick at my face. I grip the railing of Ahmed's luxury yacht as I stare at the dark waters of the sea with a growing sense of unease.

Something has gone wrong in the game I'm playing, and everything is about to come back and bite me in the ass.

Behind me, Ahmed speaks quietly in Arabic to our steward. He thinks I don't understand, but I've made it a point to learn some of the language.

He's dismissing the steward with instructions for the crew not to bother us, regardless of what they may see or hear.

Ice floods my veins, but I can't let my fear rule me. If I have any hope of making it out of this little spur-of-the-moment 'pleasure cruise' unscathed, I need to keep my wits about me.

"Meredith," Ahmed says, his voice firm. The tone is something he usually reserves for those he considers beneath him, and I've been hearing a lot of it today.

I don't know what has brought about this change, and it's extremely concerning.

"Come, have a drink with me."

I can't disobey.

Slipping my mask back into place, I relax my lips and fix a serene look on my face as I turn to face him.

Walking towards him across the deck, the breeze whips at the skirt of my flowy dress as I force myself to imagine that I love him, that he's handsome. That he's everything I want in a man and not everything I actually despise… so that warm affection fills my eyes.

Ahmed extends a flute of sparkling champagne towards me while his dark eyes roam critically over me.

Shit. I don't think he's buying it.

Fingers wrapping around the flute, I bring it up to my lips and sip from it. The sweet liquid fizzles and pops across my tongue before sliding down my throat.

I drink just enough to settle my nerves and appease him. The last thing I need right now is to have alcohol muddling up my thought processes.

Ahmed's eyes never leave me as he lifts his own flute and drinks deeply from it. In his own words, he's a 'bad Muslim'. When he leaves the Kingdom of Saudi Arabia, he likes to indulge in all the vices the world has to offer.

Alcohol. Pork. Gambling.

Beautiful women.

He has admitted that his vices have caused him to fall out of favor with his family, but it hasn't stopped him. A prince of significant power and financial means, he's not about to let a little thing like familial favor hold him back. No, he enjoys having the world at his feet too much.

It's what drew me to him in the first place.

For the past several weeks, I've been stringing him along. Slowly weaving my web around him while he's been playing the game completely unaware.

But something changed today. Something has happened without my knowledge and tipped him off.

And I can't figure out what.

My performance has been flawless. Everything has been progressing as it should. There's still several weeks left to go before I move in for 'the kill', so to say.

Ahmed sets his empty glass down on the table and

grabs me by the arm. He's draws me closer and plucks my glass from my hand.

Setting my glass down, his eyes never leave my face. They search me, probe at me, as if he's trying to see the things I don't want him to see.

Things such as my true revulsion for him. For his kind. And his nationality has nothing to do with it. He's just another man with too much money, too much power, and he's long overdue for someone like me to knock him down a few notches.

If anything, the fact that he's a prince only makes his fall sweeter.

Men like him, like my stepbrother, think just because they're rich and powerful, they can get away with anything.

Get away with lies. Infidelities. Murder.

It took me a few years to find my place in this world, but now that I have I relish in it. Growing up pampered to an excess, I have no true skills. I found higher education tedious. The hours spent studying was pointless. A waste of my life. There are so many figures in my bank account, what is the point of work? To prove I have some value beyond my looks?

I don't hunger for power. No, it's quite the opposite. I'd prefer to be without it. Power brings too many headaches and responsibilities. And it's a constant struggle to keep a grip on it. There's always someone waiting around the corner, someone like me, ready to knock you down.

So what is left?

Socializing? Boring. Treat life as one long luxury vacation? Been there, done that. It's not as fun as it sounds. Help the poor and downtrodden? With what skills? I could donate all my money, but then where would that leave me?

The only thing I seem to excel at in this life is attracting bad men then breaking them.

It's a game I've perfected over the years. The only thing that gives me a thrill nowadays, and my way of contributing to the betterment of this world.

It's simple, really, and almost too easy. The real danger doesn't come until the end, when the man's world comes crashing down, but I've grown quite adept at covering my tracks.

I reel my marks in with this stunning face God blessed me with. Then I string them along while learning all their dirty little secrets. Once I grow bored, or discover something particularly juicy, I use those secrets against them. When they fall from grace, I have the perfect excuse for leaving them and moving on to the next mark.

Ahmed draws me closer and closer, as if it will allow him to peer deeper into my soul.

My skin crawls under the grip of his soft hand and

my nose wants to wrinkle at the thick scent of his perfumed musk.

Reaching up, he tucks one of my wayward curls behind my ear. The action should be tender, but it feels more like a threat.

"Is there anything you would like to tell me, Meredith?" he asks as the tips of his fingers trail down my cheek.

Shit. Shit. Shit.

It's just as I suspected, but what does he know?

I squint my eyes a little bit, just enough to cause wrinkles to appear on my brow so that I appear confused. "Tell you? No… I don't think so."

He stares at me for a long moment then gives a nod of his head as if that's the answer he expected. His fingers suddenly dig painfully into my arm as he tightens his grip.

With a hard tug he begins to drag me towards the side of the yacht.

"Ow! Ahmed, you're hurting me!" I cry out, hoping to earn some sympathy so he'll lighten up.

It only causes his grip to dig in even deeper.

Dammit. Whatever he knows is bad.

Once we reach the rail, he uses my arm to jerk me around so that I'm facing him. My shoulder screams in agony as he then pushes my back up against the railing.

"I'm going to give you one more chance, Meredith,"

he says calmly. "Is there something you want to tell me?"

My mind races, trying to figure out what he can possibly know. I've been careful, so careful. The only way he could possibly know anything at all is if one of my former marks somehow found him.

But even then, even if they were aware of what happened, would they want to admit they had been suckered by woman?

No, it's not likely. That's why I only choose the ones with huge egos...

I search his face, looking for a hint, for anything that will give me a clue of what he knows, my confusion now genuine.

But all I see is his eyes growing darker and darker with anger.

"Have I done something wrong, darling? If I have, I'm truly sorry. I can assure you it wasn't intentional..."

Despite the pain of his grip, despite the rail that's digging into my back, I reach out and stroke his arm.

If I act afraid now it will only prove my guilt.

"I'll make it up to you, I promise," I say, flooding my gaze with heat and lowering my lashes.

His eyes begin to soften and his grip loosens a fraction.

I haven't slept with him yet, despite his rather aggressive advances. Not only because I find the thought of it repugnant, but because once you spread your legs for a man like him they're done with you and ready to move on to the next conquest.

I continue to stroke his arm, letting my eyes do all the talking for me. I think of the all the dirty little things I could do for him if he was someone I actually found attractive.

Just as I feel like I'm pulling him back into my web, his expression suddenly hardens. His hand releases my arm and he reaches up and wraps it around my neck.

Squeezing his fingers together, he leans over me and begins to push me back.

Panicked, I stop stroking his arm. My fingers scramble up and desperately claw at the fingers squeezing around my throat.

"Stop playing games with me, Meredith. I'm on to you."

He keeps pushing and pushing, looming over me until I'm nearly bent in half. I can feel the mist of the choppy waves splashing up. The drops of water that hit my nape and dampen my curls are uncomfortably cold.

I glance to the side and all I see is endless black sea.

This was always a possibility, being killed by a mark, and it's what makes the game so thrilling in the first place.

But I'm not ready to go just yet.

"Tell me who those men at the dock are," he demands and my attention snaps back to him.

"What men?!" I cry out.

I honestly have no clue what he's talking about.

His face twists into an ugly expression of rage and his fingers squeeze harder, cutting my air off. "No more lies! The two men who were following you."

I cough and cough, unable to breathe, and my heels scrape against the deck as I struggle not to fall over the rail.

Realizing I can't answer him, his grip lets up just enough for me to draw in some much needed air. I gulp at it, swallowing up as much of it as I can.

When I don't immediately answer him, he shakes me hard. "Who are they?!"

"I don't know!" I scream honestly and clutch at his forearm with both hands as I feel my heels slipping on the decking.

I have no clue why two men would be following me. It's a little concerning, but not as concerning as falling to my watery death.

Ahmed's nostrils flare as he huffs and puffs and his face is flushed an angry red.

"I swear, Ahmed, I swear on everything, I had no idea people were following me," I plead.

I don't want to die, especially when for once in my life I'm telling the truth.

Grip tightening around my neck again, he pulls me closer, until we're almost nose to nose. His hot breath hits my face and it takes every ounce of my self-control to keep from recoiling in revulsion.

"If you are lying to me, Meredith..." he threatens.

"I'm not!" I insist. "I swear."

Ahmed closes his eyes and I pray that I've been convincing enough.

His eyes slowly open and he yanks me upright. I stumble, getting my feet under me, and almost fall into him. Before I can push away from him, his hand releases my neck and his other arm wraps around me, pulling me into his chest.

"I believe you, habibti," he says, suddenly tender again. Reaching up, he brushes my hair back, out of my face. I feel so much relief tears fill my eyes. That was too damn close for comfort. "But I fear you are in danger."

I nod my head as I lean into him as if I need his strength right now. What I really want to do is slap him across his face for doing what he did to me. Instead, I give into my tears so that he believes I'm weak and stupid.

Ahmed frowns at the tears that roll down my cheeks. "Don't cry. I will protect you."

Oh, that's just rich. After almost killing me himself now he wants to 'protect me'.

I nod my head and look down so he doesn't catch the anger in my eyes.

"We will marry. I will take you as my third wife, and

we will return to my home. You will be safe in my compound."

Wait… what? He wants to take me to Saudi Arabia and marry me? And I'll be his third wife?

I shudder at the thought of being trapped in a country where I'll be essentially owned by him and forced to completely cover myself from head to ankle in public.

I can't live like that, I can't. But I also can't risk angering him again…

"You would do that for me?" I sniffle and lift my gaze, turning the full force of my glistening eyes on him.

"For you, habibti, I will do anything," he says with so much emotion I almost believe him.

But I know he's not offering this out of love, despite his little pet name. He's doing this because he wants to possess me like I'm a trophy. He doesn't know me, the real me. He hasn't even tried to get to know the fake me. I'm just a beautiful toy in his eyes, something to claim so no one else can play with it.

I do the only thing I can do at this moment. I lean into him and give him a kiss that shows how much I appreciate his declaration.

He seems surprised at first, but quickly throws himself into it. His lips greedily push into my lips and then his tongue is trying to thrust its way past them. I open for him even though I feel sick to my stomach kissing a man that almost killed me.

His tongue sloppily swipes at my tongue and I want to throw up, but somehow I muscle my way through it. I manage to work him around, turning him just a bit here and there until his back is facing the railing.

Finally, when I can bear no more, I push away from him and break the kiss.

Panting heavily, he immediately reaches for me and tries to pull me back.

"No... no... darling," I say, shaking my head at him. "I want to show you how much I love you..."

I slowly begin to sink to my knees so he draws his own conclusions.

He stares at me for a moment, and I'm not sure if it's because he's offended or if he can't believe his good fortune.

Then he asks, "Really, habibti? You would do this for me?"

I smile at him and nod.

Oh, I'm going to do it for you, buddy.

Muttering something in Arabic, he reaches down and begins to fumble with the buckle of his belt.

I start the countdown in my head.

One.

Yanking hard on his belt, he manages to undo the buckle and quickly unbuttons his slacks.

Two.

Eagerly, he pulls down his zipper and takes himself in his hand.

Three.

Surging forward, I push out with everything I have. I scream as my hands connect with his stomach, praying that it's enough.

His arms flail out and he takes one stumbling step back, then another.

For a split second, I fear it wasn't enough and I have no fucking clue what I'll do now, but then his back hits the rail and he goes tumbling over.

He hits the water with a loud splash and I rush up to the rail. Gripping it, I lean over and watch the water.

A couple of seconds pass before his head bobs up, breaking the surface.

"Meredith!" he yells, flailing about.

Yeah, I never understood why the stupid fuck owns a yacht if he doesn't know how to swim.

His head sinks below the surface and I glance nervously towards the cabins. If any of the crew appears I'll just act hysteric. After all, it was a total accident.

His servants must be very afraid of him though because none come running to his rescue.

Good for me, bad for him.

I look back to the water and try to watch for bubbles, but it's hard to see given the dark and all the waves the yacht is kicking up.

His dark head suddenly surfaces again, farther away, but he doesn't cry out. No, he's completely silent before he disappears again.

I watch and watch. Seconds turning into minutes. When he doesn't make a reappearance, I finally relax.

He's gone... and it was almost too easy. Shouldn't murder be harder? I don't know. I'll have to ask Matthew...

But no, it wasn't quite murder was it? It was self-defense. Yes, self-defense. It was kill or be killed. Because if he would have taken me to Saudi Arabia and made me his third wife, there's no way I would have survived. Once he learned who I really am, they probably would have stoned me to death.

I had no choice, really. He forced my hand.

Bolstered by my reasoning, I push away from the rail and straighten my dress.

Now all that remains is to sneak out once we dock before the crew figures out what happened.

1
SIMON

Three months after Christmas

"Hold him still, Andrew. I can barely work with him squirming around like this," I say as I wrestle with the man's hand.

The gag shoved in this fat sweaty asshole's mouth is crammed in tight, but it does little to silence the pleading squeal of his beet-red face. He's most likely desperately trying to tell us all his dirty little secrets, but it's too late for that now.

"Simon, I thought we agreed that there would be no removal of body parts..." Lucifer says quietly behind me as I hear him walk into the room.

"I'm not removing anything that belongs to him. The only thing I need is his prints," I say as I finally slam the man's hand down into the square plate. Its clear gelatin oozes around the hand a moment before I yank it back out.

Pushing the plate to the side, I motion to Andrew. "Let's get his left hand and then he can disappear."

"Thank god, this man's sweat smells like boiled fucking cabbage," Andrew says before wrestling with the second hand.

"So, you don't count his identity as belonging to him?" Lucifer asks with a chuckle, perching himself on an old metal shop desk. "It hardly seems fair... But then again he did steal from us."

"No one but our inner circle may keep their identities intact, Matthew. Anyone who run afoul of us... they lose the choice of having anything of their own," I growl out. "Embezzlers like this piece of trash go to the lowest level of hell for betraying us."

"Isn't the ninth level set for treachery? Then again, I suppose stabbing one's boss in the back, as well as stealing, could be looked upon as treachery. Though, if I remember correctly, fraud is on the eighth tier," Lucifer says with a smile.

"You damn ecclesiastical types," Andrew mutters before pushing the left hand in front of me.

Grabbing the hand, I press it firmly into the clear mold before pulling it back out. "You see, Andrew... We didn't even need to use violence to solve this little issue."

"That's fine with me." Andrew stands up as he pulls

the man sharply back down in the chair. "Stay the fuck there, Eugene."

Motioning for Lucifer, I point to Eugene Bancroft, our latest debtor. One who decided to steal from the very hand that feeds him. "All the money and information has been turned over to us. I also spoke with Marco, he's been updated and paid back his missing portion of what we've been able to find."

"Able to find?" Lucifer turns serious. "How much are we missing?"

"One point two million..." I say as I look back to Eugene. "Two hundred thousand of that went to gambling in Vegas and a long weekend of coked out crack whores."

"Jesus Christ. How the fuck do you blow through two hundred thousand dollars on crack whores in Vegas?" Andrew bursts out laughing.

Eugene begins to scream through his gag at the three of us, but it's silenced as soon as James walks into the room.

As usual the damnable playboy is fashionably late as he calls it. If Lucifer didn't have such a soft spot for the lazy man, I would have strung him up long ago.

James slaps the butt of his gun against the side of Eugene's head before walking over to the desk to sit beside Lucifer. "What did I miss?"

Grunting his displeasure, Lucifer says, "Simon was just telling us how Eugene here spent two hundred thousand dollars on a coke-fueled long weekend in Vegas with, as he put it, crack whores."

"Three hundred and twenty thousand," James says dead faced to us all.

I know I'm blinking in confusion as I ask, "Three hundred and twenty thousand what?"

"Oh, fuck me..." Andrew groans.

"Are you serious, James?" Lucifer asks in genuine amazement.

"What are you all talking about?" I ask harshly. I hate when they pull this kind of shit.

There is no possible way that James has found the money I haven't been able to track down yet. I know it's been working its way through a very complex system of funnels. So far I've tracked down fifty-two different banks it has be routed through. That this pile of human excrement has caused me three sleepless nights of searching through countless statements and business transactions....

He's crafty, I will give him that.

But it's now only a matter of time until the tracer bots running through my computer systems locate the final destination. I don't worry about that. It's James spitting out such a random number that is annoying me. He doesn't deal with this side of the business.

"Three hundred and twenty thousand dollars... I thought we were comparing weekends of regret," James says with a shrug.

Eugene groans loudly from his chair and a red trail of blood leaks down the side of his neck from where James hit him.

"How in the bloody hell did you spend three hundred and twenty thousand dollars on a long weekend?" I ask, and for once I find myself speechless at the playboy's idiocy.

"She called it the girlfriend experience," he says with another shrug, as if that's supposed to explain everything.

"Oh, for shit's sake, James," Andrew rumbles with laughter.

"James..." Lucifer says with almost fatherly patience. "What in the world were you thinking? And when was this?"

Looking up at the ceiling, James thinks to himself. "About four weeks before those girls we pulled away from the Russian's slave ring got grabbed up."

"Are you serious? I was expecting this to happen a couple of years ago, when you were still young and stupid," Lucifer laughs as he slaps James on the back of the head.

"Hey, I'm still young, and probably, stupid. At the end of the weekend, I proposed to her," James says with a weak grin.

No one says a word for a solid minute. All of us are staring at him in absolute shock.

"What did she say?" Andrew asks, finally breaking the silence.

"She didn't. She took the rock and disappeared in the middle of the night."

Running his hand down his face, Lucifer begins to chuckle. "And this, Simon, is why we love our dear James so much."

"Thank the gods he isn't dumb enough to ever procreate," Andrew laughs as he looks to me. "He's going to die in an old fuck's home with you, Simon. Alone and miserable!"

Rolling my eyes, I turn away from the neanderthals before I'm tempted to shoot one of them. Self-control is the key to my job. If I didn't have it, I would be in deep shit. Not that I'm not already in over my head.

"So, what are we doing with fuckstick?" James asks.

Setting the molds of Eugene's hands carefully into the black bag I brought and pulling off my latex gloves, I look over my shoulder at him. "Lucifer wants a message to be sent to any and all."

"Yes, we're going to be going back to an oldie but goodie, boys," Lucifer says with a grin.

"Ride with me, Simon. Andrew can drive your SUV to the site," Lucifer says as we walk out of the old sheet metal warehouse.

Grunting loudly as he walks towards James's black BMW, Andrew says, "Yeah, but I'll put this pile of shit in James's trunk. No need for him to be kicking around in the back of an SUV."

"Asshole," James grouses at Andrew.

"Shouldn't have been late, little buddy," Andrew laughs out loudly.

"I was... Ah, fuck it," James starts before cutting himself off. He slaps Eugene on the head with his pistol again before he says, "You better be fucking quiet, asshole. I got music I want to hear."

We walk to Lucifer's own SUV and climb into the backseats. The heat is blowing heavily onto us. Peter up front is rubbing his black leather gloved hands together as watches us shut the doors.

Peter leans further around the seat to look at us both. "Cold enough out there for you guys?"

"A bit too much... It doesn't feel quite like home, what with all the freezing temperatures." Lucifer grins at us both before leaning back into his seat.

Of course the boss, Lucifer, likes it hot as hell in Garden City. It's when all the crazy spills its blood over the brim of the cup. Now that we've become the largest enterprise in Garden City, Lucifer has been looking forward to another heat wave.

I think at times that he would like to watch the whole place burn, just for the amusement factor of it all.

I, on the other hand, prefer the cold and dead of winter. It's the only time the hot, sticky humidity is gone from this hellish city. Neither I, nor my computers, enjoy all that warmth and humidity in the air. Like my machines, a cold environment is good for us. It's easier to keep things sterile and predictable. Introduce moisture into any computer or electronic and it leads to instant failure.

I don't like failures, not of my machines and not from people. Why the hell we can't live in a city where it is cold and dry all the time causes me frustration. My computers and sense of sanity would benefit so much more from it.

"So where to? Still want to go to the docks?" Peter asks.

"Yes, we need to make a drop-off. Did you remember to bring the stuff I asked you about?" Lucifer answers.

"Yeah, I have it in the back."

"Good."

Peter turns back around and nods his head. "Your... sister... has been calling boss."

"Thank you, Peter. Did Meredith say what she wanted?"

"She demanded that you speak with her," Peter says as he pulls the vehicle out of the empty parking lot.

And right there I can feel all the blessed cold that

was still wrapped into my bones evaporate instantaneously. My heart rate reaches an uncomfortable level as I look over to watch Lucifer's face to gauge his reaction.

Does he feel the disturbance in the air as I do? Just the very mention of that name causes my body to react in unacceptable ways.

"And what, pray tell, does my dear sister demand of my attention?"

"Accommodations, money, accommodations... Simon is becoming unbearably restrictive. Should I continue?"

"No. I believe I get the gist of what she wants to speak about."

"Good enough. Can I let her calls go to voicemail for the rest of the night? Even I can only stand the sound of her voice for so long boss."

Rolling his eyes, Lucifer nods his head, "Yes."

Restrictive my ass. If it wasn't for my rules and way of doing things, she would be dead in a gutter in some back alley in Morocco. If I didn't have her on strict lockdown in the safe house, she would be putting herself, and by extension me, in more danger than is allowed.

I can't explain what made me take such a dangerous step in insanity. Taking her safety on as my own responsibility. Taking my self-control and throwing it to the damn wind. I don't have an excuse.

She's... she's... the damn devil's temptress.

The thought of her is as intoxicating as it is angering. She should not have this hold over me.

This... this...

I have no words for what I feel. In the mornings, since she has returned, I have driven myself to drastic measures by abusing my body in the gym. I've never pushed my body so hard before to purge itself of these desires. These damning thoughts.

If only I could quit thinking of her in my every waking moment.

Her voice is made of pure silk. Her eyes the deepest golden brown I have ever seen. Her dark, raven black hair falls down past her shoulders in natural waves. Her skin, I can find no flaws in it like I see in so many others. It's tan, but it's not one of those tans from a bottle or tanning booth. It's natural.

She has a natural scent to her when I brush by her. It's understated, but there. I never see her putting on perfume, but I smell it on her nonetheless. I'm not sure what attracts me to her more, her physical appearance or the fact that she absolutely infuriates me to no end.

I don't know if she is knowingly torturing me or if it's because I have deprived myself for so long, but I feel the delicate strands of my existence stretching far beyond their limits.

"Where are we at with her... issues?" Lucifer asks in a frustrated voice.

Meredith pains him almost as much as she does me, but for entirely different reasons.

She's been a thorn in his side since they were children. Now that she's a full-grown adult, I've been the one who's had to keep her whims at bay. She may hate her brother for her own reasons, but she's never failed to come to him with open hands expecting everything. Whether she deserves what she takes from him or not, she expects it.

"The Saudis are very upset over the loss of Prince Amir's son, Ahmed. Regardless of what happened, they're furious over the mystery surrounding it and the large amount of money he was worth to them. They want her back," I say, then hold my fingers up in quotation marks. *"For questioning."*

"The man has eight sons. From what you said, Ahmed wasn't even in favor with his father. How much are they asking for?" Lucifer asks in annoyance.

"Money isn't going to work on this, I believe. They consider this a matter of honor"

"Their honor can suck a pig's dick," Lucifer snaps. "How much did you offer them?"

"His net worth was about three million without his father's backing. It's a paltry sum compared to what the father is worth. I've offered triple the amount, and they're not biting. They are now increasing their threats to our operations," I reply.

"What kind of threats?"

"Nothing substantial, yet," I say. "But they are making threats to our well-being and our foreign interests when it comes to our holdings overseas."

"They don't have the clout for that. No one is willing to work with them. Not even the Russians. They have no real stake in our daily lives. It doesn't make sense," he says.

"They don't have to make sense to cause us trouble though," I say, shrugging.

"Simon, how the hell did this all come about? I thought you were keeping tabs on the damn brat."

"I was and am," I say evenly, but my blood runs cold. If he only knew the intensity of my surveillance.

The sheer amount of man-hours I've personally put into watching her live feeds and recordings. The men I had tailing her and watching her. The prince had his own security service, but my men were the damn professionals. They should have caught this damn mishap before it started.

That I've been watching her for the past years as an almost obsession…

"What happened, Simon? What is she not telling us?" he asks.

Looking out at the dark sky, I watch as the moon tries to break through the bleak skies, but it's no use. The forecast calls for freezing rain and then more snow. The heating bill will be going through the roof thanks to how hot the safe house must be kept for this insufferable woman.

What happened, indeed? That's the big question.

"She slipped my men and my surveillance team on the docks. She wasn't even supposed to know of our presence, and from all indications she still has no clue of the protections you and I had in place for her."

"How?" he asks, and he sounds almost as annoyed as I am about the situation.

"I've watched the surveillance over and over. I've watched from multiple angles and feeds. His team blocked ours off with expert efficiency. None of his team has shown this level of competence before. None. They aren't local thugs, but I would only put them one rung above."

"So…"

"So they expertly blocked off our men, and all the surveillance cameras on the yacht went offline halfway through their cruise."

"What's Meredith saying?"

"She won't talk. I could use…"

"No, not yet," he cuts me off.

"Have you thought about questioning her yourself, Matthew?" I ask with a chuckle.

That would be an interesting occurrence. If it's anything like Christmas dinner, it would be a rather profanity-ridden affair.

Meredith, how I loathe the crass American woman you

turn into when you aren't around the wealth and pomp you are so used to.

She turns in to a downright nasty hellcat. I'm strongly doubting my resolve not to chain her up to a bed for a good spanking.

"I'd rather not have to deal with her at the moment. Lily and the children have been begging for an addition added onto the house. They believe if we have more rooms, then there could possibly be another brother or sister in the future."

I'd rather puke than have those types of burdens. "Yes, I can see how that is an issue."

"Children aren't the evil you think them to be, Simon," Lucifer chuckles.

"If you say so, Matthew," I reply and turn back to him. "Eugene will be a complication no longer. He has also added even more of a tie for us to the Italians. We are the proverbial golden teat."

"Finding a good investment banker who knows how to launder a large amount of money is becoming harder to find," he says.

"Is this why you're having me look at another disease infested strip club?" I ask.

"Well, we do want to look legitimate," he snickers at my discomfort.

He knows my... distaste for the dirty, fluid-filled, sour smelling, unwashed attendees of these type of operations. I know he finds perverse pleasure in sending me into them for appraisals.

"There are many other establishments we could be investing in. I think there are even a couple of banks we could scoop up through one of our off-shore companies."

"How many are you thinking?" he asks as he looks over to me with interest.

I knew that would get his attention away from Meredith. I could just tell he wanted to get back into it with what's happening.

"Three. The two remaining West Liberties and the last of the Provident Banks of Garden City. This would be an excellent way to head into a more legitimate direction for Adam."

"Indeed, it would. What would be the term of ownership before we could sell them to him?"

"I'd give it fifteen years. We would, of course, be able to tap into new markets in that time. With the local unions being much more trusting of us than a banker group from another city."

"Simon, I do believe you have given Adam his twenty-first birthday gift," he smiles at me and I can see his joy.

Adam is one of Lucifer's greatest lights. The others are Evelyn and David. There is no distinction between adopted or not. In the eyes of the government, and Lucifer, they are his by blood. I would commend

Lucifer for his devotion, if children weren't so repulsive.

"So, I believe I can skip the unnecessary…"

"Simon, we can't be viewed as living the life of the virtuous." He shakes his head. "It's not good for our image. Also, we need to keep all toeholds away from any incoming Russian presence. We may be at a lull, but I can feel… that this complacency will not last."

"Agreed. Whether I want to admit such out loud at this moment, it's odd that they are keeping their drunken selves so quiet."

"We're here, boss," Peter says from up front.

"So we are," Lucifer says looking out the window. "Let's finish this up. Lily has plans for me to look over for the gathering at the end of the month."

"Speaking of that…" I say.

"You will be in attendance."

"Matthew, have I ever told you how fitting your moniker can be sometimes?" I say with a grimace.

Laughing loudly as he slides out of the door, he sounds to me like the real Lucifer when he says, "A few times."

EUGENE IS STRUGGLING MIGHTILY as we finally have the concrete mortar set around the cement blocks his feet have been stuck in.

"Eugene, I've been known to be a forgiving man in my past, but I feel that has been taken far too much for granted as of late," Lucifer says as he holds a pistol to the head of the quivering, overweight banker. "So, while I would have considered just putting you out of your misery, I've decided to be very strict with those that betray my trust."

He pushes the fat man into the water with one firm hand and we all stand on the edge of the dock, watching as the man quickly sinks down to the bottom.

Bubbles float up as the freezing cold water rushes into the soon-to-be dead man's lungs.

We don't see his last moments deep down in the dark water, but I can feel those fears slightly rushing into my own mind as I think on Lucifer's words.

2
MEREDITH

Peeling my eyes open, I glance towards the clock on my nightstand. It reads six o'clock. Shit. I've slept most of the day away...

Sitting up, I stretch my arms over my head to get my blood flowing and arch my back.

I feel a little guilty about sleeping in so late, but then again, it's not like I have anything to accomplish. No, being held prisoner in this little townhouse, I'm trapped in this kind of hellish limbo. I have nothing to do. I have no purpose.

I just exist.

Sliding out of bed, I pad my way into the bathroom, flip on the light and freeze. Struck by the sight my own reflection.

My hair is so light now, I almost don't recognize myself.

Gone is the dark color I've embraced for so long. The color that has set me apart from *him*, my wicked stepbrother.

I bleached my hair before I went to sleep, and the new blonde color makes me look like I could easily fit in with Matthew's perfect little golden family now.

How a monster like him can have and even care about a family still eludes me. It's completely unnatural and goes against everything I know about him.

I curl my lip in disdain and turn away from the mirror, hating the way I look. Hating the loss of that last distinction that set me apart.

Unfortunately, it was necessary.

Short of plastic surgery, this was the only way to drastically change the way I look. And I need to change the way I look if I ever hope to escape and evade the men after me.

Three months. It's been three long months since I came to Garden City and begged Matthew for protection. If I would have known his version of protection would be handing me off to his most trusted goon, Simon, I would have never come to this god-forsaken place.

I expected Matthew to take care of my 'problem', to wipe the family of my former and late boyfriend off the map. I even half expected him to snuff me out for even asking.

What I didn't expect was this. This... prison.

I quickly take care of my business, manage to brush my teeth without looking too much at myself in the mirror, and try to work out how I'm going to get out of the townhouse today.

Simon. Ugh. I have to call Simon.

The man has become the bane of my existence, acting pretty much like my prison warden. But given that my pleas and demands have fallen deaf on Matthew's ears, he's my only chance of getting out of this mess.

Walking into the kitchen, I grab my phone off the counter where I left it. The phone that was 'provided' to me like I needed the charity. I wouldn't need it at all if they hadn't taken everything I own away. Even now I can picture Simon's cold voice and even colder face when he handed it to me like it was some great big boon he was bestowing upon me.

The phone only dials a handful of trusted numbers, 911 not being one of them. Thankfully, they at least allow me to order my own groceries and toiletries with it.

It's the only fucking contact with the outside world I get.

I stare at the screen of the phone. Simon's number sits at the top of the contact list.

My thumb hesitates in midair, floating above his name.

If only there was another way to get away, to

escape. I've tried it all, though. I've tried sneaking out, only to find yet another of Matthew's goons guarding the front door, waiting for me. I've tried escaping through the window, and I even made it across the backyard before they captured me. I'd befriend my neighbors, but the rows of townhouses surrounding me have been bought out by them and sit empty.

Subsequent attempts have ended before they even began. I don't know how they know when I get the bug up my ass to try again, but they do.

The hair on the back of my neck rises, standing on end.

I think they're watching me.

I shiver out my heebie-jeebies and then my thumb touches Simon's name. Even if there are hidden cameras all over the townhouse, what can I do about it?

The phone rings once, twice, three times, before his voice comes through the line. "Meredith."

God, how I hate the way he says my name. It's so cold, so dead. Completely lacking in any feeling.

"Simon," I say, trying to mimic the way he said my name and failing.

"What do you want?" Straight to the point, as always.

"I want to go out," I sigh and lean against the counter. I'll try this the nice way first before I get nasty. "Being cooped up like this is driving me crazy."

"You know that's not possible. I've explained this to you before. It's too—"

I cut him off before he can say that one word he's so fond of saying to me. *Risky*.

As if I'm not already extremely aware of my perilous position. Aware that there are powerful men, very powerful and well-connected men, who want to kill me.

"I've changed my hair," I say over him and the line falls silent. I shift uneasily. "No one will recognize me."

He's quiet for so long I have to check the phone to make sure he didn't hang up on me. Then the hair rises again on the back of my neck and I get that creepy-crawly feeling that I'm being watched.

"You *what*?" he asks almost harshly, finally showing some feeling. Why he sounds so pissed though is beyond me.

"I bleached my hair," I explain, becoming annoyed that I even have to explain it to him.

Simon breathes into the phone, as if he's upset, and I can't help but find it a little unnerving. Why does he sound so upset? Is it because I've finally found a way to thwart him?

"How did you get the bleach?"

Shaking my head, I roll my eyes to the ceiling. Of course he wants to know all the dirty little details. He's so damn meticulous and uptight, it's beyond frustrating.

"I ordered it through the grocery store and had it delivered," I try to say calmly but my annoyance is getting the best of me. There's just something about him that pisses me off to no end. He's so damn stuck-up, so anal about everything, it drives me a little mad. That, and I've tried every little trick in the book on him and he's only proven to be completely impervious. "I had to because you won't let me fucking *leave*."

The breathing through the phone seems to calm and his voice returns to that cold, detached tone as he says, "You're not going out tonight, Meredith."

Those six words make me want to scream, but that won't get me what I want.

"Why? Why not? Why does he insist on punishing me?" I ask.

So the nice way didn't work. Time to switch gears and pretend to be remorseful.

"Look, I'm sorry I asked for Matthew's protection. I realize that was a mistake now and I greatly regret it. I assure you, I've learned my lesson."

"This is not a punishment, Meredith" he says slowly, snidely, once again letting some emotion slip. "This is for your own protection."

I close my eyes and take a deep breath. I knew this would be difficult, and he hasn't hung up on me yet.

"Just let me go," I resort to pleading, though it's probably lost on him.

If there were any way to sexually manipulate him,

I'd do it in a heartbeat. He's not a bad looking man. In fact, he's one of the most handsome men I've ever met. I'd take him to my bed without thinking twice about it. But Simon is beyond being influenced in that way. The couple of times in the past that I've tried with a look here or a touch there, have only caused him to shut down completely. To become even colder. More distant.

I'm not one hundred percent sure, but I think he's gay. It would explain why he seems to be stuck so far up Matthew's ass.

"I swear, you'll never see or hear a peep from me again," I add, hoping to entice him.

"*No*," he says so firmly, so strongly, I'm taken aback.

"No?" I repeat in disbelief then repeat again more shrilly. "No?!"

Fuck this shit, I've had enough. This has gone on long enough. I'm pulling out the big guns. Playing nice never works with him, he gives me no choice but to act the bitch.

"If I don't get out of this shitty little townhouse, I swear I'm going to slit my wrists and spill my blood all over *everything*. The furniture... the curtains... the carpets..."

Yeah, I'm well aware that Simon is a germaphobe and a total neat freak. It's yet another thing that makes him annoying.

He sounds almost bored as he asks, "With what blade?"

Oh, fuck this guy. Yeah, they removed everything from this house that could be used as a weapon, but I'm still pretty damn creative.

"With my *teeth*," I hiss.

The line goes quiet, and I know he's weighing whether or not he believes I'll go through with it. Just for shits and giggles, I lift my hand up to my mouth to see what happens.

"Fine," he hisses back, and I don't know whether to be relieved or freaked out. Is he really watching me right now? Or was that just a coincidence?

"Fine?" I repeat for clarification, keeping my hand close to my lips.

"I'll take you out," he grinds out like he's gritting his teeth. "But it will have to be to one of our protected properties."

That's not exactly what I was wanting, but I'll take it. "What are my choices?"

"The compound. One of the bars. Or..."

Neither of those options sounds particularly appealing.

"Or?" I press.

His voice is thick with disgust as he says, "One of our many strip clubs."

Ding, ding, ding, we have a winner. Not only because it will probably be easier to slip away in the dark of a strip club, but because it's so obvious Simon hates them.

"I want to go to a strip club," I grin and drop my hand.

"Of course you would," he says like it's supposed to be an insult or something.

I roll my eyes at the ceiling. What man doesn't like strip clubs? I was only pretty sure before, but I'm one hundred percent certain now.

Simon is totally gay.

"Pick me up in a couple of hours," I say and hang up the phone.

3
SIMON

Why not go to a strip club? It's going to be fun! We can watch the dancers, soak in the atmosphere, have a drink, and while the time away having a blast.

Except strip clubs are germ central. The dancers have STDs, the atmosphere smells like piss and old sex, and the drinks are watered-down.

Sure, this is going to be everything I could possibly hope for in a night out on the town. Diseases and piss. How entertaining. But if this is what will appease the princess, then she shall have her night out on the town. I'll make sure she gets her fill of strip clubs.

Kill two birds with one stone type of thing.

Lucifer never said I couldn't bring company with me when I inspect the properties.

"You know, for such a big SUV, you certainly are

small for it," Meredith says with a honey-laden sweetness.

She's needling me. It must be her only weapon in life, her sharp tongue.

"When I have to carry large loads, it works just fine, Meredith." I say and refocus my attention on the lights around us.

"Excuse me?" she asks in a tight tone. "What did you just say?"

"I need quiet, Meredith. I need to focus on the road."

Fucking Princess with a capital P. I don't really need to focus on the road, I know exactly where I'm going. But if it keeps her quiet, I won't complain. It's hard enough to focus with the proximity of her scent already getting to me.

It's back again, the smell of barely used perfume, so light and airy, but too faint to know what it is.

I'd shake my head or try to roll the knots that are forming in my shoulders if I didn't think she'd see that instantly as a weakness. I can feel her almost animalistic need to pounce on any sign of weakness. She wants to be the top too much for her own good, and in truth a good solid spanking would probably do nothing but make her meaner.

The way her body shifts in her seat though is driving me to desperate measures. Every time we pass under an overhead street light, I get glimpses of those long crossed legs. She should have worn a pant suit for the weather we are in. Her short, dark skirt barely reaches the midway point between her thighs and knees. She is completely irresponsible. The top under her coat shows far more skin than is needed.

Any neanderthal will now be able to ogle her to their heart's content.

Everything she is wearing is dark. The high-heeled shoes, pantyhose, tight short skirt, tight fitting top, and heavy coat.

All that dark clothing and now she has pale blonde hair to go with it. Gone is the black silky hair. In its stead is a woman who looks like she belongs right beside Lucifer in the family business.

Too beautiful to be real—that's the best way to describe her facial features. Even if she were to shave her head, she would still be the most stunning woman I have ever seen.

She's stunning and the most infuriatingly stubborn woman I have ever met.

Does she know that every time she moves or fidgets, my mind can't help but think of her? Does she know about the cameras I use every night to watch over her? To keep her safe and sound?

To keep me close to her?

Finally, I give into my body's need. Rolling my shoulders, I let my hands go loose on the steering wheel as I try to subtly flex them. My body is so damn tense my muscles are starting to ache. Ache for something, but I have no clue what.

Is it her? Is it her that would help the ache that consumes me day and night since she came back to Garden City?

Pulling into the parking lot of Lucky Tails, I breathe out a sigh of annoyance. "We're here."

Getting out of the car before she can respond, I shut the door roughly and take a deep breath of the cold night air.

It smells like shit here, but at least I don't have to deal with her scent.

The other side of the car thumps as she slams her door. Walking around the front, she doesn't even bother waiting for me as she takes off towards the entrance. I would have parked back behind the club, but she wants to come here so I might as well give her the full experience.

The sign above the club is made up of neon lights formed in the shape of a giant tiger. The tiger is lying on its stomach as its tail sways side to side in pink blinking lights. It's tacky and absolutely what I expect all clubs like this to be like.

Ugly and just waiting for the unwashed masses.

"What in the hell is that?" Meredith points to the sign.

"Matthew's idea. He believes it will bring in the crowds."

Turning her sharp gaze to me, she asks, "You brought me to one of my brother's strip clubs?"

"Of course. We must consider your safety, though we will be picking up a security detail from here. When we head to the other clubs your brother is considering purchasing, that is," I say as I motion toward the front doors.

"So he's doing what now? Franchising strip clubs? God." She shudders as she walks to the front doors and stops, waiting for me to open them up for her.

I'd rather take a bath in pure alcohol. It'd be safer than touching that handle. Who knows where people's hands have been before pulling open the door.

Knowing my luck, groping their disgusting body parts.

Staring at her intently, I say, "It's getting cold. Are we going in or should I take you back to the safe house?"

The look of pure hatred on her face as she yanks the door open is all the reward I can possibly hope for.

She storms into the place.

The security at the end of the hall stops Meredith before I have a chance to be recognized.

It's humorous to hear the door security ask, "You here as a guest or looking for job?"

"As if someone could fucking afford me!" Meredith snaps out loudly.

Walking up behind her, I say, "We're just visiting. Is Peter here tonight?"

The security guard focuses on me in the dim lighting. Recognizing me, he nods his head. "Yes, sir! Would you like me to have someone escort you to him?"

"No," I say. Meredith is still fuming as I lightly place my hand on her lower back. "Let him know we're here when you're not busy."

Giving her a light push to get her past the guard, I can feel an electrical current running up my forearm and straight to my groin. While not unpleasant, it annoys me that she is able to have this effect on me with just the barest of touches.

Through a fucking heavy coat, no less.

This is absurd.

I remove my hand from her back as she turns her head to me, her eyes beaming a dangerous glare.

"Why are you touching me?"

"So you will shut up and we can continue on our exciting journey into a filthy disease-ridden adventure."

"What the fuck is wrong with you?" she asks as we make our way into the club proper.

There are tables all around the floor. A bar is set back along the back of a wall, and the main stage has bar stools surrounding it. Mini stages are staggered around the floor for dancers who are not on the main stage to dance.

It's crowded here tonight. Crowded with a haze of smoke everywhere. Yet another issue I will have to suffer through.

Meredith stands there, looking out across the room of men and women. I'm not sure what she expected when she said a strip club, but I have a feeling she was expecting the glamorous Hollywood-type, not this.

This strip club is located between the business district and the industrial district. It pulls customers equally from both. While Lucifer may have cleaned the place up. Slapped a fresh coat of paint on it and removed a lot of the bad element that had took over this place.

It's still a *strip club*.

Again, placing my hand on the small of Meredith's back, I gently usher her to an open table. Removing my winter overcoat, I fold it neatly over the back of my chair. No doubt I will have to buy a new one after it touches this chair.

This place just feels like its crawling with germs. I can only hope a steaming hot shower and enough disinfectant to kill a horse will be enough to clean myself. My suit, shirt, and tie will need to be discarded.

No sense in keeping clothing with this kind of... filth on it.

Sitting down at the table, I look up at Meredith as she stares at me. Daggers are in her eyes again as she looks from me to her chair then back at me again.

"Yes, Meredith, you may sit at my table," I say just loud enough to be heard over the throbbing music that's being pumped over the speakers.

"Are you always such an asshole, Simon? Do you have no manners?" she hisses as she removes her coat and hangs it over the back of her chair.

"No, Meredith, it seems you bring out the best of me," I reply.

"Simon!" a feminine voice rings out.

I can literally feel my skin crawl hearing the way my name is said.

A woman with bright red hair who is wearing barely more than the strippers around us walks over to our table, trying to strut her...*goods*.

Meredith's head whips around to look at the woman who's approaching us, and at first she seems taken aback.

Then she sneers. "A friend of yours?"

Ignoring Meredith, I stand from my chair and nod my head slightly at the redhead. "Cherry."

Cherry is thankfully smart enough to know my rules of personal contact. She stops close enough to touch me, but doesn't do so.

I really do believe if she tried I might cut her hand off, and then remove any body part of mine she touched.

I simply could not handle being touched by her.

"Who's this?" she asks as she looks down at Meredith.

"A friend," I say coolly. She has no need to know who Meredith is or why she's here.

"I've never seen you with a... well... um," she says before asking Meredith. "You here for a job?"

"Why the fuck does everyone keep asking me that?" Meredith asks with some heat in her voice.

"Nope, not that then." Smirking, Cherry looks over to me and asks, "You need Peter?"

"No, not right now," I say, and I suddenly feel a small amount of fondness for the red-haired woman.

"Well, Spiderman, what can I get you two to drink?"

And now I'm right back to wanting to slit her throat with the stiletto I carry in my pocket.

"Nothing for me," I say.

I have no clue when they last washed the glasses they serve their drinks in, and I don't want to know either.

"What about you, honey?" Cherry asks Meredith with one of those smiles that seems to be so popular. It's a mixture of nasty lemon mixed with honey.

"Vodka cranberry. If you can remember that, sweetie," Meredith says back with a growl.

"Sure, whiskey sour. Be right back," Cherry says before turning to me. "I could make a pretty good dollar on her if she were to dance. With that bleached blonde hair, men would go for her being tan like that. She's a total bimbo barbie doll."

Meredith's eyes widen further. "Bimbo!"

"I'll have your cosmopolitan sent right over, girl," Cherry grins before turning to me one more time. "Her hips are probably too narrow and rigid to be a dancer though."

Flouncing away from us, I watch as she heads towards the bar.

Turning back to Meredith, I see those daggers staring right into the back of Cherry.

Whatever. I hate these social interplays. They're almost as bad as trying to read social cues.

Sitting back down at the table, I try to make sure none of my exposed skin touches anything here.

Snapping my fingers in front of Meredith, I say, "What is it you wish to do while we're here? I can arrange for you to have a dance—"

"Nothing like that!" Meredith hisses.

I didn't think so, she never put out the leanings towards women, but one never knows.

The music dies down after a moment and we both sit here, stewing in our own thoughts. I can feel the scabies crawling up my damn pants leg.

This is not the night I would like to be having right now.

Being with Meredith is a slow, tortuous affair.

I would rather be spending time exploring every single

inch of her body with my hands while I listen to her moan in ecstasy, I think to myself.

Stop it. Thoughts like that will lead to nowhere but trouble... and perhaps hell. Fuck it all. The road to hell is always paved with a lack of self-control. I may end up there because of what I do, but I will not let her break me.

"I have to use the ladies room," Meredith says, looking around the floor.

Hmm. *Lady. That's a good euphuism, Meredith*, I mentally chide her.

She keeps looking at me expectantly, so much so I have to ask, "What? Do you need help with removing those skin-tight clothes? Perhaps you should have worn a more sensible..."

"One more fucking word about my clothes, Simon, and I'll fucking break my heel off in your ear," she snaps.

So, she does have a weak spot. Figures it's clothing.

I know somewhere behind those heated eyes is a brain that could rival mine, but she doesn't like people knowing it. Perhaps that's why she dresses the way she does.

"Show me where the hell it is?" she snaps as she stands up from the table.

Looking down at my hands for a moment, I force myself to relax. Hopefully she will get one look at the bathroom and want to go home. Then I will be free of her torture and can go back to some sense of normalcy.

"Fine," I grit out between my teeth.

Standing up, I step around her, heading off towards the back of the club. On my way, I check out all those around us. I may detest this business with my very being, but it is a cash cow when I look at the numbers instead of the filth.

Stopping outside of the bathroom, I motion for Meredith to stop. "I need to check it out before I leave you alone."

Pushing us both through the door, I do a quick look through the stalls. It's empty, thankfully. I'd fucking hate to see some woman on her knees sucking a cock or snorting coke.

Meredith looks confused as I finish my search. "What the hell is going on with you?"

"Your security," I say without any other words.

Heading back out of the bathroom, I say, "The window is bolted shut."

Meredith says something, but I don't quite hear it as the door shuts behind me.

Turning my back to the door, I stand to the side of it. It's been a few years since I've stood as someone's guard, much less worked a door as security.

I watch as the crowd of people moves and flows with the strippers weaving in and out of the tables. A couple of guys follow two strippers to the private dance booths and it makes me shudder to think of sitting on those vinyl seats crusted with body fluids.

Glancing towards the front of the building, I see Peter looking frantically around the club. His face is normally as jovial as a damn caveman's, but right now he looks pissed and very worried.

Such an odd... Fuck.

He spots me and begins to race towards me with a look of something akin to fear. Shit.

Slamming the door open behind me, I race into the bathroom. Meredith is just coming out of the stall as I grab her by the wrist.

Yanking her by the arm, I practically pull her across the floor as I wrench the door open.

"What do you think you're doing, Simon?!" she screams at me over the loud music as I yank her out past the door and onto the floor.

Peter is in a full out run as he reaches us. "We need to get out of here! Bomb."

I know my eyes widen, but I don't bother asking questions. Too many times shit like this has happened for me to think he would be playing a trick.

Sweeping Meredith up and over my shoulder, I run behind Peter as he slams his body into people to get them out of the way.

Rushing through the now vacant hole of the crowd, I hear Cherry far behind us, calling out to us.

Fuck. Cherry.

Turning back to her, I wave my hand in a frantic motion to get the fuck over here.

Then I swing back towards the exit and pick up my pace again until I'm at a dead run. We're heading for the back door, not the front. It's closer and hopefully we can get clear.

Peter lifts a foot and boots the door nearly off the hinges once we reach it. Turning back to us, he motions for me to move my ass.

I hear Cherry behind us, yelling and asking what the fuck is happening, but I don't stop as I push Peter ahead of me.

Meredith, Peter, and I, get almost ten feet away from the door before a deafening whooshing noise comes from the front of the club. The fire and subsequent explosion launches Cherry out of the open door like a rag doll.

Her body lands a foot past where we were standing a moment ago.

Peter yanks his pistol from his hip holster as he looks around us.

He yells over the sudden roar of fire, "We need to get to my truck!"

Nodding my head, I follow him over to the silver Dodge Ram and plop Meredith down beside of it.

Looking into her eyes, I pant from the exertion of carrying her so far and fast. "Are you okay, Meredith?"

She nods her head numbly and points to the back

door of the club. Flames are rolling out of it hot and heavy.

Shock. She's in shock.

"I know, Meredith, I know. Let's get you somewhere safe..." I say.

Shaking her head at me, she points again behind me. "No..."

Turning back to look, I see what she's pointing at and my heart stills for a moment. Cherry is still there where she landed. Her body is crumpled on the ground, but her arm is moving almost like a flag.

"Peter," I shout. "Get Meredith in the car. I'll be right back."

"What the fuck?" he asks, but I ignore him.

Jogging over to Cherry, I can't help but think she looks like the victim of a violent train wreck. Her body just doesn't lay right on the ground. A leg is turned at an impossible angle. The good arm is still moving slightly while her other is missing entirely.

Kneeling in front of her, I look down at her mess of hair that is more blood and charred scalp than anything else. Her face has that melted wax look to it.

"I'm here, Cherry, it's Lucifer," I say in a cool smooth drawl.

Gone are any inflections that comes with the Simon voice. Now I use the smooth, unhurried voice of Lucifer.

Her eye barely moves in her skull and one is completely melted. There's this faraway look to it.

Taking her hand away from my tie where she grasps at it with blood-soaked fingers, I ask quietly, "Would you like me to do a kindness for you, Madeline?"

She's far too gone now to know who I really am. She knows only that I call her by the name Lucifer would use for her. It's her real name.

Pulling the stiletto from my pocket, I press the button and the blade shoots out from the handle.

Cherry could possibly live after all this, but she would never be right again. She would never be able to look in the mirror again.

Her lips part but no words come, only bubbles of blood.

I nod my head and whisper, "Goodbye, Madeline."

Stabbing the blade down into her chest, I push it deep down between the bones and pierce her heart.

Moving it upwards, I ensure I've severed any chance she will have to deal with this anymore.

She gives one quiet death rattle over the flames coming from the building. Then the pain-filled eye fades as the life flees from her body.

Standing up from the body, I can't help but shudder as I look down at my bloody hands. My suit, tie, and shirt are ruined.

Nothing about this day has gone according to plan, and it's driving me mad with anger.

Walking over to the truck, I see Meredith still standing beside it with Peter trying to get her to listen to him.

"Look, ma'am, we need you to get in the truck."

Meredith is not having it though. She just continues to stare at me and the hand I have holding the stiletto.

"What... What did you... do?" she stutters out at me.

"A kindness. Now if you would be so agreeable, please get the fuck in the truck," I growl at her.

Turning to the cab of the truck, she mutters quietly, "You're a monster, you all are."

Ignoring her, I say, "Peter, get me to my SUV and quick. We need to get out of here."

Once we're all in the truck, it's a quick ride around the block to reach my vehicle. In the distance, sirens wail in the background. Thankfully we don't spot anyone being too nosey as we stop in front of my Escalade.

I would try to clean myself up from the blood, but we just don't have the time.

Getting out and heading to my vehicle, I notice Meredith is still sitting in the back of the truck.

Walking to her door, I yank it open and wrap a hand around her wrist. She fights me at first, but when

I pull her arm hard enough she slides right out of the truck.

"We don't have time for this shit, Meredith!" I growl as I tug her over to my vehicle.

Turning to Peter as he looks out his window, I say, "Tell Lucifer what happened, and that I am in the process of securing his sister. I'll contact him as soon as possible."

"Got it," he says out the window before easing out of the parking lot.

Meredith must be getting her dander up again because she begins to struggle against me. Blood from me is getting all over her top and arms. Dirty disgusting stripper blood.

Motherfucker.

"Stop fucking fighting!" I shout as I pull her to the passenger door.

Opening it up, I all but toss her inside.

Pulling her belt over her lap, I snap her in before shutting her door. I run around to my side of the Escalade and get in quickly.

Starting it up, I stomp on the gas and peel out of the parking lot.

4

MEREDITH

The tires of Simon's SUV squeal as he hits the gas. Behind us, the night sky is lit up with a glow of orange as the inferno consuming Lucky Tails blazes towards the heavens. Sirens flash, red, white, and blue, illuminating the burning building.

It looks like a party in a hell, and I just barely escaped it.

I glance over at Simon. He looks... unraveled. In the three months that I've known him, I don't think I've ever seen him like this. His eyes are wild, full of emotion for once, and yet focused with a purpose. The hair he usually keeps slicked back is all over the place. His tie is askew. He shed his suit jacket, but there is still blood all over his shirt, arms, and hands.

Cherry's blood.

He killed her. I watched him lean in close to her like he was a lover and shove a blade in her chest.

Fuck. I knew it, but seeing is truly believing. He's a monster just like *him*.

Watching Simon kill Cherry was just like that day I stumbled across Matthew in the basement all those years ago, torturing that man...

The tires of the SUV squeal again as Simon is forced to come to a stop at a light.

I don't think twice. I have to get away. I can't be a part of this madness.

One hand grabbing the handle of the door, my other hand unclicks my seatbelt and I try to make a run for it.

Shoving my door open, I get one foot out the door when my hair is suddenly grabbed. I'm yanked viciously back.

"Where the fuck do you think you're going, Meredith?"

I scream and reach back, clawing at the hands gripping my hair.

"Let me go, Simon!" I screech.

"No," he growls.

He *growls*. I don't think I've ever heard Simon speak in anything but a cool, almost robotic voice before.

I guess I really do bring out the best of him.

Yanking harder on my hair, he uses it to reel me

back in. I scream again as my scalp lights up with agony.

Leaning over me, he rips one hand from my hair to pull the door shut. Then he shoves that hand into my chest, pinning me against the seat, as he straightens.

"Now is not the time for this shit," he states matter-of-factly as he looks me deep in the eyes. "I have to get you somewhere safe and take care of this mess. Do you understand, princess?"

When I don't immediately answer him, he tugs on my hair again.

I whimper at the pain and his eyes light up. Flashing with something that looks a lot like pleasure.

Fuck. Is he getting off on this?

"Yes," I somehow manage to croak out.

For a minute, we just stare at each other. Me, panting with pain and too aware of his strong hand pressed against my chest. Him, with his eyes boring into me, almost daring me to defy him.

I don't know where this new, meaner Simon came from, but I know better than to push him. I've learned from experience that the only hope I have of getting away unscathed is by pretending to be compliant.

Finally, with a look of distrust followed by something that could easily be mistaken for disappointment, Simon slides his hand out of my hair and says, "Good."

He glances down at his hand, at all the hair

wrapped around his fingers, and frowns. I half expect him to make a mean crack, but he doesn't. No, he just stares at his hand, at my hair, like he doesn't know what to do with it.

A car honks behind us, quickly followed by another. With a sigh, he leans back into his seat, shakes the hair from his hand, and throws the SUV into drive.

"Put your seatbelt back on," he says without looking over at me.

Anger flares inside me and I latch onto it. I stoke it. Needing it to get me through this.

I hate being told what to do, just fucking hate it…

But fuck, if I keep defying him, I'll never get out of this.

Gritting my teeth, I reach back, ignoring the way my scalp throbs, and grab the seatbelt, yanking it across myself.

Once the seatbelt clicks into place, Simon's shoulders slump just the tiniest of bits.

Good, he's relaxing a little. Probably thinks he just bullied me into submission.

Joke's on him.

He can yank me by my hair and push me around, but it just makes me even more determined to get away from him.

We drive in an uncomfortable silence for a couple of minutes before being forced to stop at a light again.

Simon looks over at me, his eyes daring me to try to run again.

I want to, but I'll be damned if I give him the satisfaction.

When that flash of disappointment reappears in his eyes, I can't stop the smug grin that spreads across my lips.

Oh yeah, I'm onto him now. He wants a fight. He's practically begging for it.

And he's not going to get it.

Oh no, I'll be the perfect little prisoner. I'll do everything he asks...

His gaze drops to my chest and hardens. "Remove your shirt."

"What?" Seriously, what the fuck? He can't be serious.

His voice is cold and detached again. "Did I stutter, Meredith?"

"No," I draw out, fighting off the urge to recoil from him. I will not show him any more weakness, dammit.

"Then do it."

"Why?" Why the fuck does he want me to remove my shirt? What possible reason could he have for it besides pissing me off?

"You're covered in blood."

"So are you!" I point out to him. Drops of blood are splattered along his white shirt, his pants, his tie. Not to mention all the blood on his arms and hands.

What a fucking hypocrite.

Simon glances down at himself as if he forgot and his lip curls in disgust. "Yes, yes, I am, but that is neither here or there."

I sputter, at a loss. "Neither here or there? What the fuck is that supposed to mean? It's fine for you to be covered in blood, but it's not fine for me?"

Slowly, Simon's gaze lifts back to mine, glittering with menace. "That's right. That's exactly it, *princess*."

I shake my head. He's crazier than I ever imagined. He's fucking loony. Completely and utterly mad.

The light switches to green.

Simon turns his attention back to the road. "You have until the next red light to comply."

"Or what?" I can't stop myself from snapping even though I know it's stupid to taunt a crazy man.

"Or I do it for you."

"You wouldn't dare," I hiss.

There I go, being stupid again.

He doesn't even have to say it; I can feel the words hanging in the air between us.

Try me.

Oh, I will. If he thinks I'm just going to let him remove my shirt, he's got another thing coming.

I've put up with a lot tonight and I've reached my breaking point. Tonight was supposed to be my night to finally get away, to free myself of Matthew and

Simon's clutches, but some asshole just had to go and bomb the strip club and ruin it.

Each light we pass under remains green, and I thank the universe for small miracles. That is, until we finally reach another red.

Before Simon brings the car to a complete stop, I'm throwing my hair over my shoulder, pulling off my seatbelt and pushing the door open. If I had a weapon, I'd fucking stab him. Unfortunately, I'm completely defenseless.

The only thing I can do is try to make a run for it again.

Suddenly, the car lurches forward, the tires squealing as Simon hits the gas and I almost go tumbling out the door.

"Go ahead," Simon taunts as the car picks up speed. "Make a jump for it, Meredith."

Clutching the door for dear life, it's everything I can do to keep from falling out and kissing asphalt.

As the road rolls by, my life is literally flashing before my eyes.

"You're fucking crazy! Stop!" I scream, reaching out and clawing at the dashboard. My fingers slip and slide across it, failing to find purchase.

A hand grabs me by the back of the neck and yanks me back. The door slams shut and I instantly let go of it.

"Fuck!" I scream and start shaking.

He almost killed me. The bastard almost killed me.

"Fuck! Fuck! Fuck!" I can't stop screaming.

That's the second time in three months that some asshole tried to kill me.

The car swerves to the right and I nearly go face-first into the windshield as we come to an abrupt stop.

Simon's thrusts out his arm, saving me from eating glass at last moment.

Whipping back against the seat, I blink back tears, trying to process almost fucking *dying* again. Before I can get myself together, Simon leans over me and tears the glovebox open.

My arms are yanked forward and then there's a loud click that snaps me out of my stupor.

I look down just in time to see Simon snapping a pair of handcuffs around my right wrist.

"What the fuck are you doing?" I ask, way too close to crying for comfort.

I try to yank my arms away, but he's not playing. With a grunt, he pulls me so hard he almost pops my arms out of my sockets.

"Ensuring you don't put your life in danger again," he grits out.

The second handcuff snaps around my left wrist.

"Me? Put my life in danger?" I repeat shrilly and incredulously. "You're the one who fucking accelerated! You tried to kill me!"

"Stop being so melodramatic," he sighs as he grabs

the seatbelt and yanks it across me. "You only had a fifty percent chance of dying at the rate of speed we were traveling."

"Fifty percent?! Fifty percent?! Are you fucking kidding me?"

"Even less with me prepared to yank you back."

I look down at the seatbelt and then back up at him. I don't understand him at all. I don't understand any of this.

One moment he's trying to kill me, the next he's protecting me. It doesn't make any damn sense!

Simon's eyes meet mine and I swear from the expression on his face he's about ready to crack.

Ha, crack, as if he's sane to begin with.

I take a deep breath, then another deep breath.

His gaze flicks down, locking on my breasts. His lip curls with distaste. It's all the warning I get before he reaches for me and grabs my shirt.

"No! Don't!" I plead, but he ignores me. His fingers pull and yank at the fabric, splitting it open.

I'm not ashamed of my body, not in the least, but to have him ripping my shirt off of me against my will is pretty damn humiliating.

With no way of stopping him, I close my eyes and wonder how my life came to this moment.

Oh yeah, because I was stupid and begged Matthew for protection.

Something cold and wet touches my hands, sliding up my arms. Oh god, what is that?

"There, that's better," Simon says and my eyes pop open.

"Better?" I repeat dumbly and glance down.

The fucker even wiped off my arms and hands with a wet wipe of some sort.

"Yes, better," Simon says, his eyes locked on the swells of my breasts. "Now you're not covered in that stripper's disgusting, dirty blood."

I can't even. Seriously, what the fuck is wrong with him?

He's starts to reach for me again and I jerk back, crying out, "There's none on my bra, asshole!"

Simon pauses in mid-grab, blinks, then shakes his head as if he's trying to come out of something.

After a couple of seconds, he says, "You're right," and pulls away.

Damn straight, I'm right. I have to bite my tongue though to keep from spitting more venom at him. Lord knows he deserves it, but I'm done fighting him. I've had enough excitement for one night, thank you very much.

Settling back in his seat, he rolls down his window and tosses my shirt and the wipe out like it's garbage. The window rolls back up as he refocuses his attention on the road, and we're moving again.

He's so damn calm, so damn cool, it's like nothing

just happened. I really don't understand him. I really don't understand why he was so upset there was blood on me and doesn't give a fuck about all the blood on him.

And why did he almost go for my bra? That's the part I really don't get. If he were a normal, hot-blooded man, then I'd totally get it. But he's not. He's a fucking freak. He's... inhuman. And I'm not the only one who thinks it. In the short amount of time I've spent in this hell-hole of a city, I've overheard some of Matthew's men crack jokes about him being a spider masquerading as a human.

With my hands handcuffed in front of me, the shoulder strap of the seatbelt rides up, towards my face, and I have the strongest urge to try and chew my way through it.

"What's that perfume you're wearing?" Simon asks out of the blue, his voice back to that cool monotone I'm so fond of.

I look at him sideways. Is this another weird thing he's going to use to attack me?

"I don't wear any perfume," I say slowly, cautiously. Doing my best not to provoke him.

His gaze jerks towards me. Why is he so surprised by this? Do I stink or something?

I lick my lips nervously and further explain. "I find most perfumes to be too strong, or they make me smell like an old lady."

Simon's nostrils flare and then he gives a sharp nod of his head before looking back to the street.

I watch him tense up again, his knuckles going white as he clutches the steering wheel. Somehow, someway, I've managed to piss him off again.

The rest of the drive is spent in a tense, uncomfortable silence.

The lights and cramped together buildings of the city fade away, giving way to woods. We turn and drive up a winding, secluded road, and I start to tense up. Where is he taking me? Obviously not back to the townhouse that's been my prison...

The winding road goes on for a couple of miles before a house appears in the distance like a beacon. It's white and ultra-modern. Looking completely out of place in the middle of the forest. The brick walls reach at least three stories high, and large, chrome-like windows reflect the moonlight that hits them.

We pull up in front of a gate set in a white brick wall that matches the house, and all the security cameras pointing at us makes me feel like we're entering the liar of an evil spy movie villain.

"Where are we?" I ask, taking everything in. Plotting and planning how I'm going to get out of this.

The white brick wall surrounding the house is at least ten feet high and it's going to be a real bitch trying to climb it.

"My house," Simon answers as the gate opens and we roll through it.

The gate doesn't even extend all the way out before it quickly begins to close behind us. It's made up of black wrought-iron bars and they're so close together there's no hope of me squeezing through them.

"Why are we here? Why not take me back to the townhouse?" I ask as we pull up to a garage.

Damn, I never thought I'd actually want to go back to the townhouse, but the thought of staying in Simon's house is giving me the heebie-jeebies.

The garage has four doors and is so large it appears to be its own separate building attached to the main structure.

Simon rolls up to the second door and it begins to lift before he answers like I should know the answer. "Because, Meredith, Lucifer has tasked me with your protection."

"Yeah, so? You can't do that from the townhouse?"

He gives a sharp shake of his head.

Fuck. "Why not?" I ask as we roll into the garage and the door lowers behind us.

I really, *really* don't want to stay here, and now that we're parked in the garage, I'm starting to feel a little claustrophobic.

Simon turns off the car and turns to look at me. His face is completely smooth, not giving away any emotion. "Because the closer you are, the better an eye I can keep on you."

He couldn't be creepier if he tried.

Opening his door, he slides out and then slams the door behind him. I jump at the sudden loud noise.

He walks around the front of the car and then yanks my door open. Leaning in, he unbuckles my seatbelt for me, and it's everything I can do to keep from taking a cheap swipe at him.

I have no hope of knocking him out so the move would be completely pointless.

Grabbing me by the chain between the handcuffs, he tugs me out of the car and slams the door shut behind me.

His face may be emotionless, but his actions definitely scream that he's irritated.

I doubt he wants me to stay here any more than I want to, so I try to make a suggestion. "You could always take me to the compound. I'd be perfectly safe there."

I hate Matthew, absolutely despise him. But the devil you know and all.

"Your presence would only be a burden to him," Simon says and tugs me forward.

Ouch. That kind of hurts, but yeah, I get it.

Simon leads me up to a door that connects the garage to the main house, and as we step over the threshold, the room we step into is instantly illuminated.

The lights must be on motion sensors. That's going to make getting away even trickier.

As we move deeper into the house, my nose stings a little with the smell of disinfectant.

He leads me through a gleaming, stainless steel kitchen. Through a white and gray modern living area. Then up a set of winding stairs.

Everything is done in cool neutral tones. The walls are either white or grey, and the furniture is all sharp lines and hard angles.

There's no personality, no warmth. Everything is cold and sterile. A perfect reflection of the owner.

Once we reach the second-floor landing, he leads me down a long hall and up to the third door.

Twisting the door open, he roughly shoves me in. I stumble forward and manage to take one deep breath before he grabs me and drags me over to the bed.

My eyes look wildly around the room. Searching for anything to help me. An escape. A weapon.

Simon gives me another shove, pushing me onto the bed, and steps back.

Without a word, I hear him exit the room, slamming the door behind him. There's no click of a lock and I take that as a promising sign. He probably thinks I can't get away with my hands handcuffed.

Pushing myself up, off the mattress, I just manage

to get my feet under me when he comes stomping back in.

Head whipping towards him, my eyes immediately lock on the set of handcuffs he's carrying in his hand.

"What do you think you're going to do with those?" I ask sharply in an effort to keep my panic from leaking through my voice.

"I'm going to secure you, Meredith, so I can get some work done," he says, his face still wearing that smooth, emotionless expression.

"The fuck you are," I hiss and take a step back.

He stalks towards me and I lash out, swinging my bound hands.

"Keep your fucking hands off of me, Simon!" I screech.

I get a couple of hits in before he's gets a grip on the chain between the handcuffs. Using the chain, he jerks me over to the bed and then shoves me down on it.

His body comes down on top of mine and my mind goes completely blank.

Is this really fucking happening?

Pinning me with his weight, I try to twist, try to knee him, but he's too damn big and heavy. For such a fucking geek, he's surprisingly dense.

"Stop fucking fighting," he grits out, his emotionless mask cracking as he struggles to secure my hands.

"Fuck you, asshole. Get the fuck off of me!" I scream and then I do the only thing I can do.

I lift my head up and bite him.

"Fuck!" he roars as my teeth sink into the flesh of his shoulder.

My teeth dig and dig, but it doesn't stop him. No, I feel one handcuff being opened, only for my wrist to be covered by another.

Then he yanks my arms up hard and my teeth are forced to release him.

I can taste the coppery tang of his blood as he cuffs each of my hands to the frame of the bed.

Simon jumps up from the bed and takes a stumbling step back. His hair is even more disheveled than before and his eyes are bright and wild. He glances at his shoulder and then lifts his hand up, his fingers exploring the wound I inflicted. The blood stain on his shoulder started small but is growing and growing.

I yank my hands hard but the handcuffs hold.

Fuck. I can't believe he cuffed me to a fucking bed.

"This is completely unnecessary, Simon, and uncalled for," I try to say calmly but I'm too damn pissed.

His hand drops and his eyes snap to me. "I know. The situation calls for a cage, but alas, I don't have one on hand."

My rage is palpable. I fume, yanking and yanking, but the only thing I manage to do is hurt myself in the process. A cage? A cage? Is he insinuating that I'm an animal?

"Let me go!" I scream at him. "You can't fucking do this to me."

"I can do anything I want. You're in my house now, princess."

He turns and starts walking away from me.

"Fuck you!" I scream and all my anger, all my rage bubbles forth. "I fucking hate you, Simon! I hate you," I scream and scream, even as the door slams behind him.

I thought I hated Matthew the most in this world, but Simon just placed himself at the top of my shit list.

I'll never fucking forgive him for this. And... fuck... he's going to pay for this.

5

SIMON

The door slamming behind me helps with the ache I feel in my loins. The rage of pain radiating through my shoulder does nothing to dissuade the hormonal reaction I feel. If anything, the fight I feel from her makes the pain so much more... sexual.

Sexual pain, that's a novelty if I've ever heard one.

Putting my hand on my shoulder, I pull it away only to find fresh blood bleeding up through my shirt.

That little...

I suppose first blood goes to her then.

Not that I will try to one up her. No hair will be harmed on her damn head. She might very well end up with a bright red bottom though. If she wants to behave like a child, then I'll treat her like the obstinate one she is.

Walking into the bathroom, I flip the light switch on to survey the damage of my clothes and body. Thankfully, neither Meredith or I were injured in the explosion.

Cherry was a loss though, as were all the workers and clientele.

I think this should be put down as a gas main explosion, not an attack. If word were to get out it was anything but an accident it would look very bad on us as a whole. We've stayed out of the national spotlight, and now with the governor we have in place, it's even easier to stay in the shadows.

But if it came out that we had another gang war on our hands...

Damnation. Everything we've been building up and putting in place could be put under the microscope. The current political climate does not bode well for criminal enterprises.

Walking into the kitchen, I grab a garbage bag. Then I pull my cellphone out as I head back into the bathroom.

I scroll through my contacts list and I have to scroll pretty far down before I find who I'm looking for.

Putting the phone down on the counter, I press call and turn on the speakerphone.

It's five long rings before I hear a voice. "Fire Chief Martin."

"Chief, this is Simon Whitmore," I say as I start untying my bloody tie.

There's a long pause and I can't tell if he is trying to willfully forget my name or if he's sensing the oncoming headache I'm going to cause.

"Simon, how can I help you?" he asks quietly.

"I was calling to find out more about the gas main explosion that occurred at Lucky Tails tonight."

"Gas main explosion..." he starts off and I can tell he's not happy to hear the news.

"Yes, it's very tragic that we had such an awful accident at the club."

"There's no way that it could—"

"Chief Dennis Alan Martin. You have three daughters. One's in Yale, yes? And the other two are still in private schooling within the city, I believe... Which one do you love the most?" I ask as I toss the bloody tie into the garbage.

"How dare you! You son of a bitch!" he says with a deep growl.

"Quite true. Now answer me, which one do you love the most? Is it the Ivy League child? What about the soccer star? Which will bring you the most pride? How about the youngest daughter? Nothing notable about her yet."

"The gas main explosion was an unfortunate accident, due to unforeseen circumstances," he says quickly.

"You still haven't answered my question," I press.

"Look, I'll say anything you want, Simon," he says in a rush and I can hear the terror in his voice.

"Thank you for your concern and diligent inspection during these upcoming days. I'll make sure to send a fruit basket over to your home," I say before pressing the disconnect button.

Another scroll through the contacts and then I push on yet another person's name.

Two rings this time. "Detective Sommers."

"Detective, it's Simon."

"Simon, good to hear from you. Though I have a feeling this isn't a call to see how I'm doing," he says with a sigh.

I really do wish people would be happy to hear my voice...

No, actually I don't.

"Indeed. I need you to find out what you can about the gas main explosion tonight at Lucky Tails. Names and addresses of all the visitors, any information that could help us identify the part of the gas main that exploded..."

"Got it. I'll try to get you everything as it comes in. Any issues and I'll contact you. Anything else?" he asks.

"Yes, make sure you work very closely with Chief Dennis Martin on this. If there are any issues, no matter how small, please inform me," I say.

"Will do. Have a goodnight, Simon."

"You as well," I say and push the disconnect button.

Removing my shirt completely, I wait to look at where she bit me.

I don't dread looking at what I know to be a vicious bite mark. No, I wait because I fear the exhilaration I'm sure it will give.

Why would I feel such an emotional high? I have no clue. I'm in new territory with all these emotional and hormonal threads. Long before I was an adult, I, like many others, reveled in the hormones and lack of self-control only a youth could possess.

Now I must keep a rigid control of myself. I'm not some unthinking neanderthal.

Wiping mine and Cherry's blood off on the what was once a crisp, white shirt, I notice how the blood has stained my hands.

My life of bloody hands has been over for a long time. I wear gloves if I need to cause physical damage to someone. It allows me to remain remote and professional about the matter.

Blood makes things personal when it's spilled on your skin.

Putting the destroyed dress shirt into the garbage bag, I remove my wasted pants, socks, and shoes. All go into the bag. No evidence of Cherry's blood on me will be left. I'll have to take care of Meredith's clothes, and the bedding she's laying on, but that can wait for now.

The stiletto goes in the bag as well. I'll need to grab another one of those from my home office.

Still avoiding the mirror, I push the first contact on my list and wait for him to pick up.

"Simon... Do tell me why I heard from Peter and not you about Lucky Tails and Meredith."

He's angered. Though I'm not sure which has him madder, that his club has been destroyed or that Meredith was in danger.

"Her security took precedence in the matter. Though I do not believe either her or I were the target of the bomb."

"Peter was of the same mind," he says, and I can hear Lily in the background asking what's going on.

I'm surprised I haven't paid more attention to what time it is and glance at the clock. It's almost midnight. I doubt he went back to bed after Peter called, so she's probably come to see why he left the bed.

Why he deals with such annoyances, I have no clue.

"What did Peter say?" I ask.

Knowing I didn't get more information before Meredith and I raced from the bombing irritates me to no end.

Meredith is becoming too much of a burden.

"That the location of the bomb was back by the DJ station. It had no timer, only a flashing light. He believes it was a military grade explosive, probably expert in set up."

"That fits what little I saw of the scene before we left. It was most likely remote-detonated," I say quietly as I begin to run the water of my sink.

Blood slowly comes free of my hands and swirls down the drain as I continue my thought process. "If I was to conjecture at this exact moment, we weren't the target of tonight's attack. It was a message meant to be sent to us. Now as to who... I don't have enough information to even guess. It could be anyone. Russians, Yakuza, fringe Irish. I doubt the Saudis have even had the opportunity to do something like this yet. It could have been a rush job, but it doesn't feel like it to me."

"Peter gave me the estimate of fifty-five to seventy people dead. Workers and clientele. This will be national news on late night TV, and at the very least in the morning news and papers."

"Agreed. I've got both Sommers and Martin on the same page. Gas main explosion, catastrophic failure due to anything that can help get the spotlight away from the truth. Blaming it on a gang war is the last thing we need right now."

"Good. Will they both play their parts?"

"Sommers will, of course. Martin will need to be closely watched. I plan to have a reminder sent to him tomorrow, and another will visit his daughter at Yale," I say.

The blood under my fingernails is the hardest part to get clean, and it's through sheer willpower alone that I don't rip them off just so I can get the stripper's blood off of me.

A good dose of antibiotics will be in my future.

"Tell me about Cherry," Lucifer says quietly, and I can feel his anger at the loss.

He, of course, had no emotional ties to the woman beyond favoring her brains and intellect for the business. At least that I can see.

"She was severely injured from the blast. She was so injured she would never have a life worth living again. It may have been possible to save her, but I decided to show her a kindness."

"Understood."

Taking a deep breath, I look up from my clean hands and stare at my body.

"Will you be avoiding me any further on the Meredith topic, Simon?"

"You know your sister's ways as well as I do."

"I do," he says with a chuckle. "So she got underneath the most collected man I know's skin?"

There, on my shoulder, is a bloody bite mark. She tore through the shirt and skin when she bit me. Plain and simple, she became the hellcat princess I've thought her to be all along.

She's marked me just as if she were to brand or tattoo me as hers.

She really was mad to have been able to cause that kind of wound.

"She was trapped in the townhouse for too long. She was becoming stir crazy. After this latest escape attempt out the bathroom window... I decided to give her some fresh air."

"So you took her to Lucky Tails?" His tone is neutral, but I can tell there is a smirk in there.

"She actually chose it. I offered her the option of any one of your protected properties. Compound, which I wouldn't have done. Bar or strip club. I don't think she really expected me to take her to the club, but I figured I could kill two birds with one stone. Check on Lucky Tails and then look at a couple of clubs you wanted buy. She didn't have to know you didn't own the other ones."

Finally, he lets out a chuckle. "She will pick out the most uncomfortable thing every time, Simon. She was born to push the buttons of all who surround her."

"I'm quite aware of that," I say and pick up the phone as I head out of the bathroom and make my way to my office.

I'm naked, but the blood has stopped enough on my shoulder that I won't drip. Picking up my black bag, I walk back to the bathroom.

"Where is she now?" he asks.

Fuck. I knew that this question was coming. I knew it from the moment we left the strip club in our hurry for safety. I knew this question would come and the answer I have could be very bad for both her and I.

"Here at my home. I'll be able to keep her... secure here. No more threats of ripping her wrist open with her teeth."

"Simon," he says simply. "What are you doing right now?"

Unzipping my black bag, I pull out the small suture kit I keep inside of it. This is my personal medical supply bag. It has everything I need to take care of myself. Doctors can be useful, but I find I trust myself more than them.

"Preparing to give myself eight to ten stitches on my shoulder."

"Should I send Andrew over? He can do that for you." He says it more as of a statement than a question.

"No. I'd rather grow gangrenous than have that caveman try to give me stitches."

Pulling out a fresh packaged syringe and then a small bottle of numbing agent, I set them on the counter.

"Simon, why is my sister at your house?"

"Because she infuriates me so much she can't be trusted by herself again."

The laughter that comes out of the phone is shocking, just as shocking as it is for me to admit to anyone how much she gets under my skin.

"Truly, Simon?"

"Yes," I say tersely.

"Simon, should I trust you with her? Or should I trust her with you?" There's a small amount of humor in his voice, but it could easily be danger too.

"Lucifer, have I ever given you a reason to doubt my decisions?" I ask with a huff.

Numbing the surrounding area of the wound, I pull the suture kit open and thread the needle quickly.

Dumping two different disinfectants into the wound, I savor the burn as it cleanses the bite mark.

I look at my body in the mirror. She isn't the first person to give me scars that will always be there as a reminder. I have many of them. Many of them I can't easily see from my father. My back is a mess of his handiwork.

Lots of thin white lines; coat hangers were his favorite way to teach a lesson.

Then there's the one on my thigh from a knife, and the one on my right hip from a stray bullet.

Lucifer has paused for so long that one might think he hung up, but I know better. He's running everything he knows of me in his head. He's trying to see into the future, to see all the possible outcomes of what I've said.

"Be careful, Simon. Her loyalties... She may never be trustworthy. She's not the woman she pretends to be when she has to play nice."

"Oh, I know that, Lucifer. She's the reason I'm sewing my shoulder up. She bit me."

"I..." Lucifer starts then stops.

I do believe he's speechless.

"She's in perfectly good hands then," he finally finishes. "Come to the compound tomorrow, and if you can keep her secure enough, don't bring her."

"I'll be in late in the morning. I need to stop by the office. I'm going to see if I can watch the feeds for the bomber. I should be able to see him on the cameras."

"Good, I want this prick dead. Whoever ordered this hurt me personally. I want to return the favor."

"Just a thought, Lucifer, but I would be surprised if it was the Russians directly."

"Same here. Something seems off with that thought. We need to start pulling our men home, Simon. We're spread too thin. Put a call out to Governor Norton and tell him we want paperwork done for a full pardon."

"No," I say with an angry hiss that has nothing to do with the needle I'm pushing through my skin to finish up the third stitch.

"Simon, that was not a question," Lucifer says with a deep sigh.

"We do not need to bring him back. Your hellhound needs to stay in his cage."

"Get over your issues with him. Get the process started. Have Thad brought back into the city. Call

Jude and Matthias as well. Get them to put out feelers for recruitment."

"Why, Matthew? The others I fully agree with. But why?" I ask, and the fifth stitch goes into a wider part of the wound.

Pulling it shut, I tie off the knot.

"Because I feel something of a storm coming. The priest called me personally tonight, Simon. He called *me*. Something is going on again. I'm sending you out to see him. Tomorrow night if possible. Whatever the priest needs to say, we want to listen to it."

"I'll call Governor Norton in the morning. I agree with you, Lucifer, that we've been spread too thin. But if you're bringing in your hellhound... I'm not going to hold his leash. The hellhound is all yours."

"Just like my hellcat sister is all yours, Simon," he laughs an evil sounding chuckle.

I have no clue how he knows that nickname, but he does. As much as the men call me the Spider because I can find out just about anything... Lucifer knows things that no man should be able to know.

"One thing though, Lucifer... I thought you should know she got ahold of some bleach and has changed her hair color."

"Please tell me it's a natural color, Simon. I can't deal with a purpled-haired woman in my life. I already have Evelyn asking to dye her hair her school colors."

"Oh, it's natural alright. She looks exactly like you now."

"Fuck me," Lucifer says before he disconnects his phone.

Good. He deserves a tiny bit of the heartburn she's been causing me.

What in the hell did he mean she's all mine now though? Does he know? Has he read my inner mind? Does he know the ache she has caused inside of my chest? The deep down red ball of heat that burns through my body at the thought of her?

I stand up straight for a long moment, taking a deep breath in and letting it out slowly through my nose. Looking at myself in the mirror yet again, I look at the branding she has put on my body.

On my mind, on my inner self.

I don't have a soul... or if I did, it was destroyed long ago. What inside of me has she stolen from me? What has she taken? Why does she have this hold on me? I'd pay anything to know.

Hurried thoughts of her chained to the bed rush through my head. Her eyes flaring with hatred. Her lips parted slightly, looking delicate enough to bruise when kissing. Her pantyhose with the small runs being torn by my strong hands.

A bloody bite mark on her shoulder to match the one she gave me.

A cold chill runs down my spine and it has nothing to do with the temperature of the house.

Walking over to the shower, I turn the cold water on full blast.

Stepping into the water helps me bring myself back to center. To even out my mind and body.

I'm going to need a centered sense of self if I'm going to go back into that room with Meredith.

6
MEREDITH

I scream and scream until my throat is raw, but eventually give up. I don't know if Simon can even hear me, but if he can, he's probably just getting off on it. I hate him. God, how I hate him. I despise the pencil-pushing geek with every fiber of my being.

And I will get my revenge. Somehow, someway, he's going to pay for this.

No other man has ever had the balls or audacity to do something like this to me. Not even Ahmed.

Fuck... Ahmed. His face flashes through my mind, the image of the last time I saw him. The surprised gape of his mouth. His flailing arms. His stumbling Italian leather shoes. The horror in his eyes just before he fell over the edge...

No, no. Don't think of that. Get your shit together and figure a way out of this.

Taking a few deep, calming breaths, I clear my mind as I stare up at the ceiling.

The handcuffs hold no matter how hard I yank on them. Of course the frame of the bed Simon cuffed me to just has to be made out of strong, black metal rods that show no sign of bending or breaking. As much as I wish my anger and adrenaline would give me a burst of superhuman strength, I'm actually pretty weak and helpless.

I spend a few minutes trying to slip my hands out of the cuffs, but he snapped them on so tight there's absolutely no give.

Bound to the bed like I am, there's nothing I can do but try and figure out a way to get out of this. If I want to get out of this, I know it's going to have to be by pure wit and manipulation.

But how do I manipulate a man who seems to hate me as much as I hate him?

Threats don't work on Simon. Nor do sexual advances.

Ugh. For the first time in my life I wish to god I had a dick, so I could get myself out of this mess.

Seconds tick by. Seconds that turn into minutes. My wrists and shoulders begin to ache from all the yanking I did.

What the fuck motivates the man? Money? Power?

I could try to bribe him, but thanks to him and Matthew, I don't have access to any of my accounts. Those millions from my marks are out of reach until further notice.

I could play nice, but he'll see right through it. Weak? Repentant? That will probably work better, if I can keep myself from snapping at him.

Who am I kidding? Simon brings out the worst in me. He's bound to do or say something that pushes me over the edge of insanity.

If he ever comes back.

He could just leave me here to rot. It's what I would do if I were him, but then again I'm a cruel bitch.

I stare at the blank white ceiling for what feels like an eternity. My eyelids start to grow heavy. After all the energy I've expended trying to escape, I feel utterly exhausted.

I begin to drift off.

Then the door clicks open.

My eyes flicker open just enough for me to watch Simon stride into the room through the veil of my lashes.

He's shirtless, dressed in only a pair of fresh dark slacks. His hair is soft and brushed back like he just washed it. His glasses are gone and so is his watch.

My muscles want to tighten with anxiety, with anticipation, but I fight it.

Relaxed. I must remain relaxed if I want to appear

truly contrite. I want him to think I've learned my lesson.

He pauses just inside the doorway and the door clicks behind him.

Glancing at the bed, he seems unsure. Good. If he's not set on further punishing me then there's a fair chance I can still manage to get myself out of this.

He begins to walk slowly towards the bed and I can't stop myself from admiring the way his body moves. Especially all the muscles that ripple on his chest.

So that's why he was so heavy when he pinned me to the bed...

Beneath his dark suits he's been hiding a rather impressive body. He's all lean, tightly packed coiled strength. The way he walks towards the bed kind of reminds me of a big stalking cat.

It's a sin, really, such a body is obviously wasted on him.

Stopping beside the bed, he frowns down at me. "Meredith."

Peering up at him through my lashes, I try my best to keep my expression neutral, but it's a struggle. Especially when I catch a glimpse of the stitched-up bite mark on his shoulder.

My lips want to pull into a smug grin. I did that. I made him bleed.

I fucking marked him.

"Simon," I say and then lick my lips.

I can still taste a hint of him.

Simon's frown grows even deeper as his eyes follow my tongue as it runs along my lips. If he were anyone else, I'd take it as a sign that he's interested... but I know he's not.

A couple of heartbeats pass.

Then he asks, "If I uncuff you, are you going to act civilized?"

And there he goes being an asshole again. Me? Uncivilized? He's the one who handcuffed me to a fucking bed!

Taking a deep breath, I swallow back my anger. It will do nothing but hinder me here.

Eyes on the prize, Meredith.

Simon's eyes drift down, locking on the rising swells of my breasts before flicking up again.

What the fuck? Maybe I pegged him wrong. Maybe he is interested...

"Yes," I exhale and peer up expectantly at him.

I shift just a little bit, just enough to slide my dress up even more, exposing my thighs to him.

Once again, his gaze drifts down, and my heart begins to race with excitement.

Holy shit, so maybe Simon isn't gay...

His eyes trace back up my body and lock on my face, cold and expressionless.

Or fuck, maybe it's just wishful thinking.

Reaching into his pocket, Simon pulls out a small set of keys and fingers them. It's obvious he's conflicted about releasing me, but I also think he's doing it just to taunt me.

Reminding me that he literally holds my freedom in his hands.

"If you fucking bite me again..." he warns, and again I have to hold my smug grin back.

"I won't, I promise," I say instead.

Simon gives me a look like he doesn't believe me.

He shouldn't. If I could get away with it, I'd chew through his fucking neck.

"I'm serious, Meredith. If you fucking bite me, there will be dire consequences."

Oh, *dire consequences*. I'm shaking in my boots. What's he going to do? Keep me handcuffed to this bed until I piss myself and starve to death? He can't. Matthew won't let him. My stepbrother and I may hate each other, but we're still family and there's an unspoken agreement between us.

Matthew won't try to snuff me out until I become a danger to his family or too much of a burden to him.

And I don't think we've reached that point yet.

It takes every ounce of my willpower to keep from snapping at Simon as he just stands there, fingering the keys in his hands. I want to yell at him what's taking him so long? Is he that much of a pussy? Scared of a little woman handcuffed to a bed?

But that's probably exactly what he wants so I keep myself under control. Promising myself I'll pay him back for this.

Finally, he takes a step closer and leans over the bed. Angling himself in a way that avoids any part of his body getting near my face.

Going for the hand closest to him, he grabs my arm roughly in one hand while the other unlocks it.

As soon as the handcuff opens, I just let my hand drop. What I really want to do is claw his fucking eyes out, but that won't get my other wrist unlocked, will it?

Simon hesitates. In order to unlock my other wrist, he's going to have to lean across my body to do it.

I'd bask in his hesitation if I wasn't so worried it would stop him.

Simon glances down at my face, but I just stare at him. He keeps his gaze trained on my face as he slowly leans over me.

The bed dips as one of his knees comes down on top of it. I flex the fingers in my free hand and roll my wrist to work some of the stiffness out of it.

Simon's face looms closer and closer.

So close, it would take no effort at all to lean up and bite him again.

I don't know why, but I have this unexplainable urge to sink my teeth into him. There's just something in him that brings out all these primal urges in me.

No other man has ever affected me in such a way.

No other man has ever made me feel so much that I can't contain it.

I stare into his face, into his eyes. Without his glasses, he doesn't seem so closed off. It's almost like a barrier has been removed between us.

Grabbing my cuffed arm, he struggles with trying to unlock it without looking at it.

The corners of my lips start to tip up of their own volition.

His eyes lock on my mouth and an unmistakable flash of heat, of *want*, flares inside them.

Oh shit, maybe I wasn't wrong earlier... maybe he does want me.

Partly out of curiosity, and partly because I just want to fuck with him, I arch up and close the little distance between us.

Before he can react, I press my lips against his in an experimental kiss.

He immediately freezes and his eyes widen.

A *zap* flows through me so strong I jerk back.

What the hell was that?

My heart starts to race, beating a frantic rhythm inside my chest.

I was only trying to fuck with him. I wasn't actually expecting to feel something...

Simon growls low in his throat and I watch in growing horror as the expression on his face darkens.

I try to pull away, to escape, but it's too late.

He grabs me by the hair and yanks me back.

Fuck. I pushed too far and something inside him has snapped.

His eyes flash and I experience a moment of pure terror as he growls out my name in a slow caress, "Meredith."

Before I can take a breath, before I can tell him *no, don't*, or even beg *please*, his mouth crushes against my mouth in a soul-shattering kiss.

I don't want this, *I don't*, I have to remind myself as my entire body lights up, coming alive under the press of his lips.

I don't like him, I fucking hate him, I repeat inside my head as I close my eyes and try to fight back the unwanted sensations.

But it's no use. Closing my eyes only seems to heighten my awareness and all the sharp sensations flowing through me like a current.

A current that is directly connected to him.

This is nothing like the times I've kissed all those other men. Those kisses were so cold and repulsive I could remain in my head.

When his tongue sweeps into my mouth and meets my tongue, my bones want to melt into the bed.

This is madness. Utter fucking madness.

As his weight comes down on top of me, a small, primal part of me welcomes it. Needs it, in fact. Needs him on top of me...

I don't understand what is happening. Why is my body betraying me like this?

I reach up and try to push him away with my free hand, but he grabs it and pins above my head.

Shit, oh shit.

I try to turn my head away, but with his hand in my hair I'm trapped. I can't escape him.

His tongue strokes against my tongue, hungry and demanding, and the jolt of pleasure that cuts through my core is so strong, so damn *amazing*, my hips lift off the bed.

With each suck and pull of his hungry mouth, my resistance breaks down, fleeing me. Slipping through my fingers like grains of sand.

I have to stop this. I have to put an end to this before there's no turning back. In an act of pure desperation, I bite down on his tongue.

Simon grunts in pain and rears back.

Releasing my wrist, he lifts his hand to his mouth, and there's this hurt look on his face as his fingers probe at his bloody tongue.

I feel a pang of guilt but quickly shove it away. He should be thankful I didn't bite the damn thing off.

Twisting around, I grab the set of keys he dropped on the bed. Snatching them up, I immediately and frantically try to unlock my handcuffed hand.

"You shouldn't have done that, Meredith..."

I slam the key home and nearly snap the damn thing in half as I twist it. The handcuffs click and open.

I yank my hand free and jump up from the bed.

Simon's hands come around my waist and I scream in fear and fury as he hauls me back.

"That was very, very stupid," he growls into my ear. "I told you if you bit me again there would be dire fucking consequences."

I kick and swing wildly at him as he struggles to pull me back down to the bed.

"Get your fucking hands off of me, Simon! Or I'll bite something off!"

I slam my arm back and he gives a very satisfying grunt of pain as my elbow connects with his ribs.

"A lesser man would knock all of your fucking teeth out," he curses as he releases my hips. "Be thankful I am not a lesser man."

I slap my hands at him, twisting away, doing my best to fight him off, but he still manages to get ahold of one of my wrists.

Fingers digging into my skin, he uses my arm to reel me in.

As he draws me closer and closer, my panic, my fear of what he might do to me, becomes a living, breathing thing.

Acting on pure instinct, I slap him hard across the cheek. My palm stings and his fingers dig even deeper into my wrist as his head whips to the side.

When his face turns back to me, his expression is cold, so cold, but his eyes are blazing.

I take another swing at his face. I have absolutely nothing to lose at this point.

The fucker manages to grab and stop my hand in mid-swing.

A slow grins spreads across his bloody lips. "Come here, princess. It's time to teach you a lesson."

"Fuck you," I snap at him and my panic rises a few notches.

I'm fucked. So fucked. And I don't know how I'm going to get out of this. I've exhausted every defense I have, and I've obviously only managed to piss him off more in the process.

I throw my weight back, but it's useless. He just jerks me back into him like it's nothing.

Thrown off balance, I stumble into him. He gives another hard jerk and I go tumbling into the bed.

Using my momentum against me, he manages to drag me across his lap. Then he yanks my arms behind my back, slamming my fists together.

"What? What the fuck do you think you're doing?!" I screech as I kick and struggle to both push myself up and escape his grasp.

Shoving my fists into the small of my back, he forces my upper body down into the mattress.

For a moment, I still. My body almost giving into the pressure. Into the constriction. Giving in like it needs it. Then I realize exactly where I am. I'm spread across his lap and something hard is stabbing me in the stomach.

Oh my fucking god. Is he seriously turned on by all of this?

And why does knowing that turn me on?

"You're a sick fuck," I curse and resume my struggle.

"Takes one to know one," he grunts.

Great. We're resorting to nursery insults now. How far we've come...

I kick and kick and screech. If only sheer willpower alone could free me.

He shifts beneath me and then brings his heavy leg down on top of my legs.

I buck my hips, but it's pointless. I'm completely and utterly trapped beneath the weight of his leg.

Head dropping forward, I pant to catch my breath. All my struggles have managed to do is wear me out.

I feel Simon shifting both of my wrists into one of his hands.

Shit. This can't be happening.

I give one more hard jerk of my hands but his grip sticks.

Then I feel his hand coming down on my ass, cupping around the curve of it.

No. No, no, no.

"Simon..." I plead.

I arch my back and twist my neck around to look up at him. He's staring down at my ass with an intense look on his face.

He begins to slowly slide my skirt up, almost like he's unwrapping a present.

There's so much panic inside of me now it's trying to claw its way out of my chest.

"I'm sorry! I'm sorry I bit you." And I am. Trust me, it's the biggest regret I have right now. I shouldn't have fucked with him; I should have probably just actually fucked him. Then I wouldn't be in this mess.

"Please don't. Please stop," I beg.

Fuck, I can't stand being helpless.

"You know… I think I believe you. I think you are truly sorry," Simon says, his hand pausing.

Hope swells inside me.

Then he yanks my skirt all the way up.

"But it's a little too late for that now."

I shake my head, my hope deflating. He's really going to do this. He's really going to fucking spank me and humiliate me.

Simon's hand comes down on my ass again, but this time I can feel the smooth, warm flesh of his palm against my skin.

I like the feeling more than I want to admit, and the pleasure his touch evokes wars with my anger over the situation.

Just like the kiss, the sensation of his skin rubbing against my skin is *electric*.

He gives me another squeeze and then he suddenly rips down my panties as he asks, "Tell me, Meredith, were you ever spanked as a child?"

"No!" I cry out, both alarmed and excited as my pussy is exposed.

He gives my ass one more hard squeeze and then says coolly, "I didn't think so."

I don't know what's worse, being exposed to him like this against my will, or the fact that the way he's touching me is turning me on.

It's making me want things... things I shouldn't want. It's awakening all these dark little cravings I carry around inside me. Cravings for a man who's strong enough to push me to the bottom.

I know I called him a sick fuck, but I'm really the sick fuck.

His smooth palm glides across my ass from top to bottom as if he's familiarizing himself with it and warming me up.

The way he explores me, taking his time, makes the dread of what's to come so much worse.

It's hard to ignore how prone I am. I'm completely and utterly at his mercy. Ass in the air, hands trapped behind me. Face towards the bed.

I can no longer feel his erection digging into my

stomach in this new position, and I can't decide if it's a blessing or a curse.

His hard thigh digs into my ribs and my breasts are pressed against the bed. The constriction, fuck... the constriction. I don't know what it is about it, but it's got my blood pumping so hard my entire body is throbbing from it.

It's too hard to keep my neck craned to look at him in this position so I focus my gaze instead on the blanket. Unfortunately, not being able to see his face, see anything, only makes me that much more aware of everything that's happening to my body.

The warmth coiling in my belly.

My nipples tightening into two hard points.

The slickness growing between my thighs...

Being pressed so close to him also makes me more aware of every little movement, every little change in his body.

The subtle shifting of his hips as if he just can't seem to get comfortable.

How his breath seems to hitch as his palm glides across the curve of my ass.

His hand leaves me suddenly and my muscles tighten with anticipation.

"Don't, Simon, *please*," I plead one more time, coming back to my senses and trying to stop him.

I don't know what I'm afraid of more. The humiliation, the pain, or the fact that I might like it.

His thigh tenses beneath my ribs a second before he ignores my plea. His hand connects with my ass with a hard *smack*.

My spine arches, and as the sting from the slap bites into my skin, my anger flares. The pain isn't terrible, I've felt worse. But it's the principle of the whole situation. Once again, he's stolen all my power, and almost all of my control.

"I told you, princess," he grits out. "It's too late for that now."

"Fuck you!" I curse and buck against him with everything I've got.

His hand comes down again, harder than the last time.

"I'll fucking kill you for this!" I scream.

I want to kill him for making me *weak*.

He makes a *tsking* sound. "Temper, temper, princess," he says snidely. "After all, isn't that what got you in this position in the first place?"

"Fuck you, you dickless bastard," I spit.

Yeah, it's not my most creative insult, but I'm just so worked up I can't think clearly.

My cheeks sting and the ghost of his hand crashing against them has me clenching my thighs together.

If he were any other man, this could actually be fun. I could probably actually enjoy this. But he's not. He's fucking *Simon*, the man who has become the bane of my existence.

"Have it your way, Meredith," he sighs.

His hand gives my cheek a hard squeeze and I grind my teeth together as his fingers pinch into my skin.

It's both awful and amazing at the same time. It's like the pain mixing with the pleasure is creating an entirely new sensation.

I like it so much I instantly hate it.

"This is for trying to run away," Simon says coolly as his fingers release me and his hand lifts.

I have only a split second to prepare before his hand cracks against my ass again. It's so hard I nearly bite my tongue off to keep from crying out.

"This is for biting me on the shoulder."

His hand cracks against me again and this time the pain explodes across my cheek and radiates across my entire bottom.

"This is for the *nine* fucking stitches," he says, angry emotion starting to leak into his voice as his heavy palm comes down.

Tears prick at the corners of my eyes. I must have thinner skin than I realized because that last one really hurt!

"This is for biting my tongue," he growls.

His hand cracks against me again and my entire backside burns like it's on fire. But worst of all my core throbs, wanting, aching, and begging for more.

But it's not the pain I want. It's his slip of emotion... His weakness. His anger.

His hand lingers on my warm flesh. Caressing it as if he's trying to both soothe it and cause the pain to sink in at the same time.

"Shall I go on?"

I shake my head back and forth.

His hand roams over my cheeks and his fingers are dangerously close to discovering how turned on I am.

I try to squirm away from him in a last ditch effort to protect myself. If he knows... God, if he knows, who's telling what he'll do with the information.

No doubt, he'll use it against me.

"If you want me to stop, princess, I suggest you apologize. I could go on all night..."

His grip suddenly tightens and my fists are shoved harder into my spine as he pulls me back.

I pant against the bed as he pulls my ass higher in the air.

He's giving me the power to end this. To slink away with the last shreds of my dignity in intact.

But apologize? Seriously? He wants me to apologize for the things I did to protect myself?

I can't do it. Fuck him. I just can't.

"Fuck you, Simon. Your idea of dire consequences is a fucking joke. Seriously? Spanking me like I'm child? Grow some balls... Oh, wait, that's right. You can't because they're in Matthew's pocket!"

"Fine," Simon tries to say like he's disappointed, but there's an undercurrent of excitement in his voice. "Have it your way."

Pressed so close to him, I can feel the rapid rise and fall of his chest. Oh shit, is he getting as turned on as I am?

His hand roams over my ass, exploring as if he's mapping out where he wants to spank me next. Then, before I can say or do anything to distract him, his hand is suddenly between both cheeks.

We both freeze. Me in fear and him with sudden realization.

"Fuck, you're soaking wet," he finally hisses.

My shame, my mortification is so great, I don't know what to say.

His hand pushes in, fighting through the squeeze of my thighs as I try to lock my knees together. I want to both shove him out and welcome him.

"Do you like me punishing your ass, princess?"

His fingers find my folds, lightly exploring them.

"No!" I lie.

"Liar," he hisses as the tips of his fingers brush against my clit.

My hips jerk forward and I groan into the bed.

This is the worst fucking thing that could happen.

"Do you want me to stop?" he asks, giving my clit a flick.

"Yes!" I gasp out as I buck, trying to dislodge his hand.

He clicks his tongue against the roof of his mouth. "Lying again, Meredith."

"Go fuck yourself, Simon!"

His fingers pause and then he begins to drag them away.

And I've never felt more conflicted in my life. On one hand, I do want him to stop because the last thing I need is the emotional chaos him making me come will create. But on the other hand, I really, really want to come. And fuck, I want his crazy fingers to do it.

"I rather fuck you, Meredith," he rasps, fingers stopping and poised at my entrance.

I hate that my core clenches at his admission. I hate that my entire body seems to tighten and tingle with anticipation.

I hate with every single little fiber of my being that I *want* him.

"I rather fuck a farm animal," I growl out.

Without warning, without mercy, he shoves two of his fingers deep into my pussy. Spreading me open. I bite at the blanket, trying to fight off the spike of pleasure that slams into my core, but a moan still escapes me.

He pumps his fingers in and out of me once, twice, gliding along easily with my wetness.

And then he stops.

"Then why are you so wet?"

Why am I so wet? Because he's taken control? Because he's forcing me to face the things I don't want to admit?

He pumps his fingers in me two more times and it feels so good I just want to fucking die. But it's not enough. I want... no, I *need* more.

My walls clench around him, trying to squeeze more pleasure out of him. Trying to milk out even more sensation.

"Why is your tight little pussy squeezing me, Meredith?"

Because... because... despite how much I hate him, how much I utterly fucking despise him, he makes me burn in a way no other man has before. He makes me want to swell up and explode with all this turmoil he creates inside me as I gush all over his fingers.

He pumps his fingers in and out again, but doesn't stop this time. He doesn't slow. He drives them faster and faster. Pushing me higher and higher.

"If you hate me so much..." he grunts over the wet sounds of his fingers slamming into my pussy. "If you rather fuck a dirty animal..."

Suddenly he slams a third finger inside my core.

"Then why are you so close to coming?"

I want to deny it. I try to fight off the release gathering force inside me. It feels good, yes, but that doesn't mean I have to give him the satisfaction of making me come.

In and out, he drives his fingers. Pushing me higher and higher and higher. But I can't forget who's giving me pleasure. I can't forget that it's his fingers, his touch, his will that is forcing this out of me.

Just when I think I've gotten myself in check. Focusing on my absolute loathing of him to bring me back down from that line between heaven and hell.

He curls his fingers, stroking against that little bundle of nerves buried inside me. Suddenly the orgasm I've been holding back is forced out of me. A wave of hot, all-consuming pleasure slams into me.

With a keening cry of both ecstasy and misery, I try to bury my face in the mattress as I come.

"Yes," he rasps with undisguised male satisfaction. "Come all over my fingers, Meredith. Fucking come for me, princess."

The pumping of his fingers slows, matching the deep, squeezing rhythm of my core as I clench around him. Milking, squeezing, and pulling every little pulse out of him.

"That's a good girl. That's such a good girl," he groans.

I don't know how long I grind my hips into him. Time seems to slip away. There's only me and his fingers and his praise.

But when the last fluttering spasm of my walls

fades away, the gravity of the situation slams into the very depths of my soul.

Oh god, I just let Simon make me come. Not only did I let him make me weak, but I let him completely rule my body.

And worst of all, I let him make me lose control.

Slowly withdrawing his fingers from my now overly sensitive pussy, Simon seems to draw it out, as if he's not ready to leave me.

I whimper and jerk forward until he's completely out.

I should be relieved that he's no longer inside me, that his body is no longer a part of my body, but I'm not. No, I feel a little unwanted pang at the loss.

For a few moments, we're still. Me panting, and him breathing deeply. I don't know what's going to come next.

Is he going to fuck me with his cock?

Do I want him to fuck me with his cock?

Goddammit, at this moment I think I do.

Simon's hands tense around me, his fingers digging and releasing, digging and releasing, as if he can't decide if he wants to keep ahold of me or let me go.

And then he's pushing me away.

I roll off of his lap as he stands from the bed.

"Meredith," he says, his voice trying to slip into that cool, detached tone, but failing. "I... fuck."

Rolling onto my back, I peer up at him, my mind a confusing riot of emotions.

Is he done with me? Is he satisfied? Or is there more to come?

My eyes drift down. His cock is straining against his pants as if it's trying to reach me, and there's a wet spot from his own leaking precum.

He takes one step towards me, his hands coming out as if he's going to grab me, then he shakes his head hard and jumps back.

Without another word, he spins sharply on his heel and stomps out of the room.

The lock clicks into place a second after the door slams behind him.

7

SIMON

Meredith, let me count the ways that I loathe thee.

Loathe and crave.

Should those words ever be used in the same sentence? Can I possibly loathe someone so much that I crave her presence? I remember as a child my mother telling me once that the opposite of love is not hate but apathy. You have nothing inside you to feel for another.

Love and hate can be interchangeable at times because of how much you feel for someone.

Do I feel apathy for Meredith like I do for so many others in my life? No, decidedly not.

I don't love this woman who causes me so many headaches, but I can't quantify the exact feeling I have for her. How should I know? It's not like I've ever felt anything for a woman beyond the need for sexual release.

I've never been attracted to a woman like I am to her.

It's mystifying to me. I'm not gay, like some of the men in our circle think. I prefer the female form, but I've never preferred one woman specifically.

In my life, I have quite a few restrictions for how I normally deal with these types of urges. I use a singular agency for my sexual desires. They know the girl must be clean, sterile, and above all else silent.

She is not allowed to touch me or talk to me, and must be willingly tied down.

I cannot have some willy-nilly young woman moving about while I divest myself of my baser instincts.

Lying in the bed, looking up at my ceiling, I cannot stop the replay of memories as they flash through my mind. The way her tight stomach beared down on my rigid cock. The amount of precum soaking through my pants. The round, silky-smooth skin of her ass cheeks.

The way her tan skin turned bright pink.

She needed to be spanked, I can feel it in my depths. She needed to be brought to task for her misdeeds. She's as unruly as a school girl. I truly doubt anyone has ever said no to her quite like I did tonight.

Will she learn her lesson, though, is the biggest

question I have. Can I trust her to behave, to act logical? I doubt it.

Can I trust her in the morning when I leave for work?

No.

And damn the emotions I feel running through my body at the thought of being so damn far from her.

What are they even about? I feel desire to keep her here, to stay here, and make sure she is safe. But safe from what? Me or herself?

Damnation. Closing my eyes, I start the slow cycle of counting myself down to sleep. Normally this helps in times of my mind running too fast, or if I am trying to solve an issue with the business.

But not now.

Now all I can think about is her body pressing into mine when my tongue battled hers.

Damn.

With a will that surprises even myself, I force thoughts of her aside. I need to think about the damn bombing. What do I know and what do I not know?

The Russians for the longest time have been our biggest enemy, and they've gone to ground so to speak.

After the loss of Yuri, Sasha, and the good doctor Mirov, things have gone dark.

I've already watched the video of the bombing and have spotted the two men who inserted it near the DJ booth. It was clever to smuggle it in a briefcase, but it's quite upsetting that the security men that night didn't fucking spot it.

Thankfully, Peter did.

If the men who fucked up so badly weren't already dead, I'd be seriously tempted to question them to my fullest abilities.

How the fuck they missed something as big as two fucking men setting up a damn bomb... It's beyond me.

Again and again, I've watched the insertion of the bomb. It looked like the security inside the club was deliberately looking away from those two men.

But for what reason? Were they paid off? I've met some of the men who were working there tonight, and both heads of security were solid. They were paid well and knew fully well who they worked for.

Knew for a fact what happens to those who betray Lucifer.

I'm running the computer programs I've designed specifically for tracking the banking information of our employees and nothing's shown up so far.

Nothing.

All of them are on the up and up. No bartenders skimming money from the till. Limited drug activity with the strippers, and no extortion rackets of the business. Everything there was moving along at a predictable pace.

What changed that?

The Yakuza are no more, at least in Garden City.

Italians are here, but we've got them on our side... Well, as much as anyone is on our side. The Irish don't even have a foothold here.

It all comes back to who's the most powerful.

That's us.

But who has the most to gain?

Lacing my fingers behind my head, I briefly check the gun that's under my pillow. The smooth cold metal gives me comfort as I think over the night's losses.

The two men who did the insertion had nothing special about them, at least not from what I could see in the video. No tattoos, no outstanding facial features. They didn't come up in any of my or the government's databases on facial recognition.

I'll need to refine my search in the morning, because when all else fails, start over with a bigger fucking net.

THE QUIET BEEP from my phone wakes me up instantly. It's a sound I've ensured I pay attention to. It would do me no good to oversleep through a work day. Even if I was only able to get a few hours of sleep, I need to get back on the trail of the bombers.

Heading first to the computer room that connects to my bedroom, I do a quick check on any results that may have come in through the night.

Unfortunately, but as expected, we made the late-night news, as well as this morning's news across the nation. It may be in little video bytes, but we're still out there now.

Damn. Neither Lucifer or I want this kind of attention.

I check on the scan I have running on the government's criminal database.

Nothing.

Double damn.

Tapping in a few commands into another program, I rerun the search of the security team at Lucky Tails and add the rest of the staff there as well. I run from Cherry and all the way down to the latest girl we've hired.

Heading back through the bedroom, I stop off at the bathroom to take care of my morning dealings. Then I head down to the basement where I have my personal gym set up.

Whether I feel like it or not, I make sure I never forget to do my workouts. It would not be wise to ever allow my body to slip out of its peak performance.

Like my mind, I want to know that I will always be at the top of my game.

Sweat profusely pours off me as I push my body up from another pushup. I don't want the beefy look some of Lucifer's other men prefer. I'd rather have a fit frame. One that can go for endurance rather than for pure raw power.

The beep of my watch lets me know when I'm done.

I've still not come up with any answers from last night, but if I can get back the type of explosive that was used in the bomb I will maybe be closer to knowing who did it.

Heading back up the stairs, I stop at the door for Meredith's room. Listening intently at the door, I wait to see if I can hear her moving around.

All is silent though so I don't open the door. I could just as easily check the monitors in my computer room to see if she's awake, but for now I will give her some privacy.

I head back to down to the kitchen to make myself breakfast. Looking out the kitchen window as I start up my blender, I see the dark sky through the trees hasn't changed one bit.

Walking back to my bedroom, I pick up my phone from the nightstand and head into the computer room. No calls have come in yet, but they will soon enough. I might as well prepare for the ones I need to make as well. The computer searches are still running so I head back into my bedroom and begin pulling clothes from the closet for today.

Dialing the Fire Chief's number, I listen as it goes straight to voicemail.

"Call me back," I say and then press disconnect.

He's going to be a problem if I don't do something about him.

Scrolling through the contact list, I select a nationwide florist. It's not hard at all to get a lovely display of lilies sent to his house.

Hopefully he understands I won't be sending another bouquet to him if something unfortunate was to happen to his family.

Next I call a friend I have on the east coast. It will be a couple of hours later there so I shouldn't have any problems with him being awake.

"Simon," he says, picking up on the first ring.

"Erik, how's the city life treating you?" I ask as I tuck my shirt into my suit pants.

"Good, it's the city that never sleeps. Keeps me happy. What can I do for you?"

"I need you to visit a friend's dear daughter," I say.

"Where and when? You know this isn't my type of bag anymore," he grunts.

"I know, I know. No wet work needs to happen. Just a friendly hello."

Erik is one of my more interesting contacts. A former government special forces operative, we met two years back when I needed a trusted contact in New York City. He was able to secure a very important package from a diplomatic attaché from France.

When I first saw him, I was surprised at his seemingly young looks given his actual age. Even now he would not be out of place on a college campus somewhere.

That he's especially adept at seducing women into doing stupid things with state secrets is quite useful to me.

"Where and when?" he asks me again.

"Yale, and as soon as you can get there."

"Got it. What's the time frame of personal contact? How much contact do you want? You know I don't do the rough shit to women."

"No need, just have her contact her father for you. Try to be around when it happens. Be introduced."

"Got it. Look, I've got a job coming up in a couple weeks over in Ohio. I'll be needing some intel and maybe a safe house."

"Send me what details you're allowed. I'll consider us even."

"Sounds good. Send me her information. I'll go give her the Viking charm," he says before he disconnects.

Viking charm, he is so full of himself. But I can't argue with the results. I can only be annoyed though that he's right. He looks like a modern-day Viking. Tall, built, blue eyes and blonde hair.

Shaking my head out of those thoughts, I go back into the computer room. I'm almost finished dressing. Only my tie needs to be done now. Sitting down in my computer chair, I upload the file to an anonymous email account and send it off to Erik. I don't worry about his part of the job, he's a professional.

Now on to the Priest.

"Father Coss." his gruff voice comes through the speak phone, and I can tell I've awakened him.

"I thought you of all people would be up early enough to enjoy your Lord's blessings of birds," I say with a laugh.

"Simon Whitmore. I can damn you to hell... but I figure you've already came from there."

"True enough, Father. What is it I can do for you?"

"I have not seen you since three Christmases ago. I believe it's time to come confess your sins. You can't be too careful. Never know when the good Lord will take you into his loving arms."

Fuck. Whatever the hell is going on must be a bigger issue than he's willing to talk about on the phone, especially since he called Lucifer.

"Are you sure you wouldn't like me to send Andrew out? I seem to remember he's a good catholic boy."

"Simon, come to the fucking church tonight," he says and then he hangs up on me.

Well, isn't that just special of him. Whatever it is, the last time he had one of us come in it was big. Big enough that we're still paying off the investigators for the armed Russians that invaded a school in our city. All to get to one of our men's daughter.

Damn it all to hell.

The computer flashes a bright red warning icon on my search program as it brings up suspicious information about someone from the search it's running. I have it running on all the people who worked for Lucky Tails.

There, on my screen, is a redheaded woman staring back at me from the latest picture we have of her.

Cherry, fucking Cherry.

Looking through the information, I see medium payments being deposited into her account over the last month. Each one doesn't amount to a large sum, but when added together it's as suspicious as can be.

Maybe she's the proverbial red herring? I don't know.

Rewatching the video feeds for the past week will take some time, but it can't be helped. Especially since I need to watch her specifically. Damn, it could be anything with her.

Pushing a command, I begin to break into her cell phone carrier's information banks. I need to see everything she's done for the past year on her phone.

Pulling my cellphone out of my pocket, I scroll down to Peter's name. I push connect and wait as it rings. It's not too damn early, he better be up.

"What's up, Simon?"

"Head to Cherry's home as soon as possible. I need everything you can find in the way of electronics.

Computers, safes, just about anything. In fact, grab some of the extra security guys we have and pack up the house."

"Cherry? What's going on?"

"She had suspicious deposits in her account for over a month and I need to find out why."

"Got it. I'll head over there now."

"Good," I say as I disconnect.

Turning back to the screen, I download all of her phone calls and text messages for the last year and a half. No telling how long something like this could have been happening.

I dial Lucifer. He picks up on the first ring.

"Simon."

"Cherry had some suspicious deposits. I'm going to run a full-scale dive into her life. I have Peter on his way over to her home right now."

"Cherry?" he asks, and his voice is neutral in tone, but I can tell his little mannerisms. He's perturbed.

"Yes."

"Tell me immediately what you find."

"I'll be late coming to the compound. Around lunch most likely. From there I'll head over to see Father Coss."

"Sounds good. Be thorough investigating her life. We need to find out who the fuck would turn one of my employees against us."

"That's my full intention. She may have been a red

herring for all I know, but I don't like the implications that would mean. If she was getting random deposits in her bank account, surely she would have spoken to one of us about it."

"Agreed."

"Matthew, I need to ask you once more to keep…"

"To keep what?" he asks after I trail off.

"To keep him in his cell. There is no need to have him out in the world."

"He's done his time there, Simon. Bring him home," Lucifer says with finality in his voice.

"Fine."

Disconnecting the phone, I slap it down on the table.

I shake my head. I may have web-strings all around the damn city doing my bidding, but Lucifer is ultimately my boss and I know very well he has his own needs.

If he wants the bastard brought out from the hole we buried him in, he'll get it.

Pushing a finger on the button, I wait for the one asshole even I find repulsive to pick up.

"What?" a man snaps in the phone.

"That's a very rude way to speak to one of your benefactors, Governor Norton," I say with a laugh.

"Fine, what do you want?" he asks with almost a whine in his voice. Such a petulant man now that he's been brought under our authority.

"Tsk, tsk," I say, "You really should be nicer to us. Since we are the reason you are sitting in the very chair you are sitting in right now. But that's not the matter at hand. It's time for you to try out one of the new perks that comes with your promotion."

"What?" he asks, confused.

"You're going to pardon someone, and I don't give a fuck what you have to promise to get it done. You will get it done, or we'll see how fast a governor can fall."

"There's no way I can do that. It will cause too much of a wave for me to..."

"His prison ID is 342563. He's at the supermax prison upstate. Get it done, Norton. I don't care if you have to suck the President's dick during the middle of the State Of The Union. I'll be calling you later this week to see how far along you are."

Pressing disconnect, I set the phone down.

My stomach growls loudly as I look at the blended fruit and protein drink I've left on the drink coaster.

Lifting it up to my lips, I drink it down as fast as I can and then head back out of the computer room to the kitchen.

Meredith will be needing breakfast soon.

SCRAMBLING TWO EGG WHITES, I bake a small plate of bacon with toast on the side. I've watched enough of her mornings over the years to know what she prefers after an emotional night.

Filling a glass of orange juice up, I place it all on a serving tray.

I knock lightly on the door before I push it open.

Walking into the room, I spot her there, just starting to wake up from her slumber. She looks as ravishing now waking from a long, tumultuous night as she does when she is freshly out of a shower.

Her pale blonde hair is a mess and her makeup is smeared in spots. But those pale pink lips, they look so inviting. So much trouble as well. Especially when I think of those damn teeth she has behind them.

Pointing to the door to the bathroom, I say, "There are fresh towels in the bathroom and linens in the closets. I suggest you clean yourself up. You look like you've had a long night."

An incredulous look crosses her face and her eyebrows lift almost to her hairline.

She gasps, "Excuse me?"

"I don't believe I stuttered, Meredith. You need to clean yourself up. You look like a common streetwalker right now," I sigh.

Damn. I don't think my words are coming out as they are meant to, but it's not like I'm used to talking to a woman the morning after relations.

No, I'm in new territory right now.

Last time I had a woman stay the night it was accidental... It was the night that Meredith came to Lucifer's house. I was so agitated by the whole ordeal that I called up the service I used for female company. I was so frustrated, that I forgot I left the woman tied to the bed frame.

I went to my bed without using her and woke up to her screaming to be let go.

So not only has Meredith cost me financially and mentally, she's cost me the one female service group in the city who could be held to my standards.

Damnable women, all of them.

"Are you fucking kidding me, Simon?" she asks with a hiss, and I can tell yet again I've said something too brutally honest for her.

"No, I don't kid or lie. If I have something to say to you, you can trust it will always be in full honesty. Now eat breakfast and get cleaned up for the day. It's not healthy to sit here in your own filth."

She screams out her frustration as I walk out of the room, shutting the door behind me.

As I twist the lock, I hear a thump against the door. Most likely a pillow.

"I'll make sure to have clothes for you this evening," I say through the door before walking away.

An hour later, I notice on one of my computer

screens that the shower in her room is finally in use. She must have tried waiting me out in pure spite. That's fine, she can be as stubborn as she needs.

She'll find that I'm the rock she will break against.

I frown at the screen. I've done nothing but go over Cherry's financial records for the last eighteen months. Nothing odd shows up until three months after Lucifer's ordeal with taking over his wife's former husband's financial issues...

How did we miss something like that?

Killing her was a mistake. Perhaps a costly one, for me.

Checking the clock, I notice it's getting closer to lunch time. Time to take care of the hellcat again.

I return to the kitchen and prepare three sandwiches, a bag of potato chips, and some fruit. Balancing three water bottles on the lunch tray, I walk back to her bedroom.

I open the door and check the dresser where I set the breakfast tray. At least she ate like a good girl.

I try not to smirk, but I'm afraid when I look at the aggravation in her eyes my mouth quirks up into one.

Setting the lunch tray on the dresser next to the empty breakfast one, I say, "I've prepared lunch for you and possibly dinner. I need to leave the house for a bit."

"So you're going to leave me here like some prisoner?" she snaps out at me.

"Yes." I shrug my shoulders.

"I'm bored," she says.

I point at the large flat screen television on the wall. "The remote is in the nightstand."

Turning to leave, I feel my hackles rise as I hear her leave the bed in a rush. Whipping around, I snatch the fork she has raised in her hand.

I have no clue where she was going to stab me, but I make sure she doesn't get the chance.

Pushing her hard, I send her sprawling back onto the bed. I watch as her hair falls into her eyes then I stalk forward and grab at both of her wrists.

"Meredith," I growl. "This is your final warning for the day. If you do something else, I will make sure you know last night was just a warmup for the real deal."

Her sputtering and cursing becomes so unladylike that I force both of her wrists into my one hand.

I push my free hand over her mouth and say, "Be quiet before I stick something in your mouth to silence you."

Seething with rage, her eyes try to murder me. Fat lot of good that will do her. I'm onto to her games.

"Good girl," I say, when she stops fighting my hands. "I'll be back tonight."

I remove my hand from her mouth and quickly push my lips hard against her plump pink lips. I don't dare try to taste her though.

I know the dangers of that now.

Her eyes widen in shock as I pull away from her.

Releasing her, I stand from the bed. This time I back away from her to the door and then let myself out. Locking the door behind myself, I head out to my garage and climb into the black Escalade. I need to hurry if I'm going to make it to Lucifer's compound in time.

Adjusting my firm cock around in my pants, I shrug out the tension in my shoulders.

Fuck.

Once again, she's brought out the worst in me.

8
MEREDITH

So my attempt to kill Simon failed miserably. I wasn't really expecting to succeed, but I wasn't really expecting his response either. After he left me high and dry last night, I was hoping, praying actually, that this physical connection between us was all in my head.

It was all just my sick, fuck up imagination, brought on by being cooped up so long in the townhouse without any male companionship...

But he proved that theory wrong the moment he pushed his lips against my lips.

Why the fuck did he do that? Why is he fucking with my head?

It's not bad enough that he has me caged in this room, locked up like an animal, but he also has to pour salt into the wound by exploiting my unwanted attraction to him?

Once again, I find myself struggling to understand what makes this man tick. He's smarter, much smarter than I ever gave him credit for.

And he's effectively turned me into a crazy woman.

Never in my life have I been so out of sorts. So... unable to control myself.

Control... It all comes down to control. He's effectively stripped everything away from me, and I'm desperate to get some of it, any of it, back.

My attempt to murder Simon might have failed, but he also failed when he didn't take the fork with him.

No, there will be no second attempt. Not only because I know he'll see it coming, but because, despite what happened to Ahmad, I'm not a killer. I'm not a complete fucking psycho like Matthew and his men.

That and I don't plan on being here when he gets back.

I'm going to use the fork to get out of this room. It's my ticket to freedom.

Smart as he may be, Simon really fucked up when he informed me he's going to be gone all day. Not only does it give me plenty of time to get my act together, it also gives me plenty of time to find a way out of this prison.

It takes me longer than I like to chip away at the door with the end of the fork until I can squeeze the fork through enough to push against the latch, but when I do I feel a strong sense of accomplishment.

Ha, take that, asshole.

I give one good push and the latch slides in. Another push and I'm out in the hall.

Pausing, I listen carefully. All is quiet. I tiptoe my way to the staircase and lean over the banister, checking the first floor.

There's no movement. No noise. Not even a beep.

Good, he's still gone.

Quietly, I slink down the stairs, on high alert.

It hasn't escaped me that this could be a trick. Given that I still don't understand Simon, I can't put anything past him. This could very well be another way to fuck with me.

If there's one thing I do know, it's that he seems to enjoy fucking with my head.

Reaching the bottom of the stairs, I make my way to the front door and can't help but feel like this has been too easy.

Then I spot the catch.

Beside the front door is a keypad for a security system.

Shit.

I step up to the keypad and read the display. It reads: *Armed. All zones secure.*

What the fuck does that mean? How many zones does he have?

Reaching for the door knob, I hesitate. If I try it will it set the alarm system off?

Probably. Fuck. And who knows who will show up. I doubt it will be the police. More likely it will be Simon or one of Matthew's other men.

It takes every ounce of self-control I have to keep from saying fuck it and trying the door knob anyway, but the last thing I want to do is try it and still be trapped.

There has to be another way out of the house, there has to be.

Backing away from the door, I turn around and consider my options. I don't know exactly how security systems work, but I know they're usually connected to the doors and windows. So messing with any of them right now is out of the question.

I walk through the living area, the kitchen. Searching for a phone, for a computer, for anything that will give me a connection to the outside world, but only come up empty-handed.

Simon's house is abnormally neat and orderly. The majority of his drawers and cabinets are half empty, filled with only with the necessities. Everything is sorted by color or function. I don't understand how anyone can live like this, but it certainly makes searching through his crap easier.

Makes it even easier to mess everything up for the fuck of it.

Once I tire of moving his things around, I move on to the other doors on this level. Of course there's a blinking thing by both the door that leads to the garage and the one that leads to the backyard.

The few interior doors, however, are clear.

One leads to a bathroom, the other to a closet.

The third leads to a set of stairs that I assume leads down to the basement. I really don't want to go down there, I really don't. Who knows what kind of messed up stuff he keeps in his dungeon. There could be bodies or other freaky stuff.

Besides, I doubt there's an exit.

Closing the door to the basement, I feel the need to scream in frustration. Why can't anything about this situation be easy? I'm not a stupid woman, I should be able to figure a way out of this.

Having searched the first floor, my only other option is to go back up. I take the stairs two at time, so frustrated I'm not so worried about being quiet.

Once, I reach the landing, I force myself to slow down. I don't want to miss anything because I'm upset. The clock is ticking.

There are only four doors on this floor.

One leads to a bathroom, the other to what appears to be another guest room. The third door leads to the room he kept me in.

The last door reveals the master suite.

Stepping into Simon's room, I eye his bed then take in the spartan furnishings. God, he's so boring. There's no color, no personality. Just gray, black, and white drab.

The first door I yank open leads to a bathroom. Of course it's so clean it fucking sparkles. It also reeks of disinfectant. The next door leads to his closet. All his shirts, ties, and suits are hung up and sorted by color.

I pull down one of his white dress shirts and then grab a black belt to go with it.

Simon still hasn't replaced the shirt he destroyed on the way here and I'd prefer not to walk around Garden City in my bra. I need to draw as little attention to myself as possible.

Quickly buttoning up the shirt, I wrap the black belt around my waist and check myself in his mirror. It's not the most fashionable outfit, but it will do for right now.

On a whim, I decide to push down my dirty skirt and panties then chuck them at his bed.

Bet he'll fucking love that.

Properly dressed for escape, I check the last door in this room, hoping for a miracle.

What I find is every evil genius's wet dream. An entire room full of computers and high-tech equipment.

A blast of cold air hits me as soon as I step into the

room and for a moment I'm almost dazzled by all the flashing screens. There's just so many of them. It's fucking visual overload.

Blinking, I move further into the room and count up the screens on the wall in front of me. There are ten of them. I do a slow spin and look to the other walls, counting up the screens. Ten on each. So thirty screens total in this one room.

How can he possibly watch all of them?

While the screens on the walls to my left and right seem to be live news broadcasts from around the world, the screens hanging above the desk in the back of the room look to be surveillance.

I approach the desk, a sick feeling growing in the pit of my stomach. Part of me knows what I'll find. I've had my suspicions...

Half of the screens seem to be locked on one picture, while the other half seem to be cycling through different scenes.

Sitting down in the chair in front of the desk, I start at the top and work my way left to right. The first screen shows the front gate of Matthew's compound. There's two armed security guards standing at ready in the guard shack, but otherwise nothing else is really going on.

The second screen is a little more interesting. It shows the inside of a bar or club and is actively using facial recognition to identify all the patrons. Little bits of text information keeps popping up on the screen, next to everyone's head.

The next two screens show the outside of two schools. I'd bet my left tit the two schools are Adam and Evelyn's.

The fifth screen is currently cycling but only between two images. The bedroom Simon had me trapped in and the bathroom connected to it.

That creepy fuck... I knew he was watching me. I just didn't think he'd be sick enough to watch me in the bathroom too. My skin crawls. Did he watch me while I showered? While I used the toilet?

Fuck, I rather not know.

The sixth screen is also cycling but through more images. At first it shows an empty living room then flashes to an empty kitchen. It takes me a second to recognize it as the townhouse I was living in. The screen flashes to the empty bedroom then flashes to the empty bathroom.

Goddammit.

How long has this fucker been watching me? How much has he seen?

The thought of him watching me while I was completely oblivious makes me sick to my stomach.

I suspected I was under some surveillance, but the complete and absolute violation of my privacy...

I don't even know how to fucking process it.

Is he watching me right now? My eyes quickly shift

to the next screen as the hair on the back of my neck stands on end.

The screen shows the outside of this house. Cycling from the front gate, to the backyard, to the garage, and back to the front gate again.

The next screen is static. It's focused on me sitting in front of the desk.

Shit.

If he's connected remotely to these cameras, he could be watching me right now.

And if he's watching me right now, he's probably on his way back.

"Dammit," I curse and start pushing buttons on his keyboard, hoping to trigger a command that will fuck with the cameras.

Nothing happens. No doubt he has some super-secret sequence or password to prevent someone from messing with this crap.

I grab the mouse and whirl it around, then search the screens for a pointer. My eyes fly over the screens I've already observed then stop dead on the ninth screen.

It's like some bad dream as I take in what looks to be a security check point in an airport.

The camera is focused on a man dressed in a dark suit, going through what I assume is customs. He looks annoyed, his mouth pulled down in a frown, and his gestures are short and sharp as the agent working with him glances between him and some paperwork.

I'd recognize him anywhere. It's Ahmed's brother, Asad.

Please don't be Garden City, I pray as I search the screen for a sign that will identify the airport he's in.

The agent nods his head and hands the paperwork he's holding back to Asad.

Asad angrily rips the paperwork out of the agent's hands then grabs his bag and walks through the lane he's in.

The picture changes and changes, following him as he walks through the airport. I manage to catch a glimpse of one of the signs advertising Garden City and my worst fear is confirmed.

He's close.

I knew it was only a matter of time, but I was hoping I could get away before this happened.

Now it's too fucking late. I'm a dead woman walking.

The camera sticks to Asad as he walks out of the airport to a black car that's parked at the curb waiting for him.

The camera moves away from him for a moment, zooming in on the license plate. The license plate is white bordered with red and above the random sequence of numbers it reads: Diplomat.

That's right, I remember Ahmed telling me that his

entire fucked up family has somehow found a way to secure diplomatic immunity in this country. He used to threaten that he could do anything to anyone in this country and there would be nothing to stop him.

I watch, my heart racing faster and faster, as the camera zooms back in on Asad. A driver takes his bag and pulls open the back door for him. Asad glances around himself and I swear he looks right at the camera before climbing into the car.

The driver closes the door and then heads to the back, placing Asad's bag in the trunk. The driver then walks back around the car, gets in, and the car pulls away from the curb. The camera sticks to the car until it disappears into the horizon then switches back to the airport.

I push away from the desk. Does he know where I am right now? Is he on his way to Simon's?

No. Not likely. He probably doesn't know my exact location yet, but given time and his connections, it won't be long before he finds me.

I have to get out of here. Fuck trying to be sneaky about it now.

I start to stand up when one of the static screens changes, drawing my attention. The screen that was focused on the guard shack in front of Matthew's compound has zoomed in on the front gate as it opens.

Once the gate has slid completely back, a black Escalade rolls forward. The guards in the shack are waving the car on but it comes to a stop. Then the camera zooms in even more, focusing on Simon's face.

He's staring angrily at his phone then he looks up, directly at the camera. There's no sound, but I can tell exactly what he's saying as his lips move.

"I see you, Meredith."

9
SIMON

Handful. Great word for what Meredith is. Spoiled fucking rotten by her father. Lived like a princess for most of her adult life. It's infuriating to see someone so damn unaware of her own damn self. She has no fucking control. Where I wouldn't be caught dead acting the way she does... she acts out with an almost reckless abandonment. It's like she relishes the trouble she causes. She's a complete little brat. Brat, like an ill-tempered child.

Pausing at the compound guard station, I roll down my window to show my face to the guard.

"You're expected, sir," the guard says to me.

"Yes, I wouldn't be here if I wasn't," I snap back before moving through the gate.

I know all these safety precautions are needed given the current state of our little world, but it's still a hassle for me. I remember the old days, before Lucifer became the man he is now. When we were smaller, less known to the outside world.

Small might be the wrong word for Lucifer's enterprises even back then, but then we didn't have all the strife we are currently dealing with now. It's not new to have little disagreements between rival factions, but it feels lately as if it's us against the world. The damn stress alone is causing my ulcers to go into overdrive.

Is it the stress of the fighting? Or is it the stress of having Meredith so far away, not in my safety, that stresses me so much as of late?

Pulling into a spot near the front of the house, I step out of my Escalade into the early spring weather. It's too damn turbulent, and unpredictable as can be. Snows and sun are not uncommon on the same day. I just wish it would go back to fucking full-on winter. That would make my mood so much easier to manage.

I can already hear peals of laughter coming from inside the house as I knock on the door.

Wonderful, the children are home. I had hoped with it being the weekend, Lily would have taken them out somewhere, doing whatever it is children do.

The door opens with little Evelyn smiling up at me. She has jelly and peanut butter on the sides of her mouth.

Just great, a sticky child touching door knobs and god knows what else.

"Hi, Simon!" she yells to me, even though I'm standing right in front of her.

What is it with children and yelling?

"Hello, Evelyn. May I enter your home?" I ask as I peer down at her.

"No!" she laughs out as she slams the door back in my face. Through the door I can hear her laughing loudly.

I slowly close my eyes and count backwards from ten. Ten... Nine...

By the time I'm down to four, Lily opens the door for me again.

"Hello, Simon. I'm so happy you could stop by. I see Evelyn is up to her normal, charming self," she says with a light laugh.

"Yes," I say. "She's a true gem."

Lily can see how my teeth are clenched when I say that, and it makes her laughter come out even harder.

"Oh, you poor thing," she says with only a hint of mockery. "You do know she loves you. Ever since Paul..."

Nodding my head, I keep silent. I liked Paul. He was a good man to have on our side and a very good handler of children.

From what Lucifer has said, Paul's death was quite hard on Evelyn. Her fragile mind understands death and the traumatizing way Paul was ripped away from her when he died protecting the girls. It's been hard on her and Abigail both. They have developed a support system with each other.

This is why I have formed my number one rule in my life: no children, *ever*.

"Matthew is upstairs in his office," Lily says as she escorts me in past the foyer.

Evelyn comes screeching back into the room with Abigail chasing hot on her tail. "Save me, Simon!"

Before I'm even aware of what's happening, Evelyn launches herself at my waist and she tries to climb up my body.

"What the fu—" I say, raising my voice as the girls begin screeching at me.

"If you finish that sentence, Simon, I'll have Matthew insist on you babysitting the children for the day. That includes little David."

She would too. Not that I wouldn't slit my fucking wrists the moment they left me in the room with the children alone.

Growling quietly to the girls, who keep trying to play tag around my legs, I say, "Dear young ladies. If you stop and do this around somewhere else, I will give you each a one-hundred-dollar bill."

Pulling my wallet out of my pocket, I get a very odd look from Lily. "You're so very strange, Simon."

The girls, spying the money, stop in their tracks with open mouths. I suppose they've never been bribed before. Never too young to understand how it works though.

Handing each one a bill, I watch as they race away from me, giggling like little hyenas.

"Simon, I should be mad at you," Lily says with a frown.

Grinning, I say, "Yes, more than likely."

Rolling her eyes, she motions to the stairs. "I set myself up for that. Somehow I know I did. This is going to set such a bad precedence…"

Heading up the stairs, I keep a brief eye on Lily's back as I ascend. Once I'm fully out of sight of her, I roll my eyes.

She's just lucky I didn't offer them a thousand dollars.

Walking the long hallway towards Lucifer's office, I can't help but think about the conversation with Lily. She's right about Paul and Evelyn I suppose. Ever since his death, she's been a little more…clingy to me. Like she needs a new person to torment.

Paul was her own personal guard when Lucifer wasn't using him, and she knew she could count on him to do anything for her. He even went so far as allowing her to use him as a big doll. Painting his nails. Putting barrettes in his hair.

I think it was his paternal instinct or some other foolish nonsense. I've obviously never had one of those. He did though.

Being maudlin about the situation though will do no good. Onwards and such. What else can we do, we know the lives we've chosen.

I stop outside of Lucifer's office and knock on the doorjamb. He's staring at his computer screen and waves me into the office.

Adam sits across from Lucifer. Even now he's a carbon copy of the man. Both wearing dress shirts, ties, slacks, and slicked back hair. They're often confused by outsiders as real son and father.

If I didn't know better, I would be inclined to agree.

"Are you sure about this, Adam?" Lucifer asks Adam with a raised eyebrow.

"Positive, Father. I know what my peers at school are using right now. If we invest now in the stock, we will see a large return," Adam says with a smile.

Adam. Now this is a child I can understand. He's a brilliant prodigy. As smart at mathematics as any I know, and probably more than half.

Under our tutelage, he has blossomed in his schooling. Lucifer has already had the school he attends advance him to sixth grade. I've no doubt he will be out of high school before he hits fifteen if things progress the way they have been.

"Excellent!" Lucifer says. He stands up from his desk and comes around to wrap his arm around Adam as they walk to the door. He hugs him tight to his side for a moment before saying, "I'm proud of you."

Adam beams with pride as he walks out of the office and heads back over to his own office.

Lucifer closes the door behind him and then turns to me, his smile sliding off his face like snow off a sliding off a hot roof.

"What the fuck happened?" he growls out to me as he walks back to his desk and perches on the corner.

"Someone blew up our fucking club," I snap at him as I slam myself down in a seat in front of the desk.

"I gathered that from the fucking fireball in the sky," he snaps right back.

Closing my eyes, I try to blink away the pounding tension headache I feel coming on. I have to take my glasses off to rub gently at my eyes.

"As it stands right now, I've got feeds in a five-hundred-mile radius in and around the city running. I have my programs tapped into all our government databases, combing through them as well as Interpol's. If the two men in the video I sent you show up, we'll find them."

"How is it that we missed the placement of the bomb?" he asks as he walks back to his chair and sits down.

"Perfect timing and opportunity. If you watch the feeds and pay attention to Cherry, you can see she's running interference for the two men."

"Damn," he swears as he slaps his hand down hard

on the wooden desk. "How did we miss her getting turned? Especially after Bartholomew?"

"The payments were in such increments that it looked like it could be extra deposits of her own. And when I look hard enough, she started making those deposits in cash after a couple of installments."

"Simon, this is something you should have fucking caught," his voice is almost growling as he stares at the screen on his computer.

Whatever he's seeing there isn't about this though. He's just staring at it, not reading it.

"Agreed," I say and place both palms on top of the shiny wooden surface.

The desk I rest my hands on is older than both of us put together. It came over sometime during the late eighteenth century. Its hard surface, while shined to perfection, has multiple scars from use over the years.

It was brought up by Lily once that he should have it refinished. That will never happen. This desk has been used as a warning to his men. As evidenced by the large gouge lines right were my wrists are sitting. He's taken more than one hand since he bought this desk and I've no doubt it will see many more in its future if Adam takes over the family business one day.

"Take your fucking wrists off the fucking desk, Simon," he says with a long sigh.

"It's not an offer you should take off the table so easily, Lucifer. I fucked up," I say.

"It's not entirely your fault her deposits went unnoticed. She was trusted. She could have fucking been another member of the circle if we had groomed her right."

Pulling back from the table, I sit back in my chair. I've thought about the consequences of what happened last night, and while I must agree it wasn't entirely my fault, I should have been on top of it. He pays me to be on top of things like this.

Has my head been too far up Meredith's ass to notice the things I should have?

Meredith, yet another larger issue I need to discuss today. Wonderful. Perhaps I'll just put my neck on the desk.

"I'm happy we decided against that. Especially now," I say with a smirk.

"Yes, me too. Now, where are we at with this whole mess?" he asks with a frown.

"I'm going through every aspect of Cherry's digital life. Her social media and such. Emails, texts, phone call dates and times. Peter is over at Cherry's house with a few of our security staff. They'll have it packed and trucked to one of the offices. We'll go through it all with a fine-tooth comb."

"Excellent."

"Hopefully it turns up leads we can chase down. Maybe the priest's call has something to do with this. I doubt it, but we could be lucky."

"Simon, are you believing in luck?"

"No, I'd rather not. But right now it wouldn't hurt to have some turn our way. Something is going on lately. Things are too quiet," I say, and they are.

Quiet can be good, I suppose, but when it gets too quiet I start to wonder what monster is out there scaring everything silent.

"We'll know soon enough," Lucifer says. "The priest has his ear to the masses. Let's see what he can come up with."

"Soon enough, I suppose." I don't like waiting for answers, not when it's something like this.

"Now on to a more familiar matter. What's going on in the life of my dear sister?" he asks me, and I can see a small smirk tugging at the corners of his mouth.

Why do I feel like the fly in the spider's web? Shouldn't it always be me who's laying the trap?

The hairs on the back of my neck stand on end as I say, "She put us in quite the situation with whatever her part was in the sudden death of Prince Ahmed."

"Has she given us any information we don't already know?" he asks, leaning back into his chair, his fingertips steepling in front of him.

"None. I wasn't able to question her last night after we got home, nor this morning. She was quite piqued. I should be able to get more information out of her this evening, or tomorrow at the latest," I say.

"Why weren't you able to question her, Simon? Was she that unruly?"

Just the memories of last night bring frustration to my crotch and an annoying twinge of pain to my shoulder. "She bit me quite thoroughly last night. After that, I was more inclined to be a bit warier of her."

"Surely she didn't bite you that badly, Simon? I thought you were joking with me," he says with a small laugh.

"Lucifer, how many fingers on your right hand does it take to count the times I have made a joke?" I ask in annoyance.

"So, she caused you so much damage you really did need stitches?"

"Of course, your sister is..."

"Simon, Simon, Simon... If we need to rid ourselves of an issue..." he says, but stops as I shake my head at him.

"She's not an issue we need to take care of like that. She can be brought under control. She'll reach enlightenment soon enough," I say carefully.

Lucifer looks at me for a long time. I can see the gears moving behind his eyes as he studies me. He's figuring out what my words exactly mean. He's trying to get a read of the way I react to him.

"Simon, how much of an influence are you under with her?"

"Some," I admit.

"Will this further complicate our business arrangements? I would truly hate for a second business to be blown to the ground because of something we missed."

"Hindsight is a bitch, Lucifer. You know that as well as I do. But to answer your question, no. Now that I have her here, under my thumb, things should be much easier to manage."

"Shouldn't you have said now that *we*?" he asks and there comes that slight smirk of his lips at the corners of his mouth.

He's playing me like a damn violin. He's gotten me to admit things I shouldn't have, and I feel too damn simple to have caught it.

"Stop it. I'm not some damn enemy, *Matthew*," I say as I lean forward with a growl.

Suddenly he leans far back into his chair, mouth opening up in a raucous laugh. "Simon! You of all people!"

"Yes, me, dammit," I say with a sigh.

He keeps attempting to look at me with a straight face, but each time his lips pull back to bear his teeth in laughter.

Shaking my head at his humor, I stand from my chair and button my suit jacket back up.

"I need to get going, the priest was quite adamant —" I say before I'm cut off by my phone ringing and buzzing against my side.

Glancing down at the screen, I see it's one of my

own security team calling me. "Give me a moment, Lucifer."

I lift the phone to my ear. "What?"

"They fucking took out the house, Simon. It's a ball of fire!" he shouts into the phone.

"Terry, who did?" I ask back quickly. "Why are you fucking calling me and not Peter?"

"Peter was finishing up... inside the kitchen. He saw something that spooked him and told us to run. He's gone, sir! Something blew up the house!"

"Gods below and above," I hiss out. "Get the truck with the belongings to the warehouse! I'll put extra security on your tails and they'll meet up with you."

"Yes, sir! We'll try to get there now. There's a lot of sirens coming our way."

"Just go!" I shout into the phone before disconnecting it.

"What the hell was that about?" Lucifer asks as he rises from his chair and comes around the desk.

"They took out Cherry's house and Peter was in it."

His face goes completely blank as he says, "How?"

"Bomb. Peter tried to do something, but was unsuccessful. He was able to get the security team we had with him out. That's all I know."

My phone starts going off again. Glancing down at it, I see it's the security cameras at my house.

Fuck.

Walking towards the door, I am moving before I

even speak back to Lucifer. "My house has movement on the inside. Probably your sister, but I need to check."

"I'll send Andrew to get the truck to the warehouse," Lucifer says to me as he follows behind me.

"I'll get James over to Cherry's to play coordinator. He'll have to speak with the police and the fire department. I'll have him take a supply of cash to keep people quiet."

"Good, but if people connect the names of Cherry and Lucky Tails, we won't be able to contain the mess," Lucifer says quickly.

"No chance of that. She never had her real name on anything she did at Lucky Tails," I say, as I rush down the stairs.

"Make sure of that."

"I'll try to get to the warehouse tonight if I feel Meredith will be safe."

"Make sure we put extra security on the warehouse. I don't want another explosion."

"Will do. I'll get Johnathan to bring in some of his old contacts if I can. We need more men and now, Lucifer."

"Push on the Governor. We need him now."

"I will," I say with resignation. "God help me."

Looking at my phone again, I watch as Meredith moves through the house. She's searching for a way out. Her movements are hesitant but deliberate. She won't be able to get out though, not without my help. But I can tell from the damage she did to her bedroom door, she sure as hell will try.

"Simon, this isn't the Russians," Lucifer says as we reach his front door.

He grabs me by my arm to turn me towards him.

"No, it's someone else. We'd know if it was them by now," I say, nodding to him.

"Find out who it is. I want this over with," he growls out at me.

"I have an idea I need to hunt down. Give me a bit. Can you get the priest to wait for me?"

"Of course, do what you need. Don't forget what else I've said. If she's a problem..."

"No, she's *mine*," I say as I pull my arm from his hand, turning to open the door.

"Then keep her ass under control."

I nod my head. "I plan on it."

Rushing out to my Escalade, I stop before entering.

Turning back towards the door, I yell to Lucifer, "I'm going to get a bomb squad out to the other men's houses and wherever we're most vulnerable."

"I'll be keeping the children at home for a while. Perhaps it is time for private tutors," he says as he shuts the door.

Taking a quick moment, I go through the interior of my car. Then I check the engine and underside of the vehicle. There's no way someone has had a chance to put one on me, but it doesn't hurt to be cautious.

Driving up to the gate, I keep getting buzzes on my phone the entire way out. She's moving throughout the house. Checking the surveillance, I can see that she is sitting at my computer desk.

As she looks up, I look up at the camera facing the compound's gate.

"I see you, Meredith," I say to her.

Turning my attention to the guard, I say, "Inspect every vehicle that comes through these gates. Double guards on the compound from here on out until further notice."

"Will do, sir."

Pulling out the gate, I gun the massive engine. I don't see any movement on the outside of the house. That's good.

But I need to make sure that she's safe with my own eyes.

Pulling up to the garage, my eyes scan around the outside of the house. I see nothing worth my suspicion, but I can't be too careful.

Stopping outside before I open the garage door, I step out of the car and pull my gun from my hip holster.

A quick tour of the surrounding perimeter of the house shows me nothing out of place. I run the feedback from my computer to my phone and double-check the last twelve hours to see if I've had any visitors.

Nothing. Good. I don't need to be blown up myself.

Walking back to the Escalade, I get it into the garage. Then I take a long moment to center myself.

I've seen her moving about the house. I need to be ready for anything.

Stepping out of the Escalade once I feel centered, I walk up to the door and stop again.

One more long moment of peace before the battle doesn't hurt.

Stepping into the mudroom, I can smell from here the disharmony of her actions. Once I walk into my kitchen, it's easy to see the evidence. It's everywhere. Mustard and honey is spread on top of the counters. Sugar and white flour bags have been dumped on the floor. Things like pickles and jelly have been dumped into each other's containers. All of my silverware and food preparation utensils are scattered about the room in a huge mess.

She's gone too damn far. Too fucking far.

I walk slowly out of the kitchen and work on untying my tie. Lucifer's words ringing loudly inside of my head.

Each stair I take sets my body on fire as I head up

to my room. She's in the computer room again and I swear if she has touched my children in that room I will...

I spy her sitting there in front of my monitors.

"Meredith, I know you're older than me by a couple of years... Don't you think by now that you should stop acting like a spoiled little brat?!"

10

MEREDITH

I'm playing my final hand and this could either get me exactly what I want or blow up in my face. From Simon's fiery eyes and furious expression, I'm more inclined to believe my antics are about to blow up in my face.

But what other option do I have? I've tried the doors. None would open. I've tried breaking the windows by throwing things at them. The chair bounced back and almost broke me.

I'm trapped like a rat in a cage. The only thing I can think to do, besides murdering him, is become so much of a pain in the ass, so much of a burden, he either lets me go or kills me.

And I rather he kill me if I have to choose between living and being trapped with him another day. I rather die than let him use my body against me again.

I note the tie Simon is gripping in his fist and then spread my lips in a feral smile, flashing my teeth.

"Yes, Simon. Clearly, I'm a spoiled little brat who never had to grow up. If you don't like it, perhaps you should just release me?"

Simon's right eye twitches, and I wonder if he's starting to develop a tic. I hope he is. I hope I give him so much heartburn, so much stress, he can't fucking eat for a week.

He takes one ominous step towards me and grits out, "I'm not releasing you, Meredith."

That's not exactly what I wanted to hear, but not unexpected either.

"Oh? So you like me being a spoiled little brat?" I ask and pick up the glass of water I have sitting next to me.

Simon eyes the glass and then looks to his computer equipment. Obviously, he's figured out where I'm going with this. "Meredith, I'm warning you... you don't want to do that."

"I don't?" I blink at him. "Why not? I'm a spoiled little brat, remember? I have absolutely no respect for your things..."

To prove my point, I tip the glass a little. Just enough for some of the water to slosh out and splash against his keyboard. Then I make an exaggerated 'oops' face.

Simon closes his eyes and takes a deep breath.

Such self-control. I'd admire him if I didn't hate his fucking guts.

"Just let me go, Simon. We both win if you do, and we both get what we want. This could all be over right now. Unlock the door and I'll walk away," I suggest reasonably.

"No," Simon says firmly and his eyes flash open as he takes another step towards me.

What the fuck is wrong with him? I don't understand this stubbornness. He's a smart, albeit very fucking annoying, man. Surely he can see the futility in this little game we're playing?

"Then I'm afraid you give me no choice…"

He pounces on me as I tip the glass over, upending the contents all over this desk.

"Fuck!" he roars out, slapping the glass out of my hand, but it's too late.

Torn between me and the damage being done to his beloved computer system, he hesitates before shoving the chair I'm sitting in away.

The chair rolls towards the wall and I nearly tip over as he makes a mad scramble to unplug the device. Squatting down, he curses harshly as he fumbles around then yanks a cord out.

When he straightens, he jerks the keyboard away from the desk and holds it away from him.

I can't help the giggles that bubble out of me as a stream of liquid leaks out from between the keys.

It's petty, so petty, but still amusing.

"*You*," Simon huffs as his attention returns to me. "Are going to fucking regret that."

Yes, yes, I probably will, and now would probably be a good time to make my escape...

I jump up from the chair then spin it around until the back is facing him.

Simon tosses the keyboard to the side. It lands against the floor with a loud crack as he stalks towards me.

With a scream of anger and fear, I charge forward with the rolling chair, knocking it into him with every ounce of strength I have.

Simon stumbles backwards as I use the chair to shove him into the wall.

Once he crashes into the plaster with a thump, I let go of the chair and run for the door.

"Meredith!" I hear him roar behind me, then there's a loud crash.

I manage to make it halfway through his bedroom and around his bed before I feel arms wrapping around my waist.

"No!" I flail. Kicking, punching, and screaming as he picks me off of my feet.

I know it's futile, but I'm not going down without a fight, dammit.

He's hauls me up with surprising strength and then slams me down on his bed.

"No!" I wail again once I connect with the mattress.

Clawing at the covers, I try to crawl away then his hands grab me by the hips.

I kick at him, nailing him in the chest, as he tries to drag me back down the bed.

"Goddammit," he curses.

His hands release me and I manage to scramble away a few inches before he grabs and yanks viciously on my leg, taking my knees out from under me.

I collapse on my stomach.

Pushing up with my arms, I kick at him with my other leg. But he manages to grab it and trap it before my foot connects.

Gripping my ankles, he uses my own legs against me. With a hard yank, he forces me to flip on my back.

I blink up at the ceiling in surprise. Then I start to kick at him with everything I've got, hoping I somehow manage to nail him in the balls.

His grip on my ankles tightens, going from uncomfortable to crushing. I scream at the heavens and start to sit up as his knee hits the bed.

I can't let him pin me, I can't. I know a repeat of what happened last time will completely destroy me. And besides, I'm not even sure what he plans to do... He might just very well kill me.

His other knee hits the bed and our eyes meet. His face is flushed but set with determination. Behind his glasses, I can see something dark stirring.

My fingers curl with anticipation.

This is it. Either I prevail here or it's all over...

Suddenly he drops my legs and lunges forward. I slap and punch at him. I get a few licks in on his cheeks. I even manage to knock his glasses off of his face.

"Enough!" he roars, shoving me down by pushing his hands into my chest.

"Fuck you!" I scream back as I continue to fight him. I claw at his arms, raking my nails down his flesh. My legs kick at his legs.

Not only do I want to escape, but I want to fucking *hurt* him.

"Just let me go, Simon!"

His hands move up, wrapping around my neck. Fingers flexing, they tighten and tighten until he's squeezing the air out of me.

My head fills with pressure as my breath is suddenly cut off.

Seriously? What the fuck is up with men choking me? Am I like asking for it or something?

"No. I'm never fucking letting you go," he declares as little dots start to flash in front of my eyes. "You're *mine*."

I try to shake my head, try to deny it. The lack of oxygen though is quickly taking its toll on me. My nose tingles and my eyes feel like they're swelling.

My lungs burn.

Aching for breath, for life, with every second that passes.

I focus what strength I have left on trying to dislodge his hands. Tugging, yanking, and clawing at them.

Using his grip on my neck to pull my face up, Simon's gaze bores into me.

"You've always been mine, Meredith."

Staring into his eyes, I finally realize the true hopelessness of my situation.

He's never going to let me go. Never. I can see it right there, the *possession* burning in the depths of his irises.

How the fuck did I miss that? Has it always been there, or is he just now finally admitting it?

I give one last weak kick at his leg. The edges of my vision blurs with a darkness that is slowly, but gradually, consuming me.

"And now you're right where I want you. Right where you've always belonged..."

His hands finally relax just enough for me to gasp in some much needed air.

"Beneath me."

Before I even have a chance to catch my breath, his lips push against my lips in a crushing kiss.

I struggle against him, still suffocating as his mouth blocks off my mouth.

I need air… I need air… my brain screams. I'm going to have to bite him, he's giving me no choice.

As if he's reading my mind, he pulls back just enough to give me a breath.

"I swear to God if you bite me, I'll bite you back," he murmurs against my lips.

He's so close I have no choice but to breathe him in, to suck his scent deep into my body. To fucking inhale him.

He smells clean, cool, and crisp. But there's also something about his smell, something my brain associates with danger and violence.

One hand slipping behind my head, he grabs my hair and holds me in place. His mouth pushes into mine again. So hard my neck arches back.

My senses reel. My mind feels like it's spinning. And I don't know if it's from oxygen deprivation, or simply madness.

I can't tell what's up or down. What's left from right. Do I hate this? Do I love this? Do I want to stop it?

His fingers tighten in my hair, tugging on my scalp. His lips crush into my lips so hard, my lips feel like they're bruising against my teeth.

One moment he's trying to kill me, the next he's kissing me like he can't get enough of me.

And it's confusing as fuck. But not as confusing as my own emotions.

I want more. I do. So much so that I can feel my body flaring to life with heat. It's almost like some switch has been flipped inside me.

All the anger, the frustration, and violence I want to do to him is morphing into something else.

Something that feels dangerously close to passion.

I want to slap him. But I also want to shove my tongue down his throat and show him exactly how much I hate him.

How much I fucking despise him.

How much I fucking want him.

Unintentionally, I make a needy sound and he shifts above me. His tongue suddenly thrusts into my mouth, forcing its past my lips as more of his weight comes down.

His body presses into my body, sinking me into the mattress.

The taste of him... fuck... the taste of him... I can't seem to get enough of it. His tongue lashes at my tongue and I rise to the challenge, lashing right back.

We seem to duel for what feels like an eternity. Lips, tongues, and teeth fighting for dominance. I can't give up yet, I can't. If we're going to do this, somehow I need to come out on top.

I put everything I have into the kiss. My entire being, my entire world focusing on winning. If I can just use my body to disarm him like I did to all the other men that came before him, I know I won't have to break. I won't have to lose another piece of myself.

Just when I feel like I'm getting the upper hand, that I'm overtaking him, I feel his knee nudging my legs apart.

He settles himself between my thighs and my stroke falters. A little thrill of excitement courses up my spine and I forget how to breathe for a moment.

It's all the opening he needs. His tongue thrusts aggressively into my mouth and his hips rock forward.

I'm lost, so lost, as his tongue overtakes my tongue and the hard bulge in his pants rubs against my clit.

Once again my body is betraying me. A biological weakness poisoning my will to fight back. It doesn't seem to matter that my inner angry bitch balks at the idea of submitting to him. Knowing that he wants me, that he's fucking *hard* for me, fills me with this urge to give in.

To give up.

It's like there's this little evil voice inside my head whispering that it would be so easy to just let go... *For once in your life, Meredith, just let go and enjoy it.*

But what will I lose if I do?

The possibilities are too damn terrifying. Never have I let a man rule me. Never have I let another man have this kind of power over me. Why start now?

As if he can sense my resistance returning, Simon's free hand roams down, stroking down my side.

The stroke is almost tender... until he pulls his hips back and yanks my shirt up.

My first instinct is to slam my knees together, but he's still between my thighs, keeping me spread open.

I begin to twist, fighting his grip on my hair, but it only causes his hold to tighten.

His hand slips between my thighs and my entire body jolts as his fingers touch my slick lips.

Just as suddenly as he touched me, his hand jerks back as if he's surprised.

His mouth tears away from my mouth and he growls, "Where are your panties, Meredith?"

Heartbeat in my throat, I try to regain some of my composure by giving him a smart-assed answer. "I don't know. They're around here, somewhere, Simon..."

"Around here, somewhere?" he repeats, as if it doesn't make sense to him.

His confusion though doesn't stop him from shoving his hand between my thighs again. His fingers find my folds. Pushing through them, exploring them.

I have to bite my lip and press my ass into the bed to keep from crying out as they brush against my clit.

"Have you done something malicious with them, brat?" he asks.

When I don't immediately answer him, he pulls on my hair.

"Of course not..." I gasp.

His fingers suddenly press down on my clit and I can't stop the jerk of my hips. "I don't believe you."

"Fuck," I groan as he begins to rub against my sensitive little bundle of nerves in tight little circles.

"Can't... a girl... get sick of wearing... dirty underwear..." I pant out as I try to fight back the liquid heat that's flooding my core.

"I suppose so..." he draws out as his fingers move faster. Pushing me closer and closer to the edge of losing complete control.

Sinking my teeth back into my lip, it takes every ounce of resistance I have left to keep from thrusting my hips up. To keep from chasing his fingers and the orgasm he's offering me.

Rubbing and working my clit as if he knows just how I want it, just how I like it, he drives me higher and higher against my will.

And just when I'm there, reaching an orgasm I didn't want but suddenly need, he pulls his fingers away.

Yanking his hand free of my hair, my head hits the bed as he reaches for my shirt. Before I can stop him, he's grabbing it and splitting it open. The fabric spreads open so fast the buttons pop off like a chain reaction.

"Yet, you're still wearing your bra..."

I stare up at him, trembling from the loss of my

release, and the only thing I can think to say, the only word that comes to mind is, "So?"

Where is he going with this? Why the fuck does he even care?

"So?" he repeats and then his hands move to the little thin strip of material that holds the cups of my bra together.

"So?" he repeats more angrily as he grabs the connector and yanks his hands apart.

The material snaps and my breasts spill out.

"You keep trying to play me, Meredith, like I don't know you. Like I haven't been watching you."

Simon stares down at my breasts with a dark gleam in his eyes, and for once in my life I feel utterly and completely vulnerable. Once again, I'm exposed and at his mercy. Yet somehow this is worse, so much worse, than when he had me draped over his lap with my ass in the air.

He looms above me. Confidant now that he has me right where he wants me. And I feel like prey pinned beneath a hungry predator.

I try to cover my breasts with my hands, shielding myself from him, but he just reaches down and pries them apart.

"Three months, Simon. You've only known me for three fucking months. Don't even try to pretend you have me all figured out. You don't know shit about me," I snarl up at him as he slams my fists into the mattress.

I'm pissed because despite how much I try to fight him, how much I try to resist him, he keeps overpowering me. And, of course, because he got me all hot and bothered and didn't finish the job.

My clit throbs, swollen and achy. Pulsing a heady need deep in my belly I can't turn off.

"Oh, it's been much longer than three months, Meredith," he says, his head dipping down. His mouth dangerously close to the tip of my nipple.

"Fine," I say softly, afraid to take a deep breath. Afraid of closing that last little distance between my breast and his lips. "You've been watching me for a little longer. So what? You still don't know me. I swear, you don't have a fucking clue."

"Try years..." He draws out, his warm breath caressing my breast. My nipple instantly tingles and tightens into a hard little point.

This is fucking torture, and it's obvious now that he's just fucking toying with me. He has to be. There's no way he's been watching me for years. No way. I would have known...

"I don't believe you," I hiss and try to jerk my hands up.

The corners of his lips tip up in an arrogant smirk as he easily keeps my fists pinned to the bed. "Five years, Meredith. A little over five years to be exact."

He gives my nipple one long stroke of his tongue then his head lifts, abandoning my breast.

He stares me down as my pulse starts to race. The implications of that confession fills me with cold panic. He could be lying, yes, but why the fuck would he lie about that? Why be so specific?

"Five years getting to know every little thing about you."

I shake my head and again try desperately to jerk my hands free from his grip. If only I was bigger and stronger... If only I was a man, I'd kick his fucking ass.

He suddenly yanks my arms up, pinning both hands above my head. I arch my back and buck my hips, but his hips grind back into me, pushing me down. The pressure torturing my still throbbing sex.

"I know what breakfast you eat each morning after you've had a rough night..."

And... that would explain the breakfast he brought me this morning. Shit.

He looks over my head, his eyes searching for something.

"I know that when you sleep at night you always end up hugging a pillow tight to your chest."

"Creepy fucker," I mutter and his smirk sharpens. Of course he was watching me while I was sleeping.

His face lights up with pleasure and he reaches for something above me.

"I know of the game you've been playing, Meredith. I know that you've been preying on weak, foolish men..."

Shit. Shit. Shit. Does he know what I did to Ahmed? Was he somehow watching then too?

His fingers squeeze around my wrists and I glance up as he begins to wrap something soft around them. Dammit. Fucker found his tie.

"I am neither weak nor foolish," he says as he wraps the silk around and around my hands, binding me.

"I know you never bed your prey. Which is a good thing, because then I'd have to kill them."

The silk suddenly digs into my skin as he yanks hard on the tie to secure it in a knot.

He leans back, watching me as I attempt to wiggle and pull my hands free. I have to get out of here. He's way fucking crazier than I ever thought...

He's probably going to kill me after this and wear my skin or something.

"I know that you're not due for your next period for fourteen more days. So it's impossible to excuse your behavior as PMS."

"Jesus Christ!" I exclaim and gape at him. He's keeping track of my fucking menstrual cycle too? This is too fucking surreal to be real.

Satisfied that I can't escape my binding, he sits back and begins to unbutton his shirt.

"Shall I go on?"

"Oh, please do... tell me everything about me," I say sarcastically, but he must take it literally.

"I know your favorite color is black," he says and his fingers move deftly down his buttons. Each one pushing through a hole as he states a fact he knows about me.

"I know your favorite song is *Purple Rain*. I know you were born in Saint Nicolas Hospital, and it was snowing that day. I know you lost your first tooth when you were six. You have a scar on your hip from when you fell off your bike while learning to ride it. You took a boy to prom who stepped on your toes all night. I know you would have graduated at the top of your class if you would have applied yourself better..."

"I guess you know me better than I know myself because I don't remember any of that shit!" I snap, utterly flustered and frustrated.

Simon reaches the bottom button, quickly undoes it, and shrugs his shirt off. My eyes must have a will of their own because despite all the crazy stuff he's spewing, they take a moment to admire all of his chest muscles.

Especially the way they flex with the tiniest of movements.

"Yes, I do believe I know you better than you know yourself. In fact, if you knew yourself as well as I know you, then you'd know that all you really need to reach your full potential in this life is..."

He reaches down and begins to undo his belt buckle and my eyes snap to his waist.

"A firm hand to guide you."

I roll my eyes. "Oh, spare me."

Simon yanks his belt out of his pants and my heart flutters with apprehension. Is he going to hit me now? Punish me?

"Is that really what you want, Meredith?" he says, gripping the belt in his hand. "Is that really what you *need*?"

Memories of last night rush through my head. Of being draped over his lap and completely at his mercy. The way his erection dug into my stomach... And his hands. His big, warm hands roaming over me, exploring me, squeezing me.

Then punishing me.

The spanks angered me, but there was also this... this... relief in the pain.

Simon grins as my skin flushes. My ass squirms against the bed as I remember the pleasure he brought me when he thrust his fingers inside me.

Even now, my core clenches at the memory of it.

He tosses the belt away, but I'm too messed up and fucked up in the head to find any comfort in knowing he's not going to hit me.

Then his hands move to his pants. As he starts to unbutton them I start to panic again.

In an attempt to stall him and keep him talking, I blurt out, "Is there anything you don't know about me?"

Simon's fingers pause for a heartbeat, giving me a second of false hope that I succeeded. His expression becomes thoughtful and his eyes look faraway.

Then he yanks down his zipper and pulls his cock free. Oh god, oh god. What is he going to do with *that*?

"Yes," he admits as he shoves his pants down his legs. "There is one thing I don't know... One thing I've always wondered about..."

I dig my heels into the bed and push up, trying desperately to get away.

He takes the time to completely shed his pants and socks before he pursues me.

Naked body coming down on top of my body, one hand grabs me by the back of my head and drags my face up to his face.

Staring into my eyes, he says, "What it feels like to be buried in your pussy."

Then he kisses me.

I stiffen, prepared to fight off his tongue again.

Unlike his first kiss though, he doesn't try to overtake me or subdue me. No, there's so much lust, so much desire in his kiss, the strength of it alone is enough to make me weak.

It's almost like he's trying to push all of his need into me. And there's so much *need*.

I flounder, drowning beneath the weight of his emotion. How do I fight off a man who's been waiting five years to get me in his bed? Do I even want to fight it?

I've waited so long for someone to know me. To truly know me. To look past what's on the outside and dig beneath surface.

But why does it have to be him? Why does it have to be Simon?

His hand comes down, cupping and molding around my breast. My back arches just enough to push it into his hand. I shouldn't want this; I know I shouldn't. But it feels somehow that we've gone too far now, and it's too late to turn back. I know too much now to ever look at him the same way again.

He begins to squeeze my breast, working it in his palm as his lips drag down, kissing across my chin, my jaw, then to my ear. There's something about the way he's kissing me now... something about the way his lips drag across me that makes me feel almost *cherished*.

If he'd just hurt me, or abuse me, it would be so much easier to resist. But he's grown tender all of a sudden, and I'm melting in his hands.

"Do you know how many nights I've laid in bed, dreaming about this moment, Meredith?" he exhales softly before his teeth capture my lobe and give me a little nip.

I jolt, my hips grinding up into him as goosebumps break out across my flesh.

His breath warms a path from my ear down to my

neck. And with my hips pushed up against him, I can feel the heat of his cock now pulsing against my clit.

Once again, I find myself shivering, nearly trembling. Then my muscles tense, bracing for the inevitable pain that's sure to come next as his breath puffs against my neck.

I feel his lips first. Soft, warm, almost caressing. Then his teeth.

My entire body jerks as he sinks them gently into me. There's no pain though. Only this hot, current of sensation that has me rocking my hips, gliding my wet sex across his shaft.

"How many nights I've dreamt of these breasts..."

His other hand comes down, fingers wrapping around me as his lips kiss a soft trail down my chest.

Looking down at him, watching the top of his dark head as he kisses his way down my body, I'm completely unprepared as his eyes suddenly roll up, clashing into mine.

"One thousand, nine hundred and twenty-two nights..." he says before he gives my right nipple a long lap.

There's no way... no fucking way...

I suck in a sharp breath and his hands squeeze around me hard. "I know because I counted them."

"Oh god," I groan out as his tongue drags across me again like he's trying to burn the revelation into my skin.

My entire breast feels like it's lighting up, his tongue setting me on fire. But my mind... my mind is reeling from the thought of him thinking about me for so many nights. Wanting this.

"Do you know how many hours I've spent watching you?"

He moves to the other breast and gives it long lap. I try to arch up, off the bed. This is too much... too much... but his hands keep me pinned down.

I'm breaking and he hasn't even shoved his cock in me yet.

"Keeping you safe..."

His mouth suddenly covers me and he pulls back a hard suckle. I swear it feels like the pull of his mouth is tugging on a string connected directly to my clit.

My nipple tightens and tingles almost painfully as all my blood rushes into it. Then he releases it with a wet smacking sound.

"Protecting you..."

Reaching down between us, he takes himself in his hand. His mouth latches onto my breast and he suckles hungrily as his hand guides the crown of his cock through my folds, wetting it.

Then he poises it at my entrance.

He releases my nipple with a pop and growls, "Knowing I could never have you?"

His head tips up and his eyes lock on me, trapping me with the intensity of his openness. There's such raw, naked longing in his eyes, I don't even know how to begin processing it.

"Knowing I could never have what's mine?" he says as he drives his hips forward, impaling me with the length of his thick shaft.

My back bows and my nails dig into the palms of my hands as he stretches me, spreading me open for him. It's been so long, so very long, it should hurt. But I'm so damn wet he glides into me without any resistance.

His head drops forward and he groans as his cock fills me up, stopping only when he reaches my inner barrier.

Then he just holds himself there. Panting above me. Hand coming down on the bed.

"Over five thousand hours," he finally rasps and then jerks, his head coming back up as my walls clench around him.

The way he looks at me... I've never felt so desired, so damn wanted.

He begins to pull back only to immediately sink back in like he can't bear to leave me. He pushes so hard, so deep, he grinds against my clit, trapping it between us.

I cry out, throwing my head back as he grinds me into the mattress.

"You can fight me, Meredith. You can try to run, you can try to hide," he grunts as he rolls his hips, punctuating each word before he finally pulls back. "But I'll always fucking find you..."

He slams into me. "Now that I have you, I'm never letting you go. Only death can come between us..."

My body rocks back from the force of his thrust and my breasts jiggle against my chest.

Grabbing me by the hair, he forces me to look up at him as he pulls out and slams into me, again and again.

"And even that might not be enough to free you from my grasp," he declares as he starts to fuck me into oblivion.

In the very marrow of my bones I know he means it. He means all of it. And god help me, staring up at him, I don't even want to fight it. I want to fucking revel in it. Revel in his obsession, in his fucking madness, because *I* caused it.

"Your body was made to take my body..."

It was, I nearly agree, but thankfully I'm so close to my release only a moan spills from my lips.

More of his weight comes down on top of me but his fingers continue to tug on my hair. Keeping my attention focused on his face, even as the force of the orgasm building inside me threatens to shatter all my senses.

"I'm going to fill every fucking hole in your body with my cock, Meredith," he moans.

He fucking moans.

"And I can't wait to take your ass."

His hips slam into my thighs so hard I know I'm going be bruised in the morning. But the pleasure he's inflicting makes it worth it. So worth it.

"Fuck, your pussy feels so good..." he grunts between pants. "Even better than I imagined. So much fucking better..."

My walls squeeze around him suddenly and that confession alone is enough to send me spiraling over the edge.

Knowing that's he wanted this for so long, that's he dreamed about it... that he's imagined it again and again... has me screaming out his name as wave after wet wave of orgasmic bliss crashes into me.

Overwhelming me.

Shutting out everything else in the universe until only the two of us exist.

There's only his body connected to my body. His cock pounding into my pussy. Swelling. Growing.

And now pulsing as he roars to the heavens.

Screaming out my name as his own orgasm hits him.

"Meredith. Fuck. Meredith..." he roars, pumping me full of warmth.

But he doesn't slow. No, he yanks hard on my hair as my eyes start to close, forcing me to keep my attention focused on his face. Focused on the moment.

Trapped. Held by his penetrating gaze, I watch the

last of his mask finally slip away. The true Simon revealed as he drives himself into me as if he never wants this to end.

Every word he spoke, every truth he revealed, is reflected right there in his eyes.

And it's so much, so fucking much, I have no fucking clue what to do with it.

But I do know one thing as his mask slides back into place and his pumping hips begin to slow...

If I ever want to escape him, I'm going to have to kill him. And after everything that just happened, even if I was a cold-blooded murder, I don't think I could do it.

Shit.

11

SIMON

Too many nights I've remained awake, unable to sleep, wanting something like this to be a reality.

In *my* bed, completely naked, Meredith is sleeping on her side with her cheek on my chest.

Her light breathing tickles my chest hair as she sleeps the night away.

And now I have what I've been internally aching for, the ultimate prize in the game of life. A woman who matches my ferocious desires, who challenges me in so many demanding ways...

She's the moon to my sun.

I don't simply want her to be my broken puppet. No, never that. Her spirit and fight are far too precious for that. If she can simply channel that energy into something more along the lines of what I want, she will be an unstoppable force.

Answering to no one, but me.

I will be her lord and master now.

Damn, how surreal it is to have what I've longed for, and yet now I worry about what it will do to me. Will it burn me out like a neutron star? Will I collapse into a black hole if I were to somehow lose her?

I can't let her go. Not ever. She will be with me for as long as I can hold her to my side.

I want her to remain the woman who enthralled me so painfully that I could barely breathe. But she cannot remain that woman, the black widow of powerful men. She brought too many men down to their knees, never giving quarter. She used her striking femininity, her analytic brain, and a ruthless cunning that rivals even her brother.

She may hate the relation she shares with Matthew, but she is cut of the same cloth.

Hedge fund masterminds, CEO's of banks, even soccer stars. No one was safe from her wrath.

Ahmed being the only one to turn deadly... at her hands.

If I were to use any type of psychological analysis on her, I would say she has deep down 'daddy issues'. Her father was a hard man and he had very little in the way of showing compassion.

He was a product of his own vices. He lived hard

and played dangerously. He ran the largest crime syndicate in the state, but couldn't manage to get past the dark ages. If he hadn't died when he did, I believe I wouldn't be in the position I'm in now.

Lucifer pulled the family out of the dark. He kept his cool under the storm that his father's death caused. He ruthlessly removed any who challenged him. Perhaps because she was seeing the man her brother was about to become, cut from the same mold as her criminal tyrant of a father, she seeks to punish them both by proxy through the men she has destroyed.

The buzzing sound of my phone pushes away thoughts of her killing her own father. I wouldn't have put it past her, though ruining men is more her style than actual murder.

Pulling my phone from the nightstand, I push the connect button, but don't say anything as I quietly slide out from under Meredith's arm and head.

As I move away from the bed, I don't give myself a chance to look at her naked spine. If I did, I wouldn't be able to resist going right back to bed.

"James, do you have the boxes?"

"Yeah, I have it all in the back of the SUV. What the hell am I now, a fucking errand boy?" he bitches to me.

"I'll meet you at the garage door," I say then push the disconnect button.

Risking just the smallest of glances back, I see that she's curling into a small ball around an errant pillow.

Her naked torso wraps tightly around the pillow as if it's a lifesaver.

Bits and pieces of our night flash through my mind in a chaotic mess of thoughts, desires, and actions.

I have no clue if Lucifer knows just how fully I plan on keeping Meredith to myself. Does he know that I had more than simple carnal desires for her? That I've come to need her like I need air to breathe?

Pulling on my slacks from last night, I hope the creases I so carefully maintain in my clothing holds. It would not do for anyone from the inner circle to see me so ruffled, even if it's by a woman.

Perhaps especially if it's by a woman.

I have a reputation to uphold. One of stiffness and sobriety. It does not do for those around me to see what's inside of my own mind. It's enough that they can barely control themselves, there's no telling what they would say if they knew I had my own demons inside that I struggle to control at times.

Slipping a fresh dress shirt on quickly, I slide a pre-tied tie around my neck. Feet into my dress shoes and I head out of the walk-in closet, making my way towards the kitchen.

I've already made James wait too long. I didn't plan on being in bed so late in the morning, but after a wild night of passion with Meredith, five-thirty came way too early for me. Even if I was awake by five, I'd still need more time to enjoy her sleeping on my chest. It was a constriction, of choice.

One I can feel slowly wrapping around my throat as surely as a noose.

I'm one hand away from tipping off the gallows. I wonder when it snaps my neck if I'll see God or Lucifer's smiling face?

All these dark thoughts and it's only six a.m. I need to get a move on if I'm to meet up with Father Coss. I have no doubt it will take Meredith her usual thirty-seven to forty minutes to get fully ready.

Opening the garage door for James, I walk through the dark room and stand there as the door rolls up.

"What the fuck, Spider? Can't you afford electric?" James asks as he investigates the dark garage.

"Would you prefer I light up the place? I'm sure if someone was standing about five hundred yards from here with a rocket launcher we would be small enough targets," I say as I point to the wall. "Put the boxes there."

"Fuck me," he growls as he hefts one of the clothes boxes from the back of a small SUV. "If there is some asshole out there with a rocket launcher, he isn't going to wait to see our asses with a fucking garage light."

"You may have a point," I say as I walk to the back of the SUV to grab a box myself.

"Peter's remains, or well what little they could find, are going to be interred at the same cemetery his grandmother was buried in. Father Coss will be doing the wake and service at Saint Michael's," James says as he passes me with the next box.

"Who's arranging it all?"

"Me. I asked Lucifer for the job," he says.

Hmmm, that's interesting... and probably for the best. James knew Peter the best, so I'm not surprised. Though it's odd, usually Lucifer handles things like this. He says it's his job to take care of his men when they pass. He calls it passing away, as if dying to a bomb is an everyday occurrence.

"Do you need assistance with it?" I ask.

"No, I got it. Need to take on more responsibility, as Lucifer likes to remind me. Besides, I know how Peter would want to be taken care of."

Nodding my head, I grab the second to last box and watch as James grabs the last. We both head back into the dark garage.

It's starting to grow light out and I can see the sky lightening up slowly.

Setting our boxes down, I look to him. "I've got an appointment with Father Coss today. I'll make sure all the fees are taken care of."

"Thanks," he says, then he looks at me with his head tilted sideways. He almost looks like a stupid dog showing confusion. "Why aren't you wearing socks, Simon?"

Looking down at my feet, I suddenly feel the tight leather of my dress shoes surrounding my toes. Damn.

"Fuck off, James," I hiss as I walk into the garage.

His loud laughter comes echoing through the dark recesses of the enclosed space. "You finally got some ass!"

He's still fucking laughing as he gets into the black SUV and turns over the engine.

Damn. Shit. And fucking rats of hell.

There's nothing to be done though. Pushing the button to close the garage door, I turn on the light. Time to start hauling in her belongings.

Collateral damage.

That's what James will be if I find out he tells anyone what he saw.

✝

CARRYING a breakfast tray into the bedroom, I set it down gently on the nightstand beside Meredith. Reaching over to her shoulder, my hand hovers barely a hair's breadth away from her.

This is it.

Last night could be considered a mistake of passion and lust. If I touch her bare, tanned shoulder, I'll be the one that's putting my head into the noose.

I'll have no more excuses within myself or for her brother.

Her breathing stops suddenly, and I can tell she's snapped awake. Her body fully tenses.

This is it.

Make the choice or have it taken from me.

Laying my hand on her shoulder lightly, I say, "I've brought breakfast."

Her body doesn't exactly relax, but it doesn't tense any further.

"Tha—" she starts but clears her throat quietly. "Thank you."

Her skin is so warm and silky to the touch, the small push of electrical current I can feel through our bodies runs straight to my cock. Stiffening from the memory of her tight walls of bliss, I fight off the shudder that wants to run through my body.

Standing up from the bedside, I walk over to my dresser to remove a pair of black socks. "Your clothing is in the closet, hung up next to mine. I've begun unpacking all of the boxes, but there are still more to go through."

"You, what?" she asks.

I can hear her sitting up on the bed. The rustling of the sheets lets me know she's covered her wondrous breasts.

Turning to face her, I say, "We have an appointment today. I need you to eat breakfast and get dressed. Something respectable."

Turning away from her gaping her mouth, I start to head out of the room only to stop to warn her.

"Don't push me on this, Meredith. We need to go to church and I promise you, if you embarrass me you will not like the consequences."

"Asshole!" she shouts at me as I walk out.

SHOULD I be surprised or worried that she heeded my demands to dress respectfully? Either way, I find that I'm enjoying it too much to be too worried. If she misbehaves, we can always revisit the night I spanked her.

The way her bottom turned pink gives even more life to my now constant semi-erect cock.

It seems my body has decided to betray me. No matter what I do or think about, a small glance of her, or the faint hint of her scent, and I become aroused.

I feel like a damn teenage boy, raging hormones all over the place.

Wearing a modest black dress, her hair is pulled back into a severe ballerina bun. Her long, graceful neck is adorned with a simple white gold necklace. A small cross hangs down in front of her tastefully hidden cleavage.

Tastefully hidden cleavage... What the hell is

wrong with us both? Her for being so damn placating right now and me for thinking those words.

Pulling into a parking space close to the front of the old massive gothic church, I place my hand on her lower thigh.

Looking over into her eyes, I soak in her shock at the contact of our skin. Even now I can barely keep myself from ripping the sheer pantyhose from her thighs so that I can feel the heat of her skin on the palm of my hand.

"Simon?" she asks in a low questioning voice.

Moving my hand from her knee, I lean forward and open up the glovebox. There, inside, is a velvet jewelry box.

Motioning for her to grab it, I say, "Please wear that. It has a locator device installed inside it in case of emergencies."

She pulls the thick, silver bracelet from the box and looks down at it, hefting it gently in her hands. "It's heavy."

Nodding my head, I watch as she fastens it around her right wrist. Thankfully she puts it on that wrist like I had hoped. The left wrist could have been a disastrous.

"Let me get out first, Meredith," I say as I climb out. "I'll come to you."

Taking in my surroundings, I check out the few cars parked in the lot. There aren't many this early in the morning. Especially with the slushy mix of melting snow and the grimy blackness of road soot.

Coming around to her side of the Escalade, I take another look around. Nothing stands out as a threat and I don't have any telltale gut instincts ringing alarms in my head.

Opening the door, I take her hand as I carefully assist her down from the seat.

She looks radiant. Like an angel gracing this world of shit, just fallen from heaven.

"I really didn't think you were going to take me to a church, Simon," she says as she looks up at the spires reaching into the ugly gray skies.

"Meredith, as soon as you realize I rarely, if ever, joke, you will see that when I say something I mean it."

Rolling her eyes, she lifts her wrist. "This bracelet is really heavy, Simon. What is it made of? Pure gold?"

"No," I say with a small smile. "That's the small electrical capacitor that's also installed inside it. I have an app on my phone that will immediately send the same current from a taser shot into your wrist if you should decide to run."

"What?!" she squawks at me, her eyes widening. Looking down at the bracelet, she tries to unfasten the clasp.

"I wouldn't do that. It's set on a trigger to go off once it's been sealed. If broken, you or whoever tries to take it off you, will get a nasty shock," I say as I come back to her side.

Putting my hand on her lower back, I feel her spine go rigid through her wool coat.

Turning her head back to look at my face, she says, "You joke."

"Meredith, what did I just say about joking?" I ask as I usher her towards the door. The wind has taken to a chilly gust. It pushes at both of our backs.

"I—" she starts.

"I keep what's mine safe, Meredith. Never forget that, ever. I will protect you, even if I have to protect you from yourself."

Though I'm not entirely sure what will happen to her hand if that taser goes off. There have been reports it could ruin the appendage completely.

Good thing she put it on the right wrist. I might have plans for the left hand.

Pulling open the huge oaken door, I all but have to shove her in and over the threshold.

I wonder if I would have to push her down the aisle if we got married?

Now that's a horrendous thought. Marriage. The death nail of any coffin. Maybe... Perhaps...

Who knows?

Ushering a now very shocked and silent Meredith down the aisle between the pews, I seat us in the fifth row from the front.

Spread out around us are men and women of varying ages, all either sitting or kneeling. Some with their heads bent, others looking up at the man on the cross.

We all have our crosses to bear, I guess. Though mine is more of the flesh than wood.

Meredith, how do I count the ways I want to possess you?

A small, older man comes out of the confessional booth and walks over to sit next to his equally old wife. Both sit silently as they look up at the church's ceiling. When they stand up slowly, taking each other's hand, and walk down the aisle, I catch Meredith with a small smile at the corner of her lips.

She has some romantic thoughts after all it seems.

Standing up from the pew, I motion for Meredith to remain seated.

"I'll be right back. I need to make a confession," I say with an annoyed sigh.

"You... Confess? Ha." she snorts quietly. "To which of your many... sins."

I just know she wanted to say *crimes*.

"Too many to do today," I say and walk away from her.

Turning back to her as I enter the booth, I look at her and then motion to my wrist. She gets the message, I hope.

Yep. The middle finger she shoots back at me ensures me she got it.

What a classy lady.

Pulling the curtain behind myself, I lean against the kneeling post and wait for the priest to open the little sliding door to address me.

When it slides with that unmistakable rasp of wood on wood, I say, "You summoned me, Father?"

"Do you have any respect, Simon?" Father Coss growls out from behind the partition.

"Respect for what?" I ask in confusion.

"Leaning against the post like a common hoodlum."

"Ah, forgive me, your eminence," I grumble out as I kneel.

"That's better."

"What did you want?" I ask.

"The damn city is tearing itself inside out trying to keep the peace, and it seems Matthew and you both won't let sleeping dogs lie," he says, and I can hear the anger in his voice.

"Us? What the hell do you mean?"

"Don't you use that word in here, Simon. I'm not nearly too old to slap you around this church."

"Try it Father and I'll remove your fingers one at a time with a pruning shear."

"You foul little demon."

"Yes, I know..." I sigh.

It's like this every time he insists it's me who comes to this damnable place.

"The Russians have reached out to me, Simon," he says after some time.

"Oh. When?"

Why in the world would they want to contact him?

"Eight days ago."

"That was before the bombing..." I say quietly.

"Yes, it was, and they were requesting a sit down with Matthew."

"What?" I ask in confusion.

"They didn't have a hand in the bombing, and they contacted me again to make sure that you knew that. They have no clue who did it and want that made clear," he says, and I can hear his voice clearly.

He's being emphatic, he really thinks they're being honest.

"Why the sit down?" I ask.

"Because the death tolls are getting too high."

"Yeah, on their side. They shouldn't run slave rings in our city. It's bad for their livelihoods," I say with a chuckle.

Our casualties... none. Theirs were far too many for them not to worry about.

"I agree, but that's not the damn point. They are trying to broker a peace and I want you and Matthew to hear them out. I don't care what you have to say about it. Just do it."

"Listen carefully, Father. This is your sanctuary. At our good fucking graces, it's yours. Don't push too hard. But I agree, we need to sit down and talk with them. Especially if they are claiming innocence in the bombings."

"Simon..." he starts to say, and I can feel his anger through the wooden wall between us.

"We'll talk to them, get a time from them, and we'll set the place. We'll make sure it's on neutral territory."

"Good, because I'm tired of the funerals that have been popping up recently. The loss of Paul and now Peter... I had a lot of hopes for Peter..." he trails off.

"Just because of his attendance to church, Father..." I start to say

"He was one of the fallen who had a chance of redemption, Simon. The same chance you've all had. Dammit. All of you have had a chance at one time or another. He was one of my flock."

Closing my eyes for a moment, I breathe in and out, then ask "What does that make us? The Fallen? Lucifer's merry little band of Fallen men?"

"Don't use that name here," Father Coss says and for the first time that I can ever recall I hear a tinge of sadness in his voice.

"Don't you want to try and redeem me?" I ask suddenly, and for the very life of me I can't think of why it would even matter.

"Would you even want it?" he asks back.

"Any and all costs for the funeral should be sent directly to me," I say as I stand from the post.

"Simon," Father Coss says, but that's all I hear as I pull the curtain shut behind me.

Heading down the aisle, I walk with long strides and grab at Meredith's wrist. Pulling her up from the pew, I watch as she must be debating on whether to make a scene.

Thankfully she doesn't.

Pulling her behind me, I cannot walk fast enough to get me out of this dark depressing place.

Almost bursting through the doors, I feel like I can finally breathe again.

Looking up into the sky, I smile for the first time today. Taking a deep breath of the freezing air, I smile. I hate this fucking city.

"We need to go," I say as I look back down at Meredith.

"Okay..." she murmurs as if she's not quite sure what to do with me.

Pulling her to the car, I first seat her then walk briskly around to the driver's door. Checking out the lot, I still don't see anything of concern, but the hairs on the back of my neck stand on end.

Damn.

Two choices. Get in the car and risk an explosion or search the car quickly and risk being shot.

Squatting down close to the dirty asphalt, I do a

quick bend over and search beneath my car. Nothing's there. No little telltale signs of a bomb. Opening the door quickly, I pop the latch of the engine hood.

My hand goes to the pistol under my arm, yanking it out of the leather holster when I hear a loud noise.

A high-pitched motorcycle whine pierces the air as I pull the door closed across my chest. I hide my head behind the window. I don't have enough time to jump into the vehicle as bullets draw a bead across the glass.

Six well placed shots slam into where my head is at and I flinch as each stops dead in their tracks.

Bulletproof windows, assholes, I think and then lean my arm around the protective barrier of the door.

The motorcycle starts to peel away from us and I can spot two riders on it. The one who was shooting is turned around, aiming his Uzi directly at the door again. I doubt he realized the shots were stopped by the glass.

I place three shots directly in the center of his side and spine.

The bike begins to waver as I place one more shot just the below the bottom of his helmet. I watch as blood bursts out from the collar of his tight-fitting leather jacket.

The guy that's driving reaches back to try and hold the dead shooter on the back, but it's too much of strain for him. He let's go of the man and slows as the body falls off the bike and onto the pavement.

I shoot three more times, trying to hit the guy racing away on the bike, but only one of the shots comes close. It grazes his left shoulder. It might have hit his skin, but with the leather jacket he wears I can't tell.

"Damn!" I shout as I stuff myself into the Escalade.

Slamming my key into the ignition, I debate for only the briefest of seconds on whether I should start it or not.

Flipping over the massive engine, I don't give it time to settle in as I shift into drive.

"Simon!" Meredith shrieks as she grabs at my shoulder. "What is going on!?"

"Give me a moment!" I growl as I push down hard on the gas pedal.

Luckily the parking lot is empty as I fishtail the armored Escalade around in a circle. Heading in the direction of the body, I slam on the breaks as soon as I near it.

"What are you doing?! We need to run!" Meredith shouts.

Shaking my head, I hop out of the door.

The body is lying in a large red slush of blood and snow.

Squatting down, I rip the helmet off his head and frown. Japanese. He's fucking Yakuza.

Damn.

There's sirens far off in the distance, and I can tell

they'll be here sooner than I'd like. I can't get the damn body into the car.

Shit.

Rifling through his pockets, I don't find anything of importance. Just a pack of Japanese cigarettes and a cheap lighter. Pulling up the right sleeve and then his left, I find tattoos. Damn.

Flipping his body over, I start to unzip his jacket when Meredith rolls down her window. "Simon what the hell? I don't want to die so you can get some cheap thrills!"

"Very funny, Meredith," I say with a laugh and smirk.

Ripping the shirt up, I expose his chest. He has the tattoos I was expecting there. No telling who he's working for on tattoos alone, but it's a damn good way to guess we've got another headache coming.

Pulling my phone out of my pocket, I take three quick photos of his face and a couple of his chest tattoos.

Running back to my car, I jump into the open door. Hitting the gas pedal, the car door slams itself shut as we screech away from the body.

Pulling a burner phone from the center console, I dial 911. "There was a shootout at Saint Michael's church. Some guy on a motorcycle wearing black clothes shot at another guy in a tan Tahoe."

That should get them looking for someone besides my black Escalade.

Disconnecting the phone, I hand it to Meredith. "Toss that out the window."

While she does that, I pull my regular phone from my pocket and press the Bluetooth function on my steering wheel. "Call Sommers."

The phone rings quietly through my speakers. "Detective Sommers."

"The shooting at the church, I want any and all information you pull off the corpse. Also, if you get lucky enough to catch the motorcyclist, give me access to him."

"Jesus, Simon. Could you go a day this week without having a major incident?"

"No," I say before pushing the disconnect button.

"Did you just call the police and tell them to give you information?" Meredith asks.

"Yes," I say as I slow my vehicle down.

Pressing the Bluetooth button on my steering wheel again, I say, "Call Matthew."

"Simon," comes Matthew's slow drawl.

"I was just ambushed at Saint Michael's by a Yakuza shooter," I say without preamble.

"Are you sure?"

"Yes. I have pictures of his head and chest tattoos. He's covered, and from a quick look they seem to be authentic."

"How did they find you?" he asks after a moment.

"I'm not sure yet. No tails this morning and I didn't spot anything before we went into the church."

"We?" he asks slowly.

"Yes, I brought Meredith along. I wanted to keep her protection under my care. Right now I'm starting to suspect I may have a tracker on me that I haven't noticed. But I'll have do a search for it, and then I'll need to switch out vehicles until this one is repaired."

"I see. I'll talk to Andrew. He should be able to scramble a private security service until we can get this matter settled," he says after a moment.

"Okay. I'll use Johnathan as a lookout while I do the search of my SUV and switch it out."

"As soon as you can, get on top of finding out which Yakuza boss we've seemed to upset," he says.

"Don't worry, that's going to be my primary focus very soon," I say and then push the disconnect button.

By the time we finally make it back to my home, Meredith looks as exhausted as she must be feeling. Her eyes struggled to remain open for the last couple of miles. The black Tahoe in front of me and the two following me have stayed as tight as they can which gives me some comfort.

Thankfully my computer systems have showed

nothing in the way of my security systems being compromised.

Pulling through the gate, I wait as the car ahead of us rolls to a stop. Four large men in black coats and military fatigue pants ease out of the vehicle. The car directly behind me pulls in past my surrounding wall, and the last car stops just outside of it.

The men in the front car pull their semi-automatic rifles out with them as they start to spread out around the front of the house. The men in the car behind us quickly get out as they spread around the yard.

"Is this protection really going to help?" Meredith asks quietly.

Nodding my head at her, I say, "Yes. I've used Twin Star Security in the past and I trust their men to do a thorough job."

"Simon, I'm... scared."

"Don't be. I told you already, you're mine and I take care of what's mine."

Getting out of the car after the lead security man motions for me, I say to him, "Ensure we're not disturbed."

Nodding his head, he asks, "Would you like us to go through the house, sir?"

"No, it won't be needed," I say as I come around the door to escort Meredith out of the Tahoe I've taken over.

"Very well. We'll have another car here soon. It will be roaming in a sporadic perimeter."

"Good."

It's only early afternoon, but I can already tell the day has worn my poor Meredith thin. Escorting her into the bedroom, I sit her down on the bed's edge. Kneeling in front of her, I look up into her tired eyes.

"The excitement will die down soon enough," I say as I drop my eyes down to her heeled shoes.

Taking them off slowly, I lift her feet up on the bed and pull the comforter over her body.

"Promise?" she asks after a weary yawn.

"Yes," I say, and then head into my office off the main bedroom.

Heading to the closet inside the room, I pull a new keyboard out of the box. I normally replace them after a couple of months. It's just too hard to get all the lint and refuse out from under the key buttons for them to be worth keeping.

Plugging into the system, I begin my work.

I need to figure out who the hell is trying to kill us off. It's the Yakuza, I'm willing to wager. But why now and what for, is the question.

The fucking tracer on my Escalade has been there for a small time. Maybe since the night at the club. Though with how sophisticated it is, I'm willing to bet I can trace it back to a manufacturer, or at the very least who built it.

12

MEREDITH

I wake up clutching a pillow to my chest and then immediately shove it away in disgust. Disgust for myself or for Simon, though? I'm not sure and it bothers the hell out of me. Ever since last night, I feel completely unbalanced.

Simon not only did a number on my body, he did a number on my head.

All those things he said... fuck. I honestly don't know how to process it.

Sitting up, I glance around the dim bedroom. It's empty, but I can hear fingers tapping rapidly against a keyboard coming from somewhere close. It must be his computer room. He left the door wide open.

Why is my first instinct to go to him?

Pushing that instinct away, I throw the blankets aside and slide out of bed. My thighs ache as my feet hit the floor and my mouth goes dry as I remember why.

Water. I need water. And perhaps a lobotomy, so I can forget that last night ever happened.

I glance towards the nightstand, checking the clock, and spot a glass covered in condensation.

Fuck. Did he know I'd be thirsty when I woke up?

Of course he did. He's been watching me for five years. Apparently he knows everything about me. Too bad I know jack all about him.

I grab the glass and drink deeply from it. Then I set it back down on the nightstand, purposely avoiding the coaster. It's a small, petty, rebellion, but still a rebellion nonetheless.

Every little bit counts, especially since that pit of raging fire I've carried around in my stomach seems to have extinguished. I want to be angry at him. I want to fucking rage at him and fight him.

But I just can't...

It's like when he fucked me he broke something inside me. He broke my ability to hate him.

Shaking my head at myself, I head into the bathroom to take care of my business. When I step up to the mirror to wash my hands and fix my hair, my eyes are drawn to the counter and all my toiletries.

It was unnerving as hell to walk in here this morning to find everything I need, everything I like to use waiting for me. Mixed in with his things.

And the devil's in the details, isn't it? Not only is all my stuff here, but he has everything placed exactly where I need it. My soaps are in the shower, my cosmetics and brushes are on the counter, and in the cabinets beneath the sink I found my tampons.

It's creepy as fuck, but also, strangely, a little flattering. He set this all up while I was asleep, and then brought me breakfast in bed, again. If I didn't know any better, I'd think he actually cares about me…

I shudder and turn off the tap. That's a terrifying thought. I know he's obviously obsessed with me, but to think he has real feelings… No, a man like him could never truly care about me in that way. I know his type. I've spent my entire life surrounded by them. Men like him, they only care about themselves. Their own personal wishes and desires will always come first. Sure, they might marry and have children. Take Matthew for instance. But ultimately their families are simply an extension of their possessions.

Things they acquire and hoard, until they grow bored of them.

And eventually they all grow bored of them.

With that sobering thought, I head back into the bedroom. I can still hear Simon tapping away. Sounds like he's very busy. It would be a great time to try and make an escape… if there wasn't a patrol of armed guards roaming the property.

And of course, this stupid bracelet on my wrist.

I still can't believe I put it on without really thinking about it. He just asked so nicely... fuck. Obviously, sex makes me stupid.

Approaching the computer room quietly, I pause at the doorway and peek my head in.

Simon is sitting in front of his desk, typing furiously while staring at the screen directly in front of him. The screen is black, but there's dozens of lines of what appears to be code in white text flowing across it.

The code scrolls by just as fast as Simon is typing.

I try to make some of it out, but the type of the text is too small to read clearly from here. I could move in closer, but even if I could read the text, I doubt I'd understand it.

Simon seems to be completely oblivious to my presence so I take this opportunity to observe him in his natural environment. Hunched over a little in his chair, the muscles of his arms and shoulders strain against the white fabric of his shirt as his long fingers dance across the keyboard.

His fingers move so quick, so sure, it brings up memories of when they were inside me. Driving me towards that release that was both wanted and unwanted. Before I can completely shut the memory down, my blood starts to pump a little faster and everything below my waist stirs, awakening.

"You may come in, Meredith," Simon says over his

shoulder, his fingers still tapping rapidly on the keyboard.

Caught spying, I hesitate. I wasn't planning on joining him. In fact, I think I'd prefer some distance between us so I can get this shit in my head figured out. Right now, I'm so out of sorts, I'm afraid I'm going to make another stupid mistake.

Simon's fingers slow and he finishes his work with a couple of clicks on the mouse. Then he turns his chair to face me.

His eyes peer at me expectantly behind the lenses of his glasses.

Never one to back down from a challenge, I lift my chin into the air and slowly approach him. I school my features into an expression of boredom even though my body feels like it's being drawn towards his body like a magnet.

"Did you sleep well?" he asks as I stop a whole foot away from him.

The air between us seems to crackle with tension. His fingers curl around the arms of his chair and his jaw tightens. He glares at the space between us as if it has somehow offended him.

What did he expect me to do? Throw myself at him? Kneel at his feet?

Not happening.

"Yes," I answer coolly and then raise my right hand.

"But this bracelet is growing uncomfortable. Will you remove it, please?"

Simon's eyes flick towards the bracelet, and either he's getting worse at hiding his emotions or I'm getting better at reading him because I can tell right away he doesn't want to remove it.

I let out a soft sigh and admit, "I'm not stupid enough to run now."

Both his eyebrows quirk up and I scowl. Of course he doesn't believe me.

"Seriously. There's way too many guys patrolling outside, and besides, this house is impossible to get out of."

Simon stares at me for a long moment and I can't stop my eyes from drinking in his perfect bone-structure. How did I not notice he's such a fucking handsome man before? Take off his glasses and ruffle his hair a bit and the man could pass for a fucking supermodel.

Finally, he lets out his own sigh, like I'm putting him out or something, and says, "Very well."

Reaching out, he grabs me by the hand and pulls me closer. I clench my teeth together as his fingers wrap around my wrist. His touch, just the press of his skin against my skin, still affects me in unwanted ways.

Ways that make me want to throw myself at him instead of ripping him into pieces.

He begins to turn back towards his desk and I have

no choice but to follow him. In a way, I kind of feel like a dog being led by a leash.

I could fight him on this, but what would be the point? The rage is gone, lost in the things he did to me last night. Pissing him off now would only trigger another unwanted physical confrontation. The best thing I can do is pretend compliance and hope I can slip away without another incident.

Grabbing his phone from beside the sparkling new keyboard, I watch closely as he unlocks the screen. It would be useful to have his password when I do get another chance to escape. But after pressing his thumbprint against a glowing circle, his thumb moves across the screen so fast I have no clue what he typed.

For all I know, it could have been 'Meredith is bitch' or 'Lucifer is the bestest'.

He pulls up an app that looks like one of those radar maps that shows thunderstorms in the area and slides a button from 'armed' to 'disarmed'.

Jesus. He locked a fucking *weapon* around me. No wonder the thing was so damn heavy.

With a click, he unsnaps the bracelet, and I find myself holding my breath as he works it gently off my wrist.

Once the weight of the metal is completely gone and the bracelet is tucked inside the top drawer of the desk, I finally relax.

I give a little tug on my hand, expecting him to

release me, but he tugs back, pulling me closer. My thighs bump into the side of his chair and I nearly fall over it.

"Are you hungry?" he asks, his thumb stroking against the sensitive inner skin of my wrist as I straighten and get my balance back.

I shake my head, fighting to keep my toes from curling into the floor. The way he's stroking me makes me want to arch my back and purr like a cat.

It's absolutely fucking ridiculous. Without my hate, I'm entirely too aware of my body's responses to him.

"Are you sure? It's past the time you usually eat lunch."

My stomach flutters, but it's not because of hunger. I don't want to eat. I just want to get away from him before I do something stupid. Like act on a physical impulse.

"No. I'm not hungry, Simon." I frown and try to ease my hand out of his grip.

His fingers clamp down on me, not letting go. "Fine, then you can keep me company while I finish my work."

He gives a hard tug on my arm and forces me to stumble into his lap before I know what the fuck is happening.

I immediately try to pull away, but his arm wraps around my midsection and locks around me just as tightly as that bracelet.

"I rather not," I protest and squirm.

"This will only take a few minutes," he says, ignoring my struggles as he rotates his chair back towards the desk and grabs his mouse. He starts to click around.

I don't know what's more infuriating, that he can keep me trapped so easily with one arm or that he's focusing on his work.

Pushing my feet into the floor, I try one last time to stand up and free myself from his grip.

His next words stop me cold. "If you continue to squirm like that, I can't be held responsible for what happens."

I immediately freeze in place.

"That's better," he coos and his arm tightens around me once more, pulling me down until my ass is completely on his lap.

Once he has me settled exactly as he wants me, he resumes his clicking. His arm sliding against my arm as he moves the mouse around on the desk.

So much for slipping away without another incident. Fuck.

This is exactly what I was afraid of. Exactly what I was trying to avoid. Him forcing proximity again. His space invading my space.

His simple fucking presence messing with my head.

And I don't have anything to protect me now. He's

stripped me bare. He ripped away every preconceived notion I had about him. Every opinion I had and used to justify my actions is gone. Burned to ash by the flames of his want.

After last night's revelations, all I have is a taste of the truth and a bunch of confusing emotions. My resistance is hanging on only by a thread. A thread that's so stretched, so taut, that it could snap at any moment.

Shaking my head, I give up. What's the fucking point? He's the one in control here and apparently he can do whatever the fuck he wants.

I begin to relax against him and his hold around my midsection loosens. I turn my attention to the screens and try my best to ignore the way my body seems to fit perfectly against his body.

All our bits and pieces fit together as if they were always meant to be connected.

His heat is at my back, warming my spine, and his strong thighs are pressing into my ass. Even seated as we are, he's more than a head taller than me. His breath puffs against my crown, tickling my hair and threatening to drive me to distraction.

The screen directly in front of us changes, flashing to a desktop then to a surveillance feed. Simon clicks the mouse a couple of times and the picture zooms in on the men roaming the perimeter of his house.

If this is his way of reminding me that attempting to escape is hopeless, he's wasting his time. I'm not stupid, I fucking get it. What I don't get, however, is how he thinks I'm safer with him than out on my own. Especially when he has crazy people on motorcycles trying to kill him in church parking lots.

The screen remains on the roaming perimeter guards for a couple of minutes. With another click the picture changes. The outside of Lucifer's compound pops up. We watch the two guards in the guard house dig into their lunch and my stomach rumbles a little bit.

I guess it is past the time I usually eat by now.

Simon sighs. "Once I finish this, I'm preparing your lunch."

"I'm fine," I grumble out of sheer stubbornness. I don't want him 'taking care of me' and preparing food and stuff for me like I'm a fucking child.

"You're not fine, Meredith. You're hungry. And denying it is exactly why you need someone like me to take care of you."

I gasp and twist in his arm to glare angrily at his face.

His attention remains focused on the screen. The blue glow reflecting off of his glasses.

"I'll eat when I want to eat, Simon."

He doesn't even look down at me when he says, "You should eat when you *need* to eat. You're far too thin, as it is. Perhaps I should increase your calorie intake?"

Too thin? Is such a thing even possible?

"If you do that, I swear I'll go on a hunger strike," I promise him. And I will. I have to draw a line in the sand somewhere.

The corners of his lips twitch as if he finds the prospect amusing.

"There are ways to get around such reckless foolishness."

Why do I get the feeling he's already thought of this before?

I just have to ask, "What ways?" So I know exactly what I'm dealing with.

His arm flexes around me and his eyes finally drift down.

"Temptation. Force feeding. Feeding tubes... The possibilities are endless. In fact, I do believe there are contraptions specifically designed to keep a subject's mouth open against their will. Should I purchase one, Meredith?"

I blink at him and the corners of his lips pull up even more. Fucker is getting off on the idea, I know it.

"No," I answer and jerk away. Twisting back towards the screen so he can't see the utter defeat in my expression.

His lips drift down to my ear and I sense him breathing in the smell of my hair before he says, "Good. You know I will do everything in my power to take care of you. Even if it means stopping you from your harming yourself."

I clench my teeth together. I'd bite my tongue, but I'm so annoyed I'd probably bite right through it.

What he really means is that he'll do everything in his power to control me, and if I fight him, he'll make my life even more miserable.

Click. The picture switches to a view inside some man's car. I recognize the man instantly as one of Lucifer's men though his name eludes me at the moment. The man seems to be ranting and raving at himself.

"What the fuck is he doing?" Simon hisses.

Click. The picture changes, switching to what I figure must be traffic cameras. The exterior view shows a black BMW driving around a block of streets in circles. We watch the car drive the same four streets for a couple of minutes before Simon switches the live feed back to the interior view.

Stopped at a light, the man bangs his fists against the steering wheel and his head drops down in defeat.

"Who is that?" I ask.

"James," Simon answers, his cold, wintery tone alone showing his distaste for the man.

I instantly decide I like this James, even though I don't know him yet.

"He works for Matthew?"

"Yes."

"Looks like he's upset about something..." I point out the obvious.

Simon sighs. "Yes."

"Perhaps you should call him and find out what's wrong?"

"I rather not," Simon mutters. "I can never talk sense into his stupid, young brain."

The picture zooms out again, but from farther away. It almost looks like we have an aerial view. Is he tapping into a satellite?

"Why the fuck is he driving in circles around a college campus?!" Simon says angrily.

The picture zooms back in to the interior view. James is no longer ranting and raving though, and he's not driving in circles either. No, he's stopped and staring at something through his windshield.

Through his windshield, I can make out a group of young men and women standing on a curb, waiting to cross a street.

"Fuck!" Simon curses. "She's the fucking police Commissioner's daughter. If he... I swear... I'll fucking castrate him."

"Oh, that sounds serious," I smirk. "You sure you don't want to call him? Before he does whatever it is you're afraid he'll do?"

I don't have to look up, I can *feel* Simon's glare. With another angry curse, he snatches his phone off of the desk and types something in quickly one-handed.

There must be little or no delay with the live feed because once Simon stops typing the man in the car glances to the side, towards his phone on the middle console.

I watch him mouth Simon's name, scowl, and turn his attention back to the windshield.

"Looks like he's ignoring you..." I can't stop myself from chuckling.

"Yes, I can see that, princess," Simon hisses.

Oh, he called me *princess* again. He must really be pissed.

"Just call him."

"No," Simon growls, but he dials a number and presses his phone to his ear.

I hear a deep, rumbling voice bark something on the other line.

"Johnathan," Simon says with undisguised annoyance. "James is about to do something stupid. I need you to get over to GCC's campus and—"

The deep rumbling voice cuts Simon off before he can finish. Simon sucks in a harsh breath and his entire body tenses beneath me.

"Look, you knuckle-dragging Neanderthal," Simon seethes from between his teeth. "I don't care about some stupid curse—"

Out of the corner of my eye, I watch Simon pull his phone away from his ear and glare down at it.

"He hung up on you?" I guess.

"Yes," Simon snaps.

"I don't think the men respect you, Simon," I snicker.

Simon growls and movement on the screen draws my attention. James is unbuckling his seatbelt.

"Oh, I think he's going to get out of the car!" I say cheerfully.

"Goddammit," Simon curses. "I don't need this shit right now. With everything else going on…"

I don't know why I feel bad for Simon, but I do, and I feel the need to help. "Dial him and give me the phone."

Simon snorts.

James starts to pull open the door of his car.

"Okay. Don't do it. Do you have any popcorn around here? This should be interesting…"

"Fuck," Simon grumbles, and his thumb dances across the phone before he shoves it in my face.

I accept the phone happily and watch as James freezes with one leg out of his car and glances towards his phone.

He scowls again, and I'm afraid he's going to ignore my call, but he must think better of it. Snatching his phone off the console, he jerks it up to his ear as he exits his car.

"What the fuck do you want, Simon?"

"Hello, James…" I smile and purr out in my most seductive tone.

Simon's arm tightens around my midsection. He definitely didn't like that, but this is all about diplomacy. Something he clearly lacks and doesn't understand.

James's brows furrow together in confusion and he pulls the phone away from his ear, double-checking the screen, before he asks. "Who's this?"

"Meredith, Lucifer's sister," I say, my smile sharpening into a smirk.

It's been years since I've thrown Matthew's name around, and yet I still experience that old, familiar satisfaction over how just invoking it and my connection to it causes the recipient to react.

James's eyes widen and his entire body stiffens.

Splendid, I've got him exactly where I want him.

"It looks like you're having a rough day..."

James's snorts. "You can say that again."

"And you're about to make a very poor decision. A decision you will regret."

James's eyes dart around and he turns in a small circle. "How do you know?"

"Simon has eyes everywhere," I say elusively. No point giving away the secret. In fact, it's best he believes the worst.

"Fucking Spider," he mutters.

"You can say that again," I sigh heavily, hoping to evoke feelings of camaraderie.

James grins. I guess it worked.

He leans against the side of his car. "You know, when I stopped by his place this morning to drop off your boxes, he was wearing dress shoes without socks. I've never seen the uptight fucker with a hair out of place, let alone missing a piece of his wardrobe. Your doing?"

"Oh, yes," I confirm almost gleefully.

He laughs. "I hope you're giving him hell."

"Oh, I am," I chuckle back.

James's shoulders start to relax and I pounce. "Listen, James, things are very... chaotic right now for the family."

Referring to Lucifer's little criminal gang as a 'family' makes me want to puke a little in my mouth, but I know it's one of the tactics he uses to ensure his minions are loyal and feel like they belong.

James sighs and nods his head. A good sign, so I go on.

"Now is the time for all of us to come together. To support each other. Whatever decision you're about to make, whatever thing you're about to do, will affect all of us."

James takes a deep breath and pushes away from his car. I watch him glance towards the group of people who had crossed the intersection and now stand together, chatting on the curb of the sidewalk.

If I had to guess, I'd say he's looking directly at the pretty, young blonde.

"Besides, don't you think whatever you're about to do would be done better in the dark?"

"Meredith," Simon hisses.

I ignore him.

"And with less witnesses around..."

James blinks in surprise and for a second I'm afraid I've lost him, that I've gone too far.

"Give me the phone," Simon whispers angrily, but I jerk away from his grasp.

James is staring off in the distance as if he's in thought. Then his lips curve into a slow, almost seductive smile. "I suppose you're right."

I've planted a seed, and I have no clue what it's going to grow into and I don't care. For the moment, the disaster seems to be averted, and that's all that really matters right now.

"I always am..." I drawl out and then chuckle to show him I'm not really serious.

"Was that Simon I heard in the background?" he asks as he climbs back in his car.

"Yes," I sigh.

"He sounded pissed," James chuckles and shuts his car door.

"Oh, he is."

"You should help him yank that stick out of his ass," he says as he starts his car.

"Unfortunately, I'm not a miracle worker," I respond dryly.

James laughs and throws his car in gear.

"Look, James, I need to go. But if there's anything you need… anything at all, don't be afraid to call me."

"I just dial Simon, right?"

Ugh. "Yes."

"Alright. I will."

"Goodbye, James."

James's grin grows and his voice has a slight husky quality to it as he says, "Goodbye, Meredith."

13

MEREDITH

Simon yanks his phone out of my hand. Yeah, I pissed him off and I'm probably going to get it now.

I tense up, expecting him to grab me or do something to hurt me. His arm flexes around me and he lets out a long sigh.

Then he asks, "How did you do that?"

I blink in surprise. "Do what?"

He leans forward, forcing me to lean with him, and sets the phone down on his desk then motions to the screen. "That. How did you talk him out of acting stupid when you don't even know him?"

On the screen, James is pulling his car out into the street. He glances briefly towards the group of young people once last time then speeds off.

I lean back against Simon as he leans back and consider the best way to answer him.

Shrugging my shoulders, I say, "I read all his cues, and then just ran with them."

Simon makes an irritated sound. "What cues?"

Is he really that oblivious?

"Are you recording this?"

"No, of course not," Simon grumbles. "It would be a waste of resources."

"Okay," I drawl out. "That will make explaining this a little bit more difficult, but we can work with it. Do you remember when you first started spying on him, and he was ranting and raving?"

"Yes," Simon says impatiently.

"Well, that was the first cue right there. He clearly was upset about something."

"Obviously," Simon snarls, but I don't take it personally. This entire situation is no doubt frustrating the hell out of him. I don't know how the fuck he's survived this long if he doesn't know how to read people though. "But how did you know what he was upset about?"

"I didn't know. I still don't know."

"Then how the fuck…"

I smirk and shake my head. "I used his body language to make a lot of assumptions. I had a fifty-fifty chance of being right…"

"So it came down to luck then?"

"Yes, and..." I trail off with a snicker.

"And?" Simon asks pointedly.

"Well, it was easy to pick up on his dislike for you. Really, you should be nicer to your men."

Simon snorts against the top of my head, fluttering my hair, but I sense his body beginning to relax.

"He either changed his mind because I talked some sense into him. Or he did it simply because he picked up on how pissed off you were that I was talking to him."

"What do you mean?"

"I mean, I'm more inclined to believe he stopped what he was doing and heeded my so-called advice because he knew it would piss you off. As opposed to trusting a complete stranger he's never met."

"Meredith..." Simon growls.

"Are you almost done here?" I ask and purposely squirm on his lap.

His chin hits the top of my head and I listen to him take a deep, calming breath. "Yes," he says.

Arm rubbing against my arm, he grabs the mouse and clicks a few times. The image on the screen changes.

"Another one of your men?" I ask as a man with long hair and a thick beard appears on the screen. I think I recognize him from Christmas at Matthew's, and he helped Simon today with his car, but again, for the life of me I can't remember his name.

"Yes," Simon answers simply, not providing a name.

The man with the beard is tossing a baseball with a young boy in what appears to be a backyard.

I yawn and snuggle closer to Simon, bored off my ass watching them.

"Tired, princess?" Simon asks, pulling me closer to him.

"No, just bored."

"Almost done," he says and double-clicks his mouse.

A big, beefy man covered in tattoos appears on the screen. The man is roaming around the outside of an ugly industrial warehouse building. Checking the doors, windows, and perimeter.

I suppress another yawn. "Who's that?"

"Thaddeus."

"Are you checking on all of your men?"

"Yes."

"Do they know you're checking in on them?"

"Doubtful."

I snort softly. "So I'm not special, am I?

Simon sounds genuinely confused when he asks, "Why would you think that?"

"You watch everyone, Simon." I point out.

Which makes more than half the shit he told me last night absolute garbage. Gah, I can't believe he made me feel like his watching me was so much more than it was. And I really don't know why that it bothers me that it's not, but it does. If anything I should be relieved, not annoyed with him.

"Yes, but only because we're in a time of crisis."

I shake my head and roll my eyes. "It's still the same."

His hand leaves the mouse and he grabs me by the chin, forcing me to look up at him. "You think I watch the men like I watch you?"

A slow smirk stretches across my lips. He walked himself right into that one. "Yes."

His eyes narrow and his grip on my chin increases. "You're wrong."

"Prove it," I dare him.

I want to see what the hell he has on me. If he has anything.

Simon stares at me long and hard, and so many emotions flicker in the depths his dark eyes my chest tightens.

"Very well," he sighs with a look of resignation.

His fingers release my chin and he reaches for his mouse.

I turn, settling myself comfortably on his lap with my back against his chest, and look to the screen. Both eager and a little apprehensive to see what he's about to show me.

He clicks around with his mouse and his other arm unwraps from around my midsection so he can type on his keyboard. His body curls around mine as he leans forward.

"I have six hard drives dedicated specifically to you. One for each year," he says as he types something in one-handed. "And everything is backed up on a secure cloud service."

The screen flashes to a desktop then several windows pop up, each one a different folder. The folders are named in code, each beginning with an 'M' followed by a long set of numbers.

"What would you like to see?"

I stare at all the files stuffed in the folders, unable to tell what any of them hold. There's no previews, no clue of the contents in the file names. It's all some weird system only he must know.

Five years. Over five years of my life is at his fingertips, if he can be believed. I try to think of some special moment I'd like to relive again, but only come up empty.

I finally settle on, "Show me your favorite."

Simon's body tenses around mine. I guess he wasn't expecting that.

This should be good. I almost wish I had that popcorn now. If I had to place a bet, I'd bet his favorite moment is probably me in the shower.

The mouse circles around and around on the screen. No doubt he's carefully considering what he wants to show me. He's probably trying to figure out what I *want* to see.

Finally, he double-clicks on a file in the dead center of the first folder. The scene that pops up confuses me at first. It takes me several seconds to place it.

But when I do, I turn to look up at him in shock. "This is your favorite?"

Simon's chest rises against me as he sucks in a deep breath.

"Yes," he exhales slowly, looking at the screen and not at me. Purposely avoiding meeting my eyes. "Out of all the moments I've watched of your life, this is by far my favorite."

I look back to the screen, my skin tingling and my breath quickening. If this is truly Simon's favorite moment, then I've read him wrong. Very, very wrong.

On the screen I'm leaning against a balcony, watching a sunset with a serene expression on my face. A breeze teases my then dark hair and the corners of my lips are tipped up as I gaze at the horizon.

The backdrop is absolutely gorgeous. A white sandy beach stretches below the balcony, and foamy, white waves lap at the sand. The sky is painted in vivid blue, warm orange, bright yellow, and deep pink.

I remember this moment very well. In fact, it's one of the most peaceful moments of my life. I was in Barbados, taking a breather after destroying my first mark and contemplating my next move.

The man I destroyed was a despicable weasel of a man by the name of Russel Clay. A Real Estate banker, he liked to prey on the elderly and poor by issuing them predatory loans and then foreclosing on their homes.

Taking him down and completely destroying him was a small victory in the grand scheme of things.

It was a drop in the bucket, but it was still *my* drop.

I was feeling pretty damn pleased with myself as I watched the sun sink lower and lower. I had finally found my purpose in life. After floundering for so long, lost, I finally found the thing I was always meant to do.

My way of contributing to the betterment of our world.

And if this is Simon's favorite moment... he knows me better than I ever dreamed.

But perhaps it was simply a fluke. A lucky guess on his part. Despite what he said.

"Show me another," I demand softly.

I doubt he'll get lucky twice.

The folders pop up on the screen and the mouse navigates deeper down the long file list. Without speaking a word, a new video begins to play. This time I'm seated outside a café in Paris.

Damn.

Once again, there's a smile on my lips as I sip my coffee and watch the people around me. After a few seconds, my entire face lights up as I watch a mother with her young daughter stroll by. They're both dressed in the highest fashion.

My eyes trail after them, and then I sigh once they disappear around a corner. I remember thinking at the time how much I would love to have my own little girl. To dress her up and take her shopping.

I twist in Simon's arms and peer up at him. I don't have any words. I'm absolutely fucking speechless.

"Would you like to see another?" he asks, his attention still riveted to the screen.

Somehow I manage to nod my head.

I see the image on the screen change in the reflection of his glasses before I can manage to tear my gaze away from him.

On the screen, I'm lying naked in a bed. Simon's bed. The sheets are tangled around my legs and I'm clutching his pillow to my chest. My hair is a wild mess and I'm asleep, but I look completely at peace.

Sated even.

A dark shadow appears at the bottom of the screen and then Simon walks into view. He's completely dressed. He stops at the foot of the bed, watching me. The way he looks down at me... no man has ever looked at me like that before.

He looks at me like I hung the fucking moon.

"Simon," I gasp and twist around in his lap.

I peer up at his face, but he's still avoiding my gaze, keeping his attention locked on the screen. Needing answers, I grab him by the cheeks and force him to look down at me.

Despite what he just showed me, his face is an unreadable mask.

The man just bared his soul to me... surely he feels something?

Sliding my hand down, across the crisp white fabric of his shirt, I press my palm against his chest and feel his heart thundering.

And I thought I was good at hiding my emotions...

Looking back up at his face, I meet his eyes, but there's nothing there. Just dark emptiness. If I didn't feel his heart pounding against my hand, I might think he's dead inside.

He's so closed off... so distant... I do the only thing I know how to do to shatter his mask.

I arch up, press my mouth against his mouth, and kiss the fuck out of him.

As I push everything I have into the kiss, determined to get a reaction out of him, to get *something* out of him, a low, rumbling groan comes pouring out of his lips.

I swallow up that groan. I fucking devour it and savor it.

Whether he knows it or not, he's just given me everything I've ever wanted. Everything I ever longed for. Everything I didn't know I needed.

"Meredith," he growls and then his hands grab me, dragging me closer.

Our tongues clash, dueling for dominance.

In his obsession, I've found my power again. To be fucking worshipped from afar and not even realize it...

It's the strongest drug I've ever tasted, and I want more of it.

My teeth find his bottom lip and I can't fight off the urge to sink them into him. I give him a little nip and he jerks back.

Then he growls again and grabs me by the ass. Fingers digging into the flesh of my cheeks, he tears his lips away from me.

"Simon..." I moan, arching my neck back as he nips and nibbles his way down my lips, my jaw, and my throat.

"Yes, princess?"

His nips me, pinching my skin hard.

I jolt in surprise and my hips jerk.

He grinds his hard cock into my sex and his mouth kisses my throat.

"Did you ever watch me when I was..."

His lips kiss a searing trail down my neck until he reaches my collarbone.

"When you were what?"

He begins to kiss and nip his way across my shoulder, and I shiver, my hands clutching at his shirt.

"When I was naked."

His lips reach the exact spot I marked on him and I tense, expecting the worst.

"Oh yes," he exhales, his hot breath caressing my skin.

"Show me," I demand softly just as his teeth sink into me. He nips me hard, but not hard enough to break skin.

"Show me what got you off," I pant.

I want all of his dirty little secrets. I want to see how deep this crazy obsession of his goes.

His eyes roll up to mine and it's like looking into a smoldering pit of hellfire.

I did that. With just a kiss, I unlocked the man he keeps chained inside him. The man he won't show the rest of the world.

Hands releasing his grip on my ass, they grab me by the hips and gently guide me, turning me until I'm facing away from him.

Then he pulls me back until I'm leaning against his chest and his erection is digging into my sex.

I squirm, unconsciously rubbing my clit against him.

His arm comes up quick, locking across my chest to still me. "If you want to see, princess, you must remain still."

I sigh and he chuckles. "If you move, I'm going to bend you over the desk and fuck you before you get what you want."

That threat sends a little thrill through me and I'm tempted, so tempted to disobey him, but ultimately my curiosity wins out.

He waits, testing me, before his arm reaches out and his hand covers his mouse. Clicking around, he pulls up a new folder and scrolls down a list of files.

"What do you want to see?" he breathes into my ear and then gives my lobe a little nip.

It takes every ounce of self-control I have to keep from jolting in his grip.

"I want to see your favorite."

"You've already seen my favorites."

I snort and he chuckles, then he nips my damn ear again, seriously testing my patience. Maybe this was a bad idea, especially because he seems to believe he's in control again...

"Say it, Meredith. Say you want to see the videos I've saved of you touching yourself."

I take a deep breath and my breasts rise, pushing against the constriction of his arm. I don't have to say it, I could easily back out now.

But then I might never again get a chance to see the moments in my life that awakened this twisted desire he has for me.

"I want to see the videos of when I was touching myself," I groan.

He rewards me with a kiss on my neck and a double-click of his mouse.

Instantly, the screen fills with a scene of me stripping off my clothes and getting ready to step into a shower.

"There are so many videos..." he taunts. "Do you want to know how many times I've watched you get yourself off?"

My cheeks burn with heat as I think about every time I must have masturbated over the past five years, completely unaware he was watching. "I'd rather not."

"Are you sure?" he asks, as my naked body on the screen steps into the spray of water. "It's a rather impressive number."

Oh god. This was such a bad idea. What the hell was I thinking? He's completely turned this thing around on me. He should be the one feeling humiliated and embarrassed. And yet, he's showing no shame at all.

"I'm sure," I grit out.

"Very well," he sighs as if he's disappointed, and then the hand that was on the mouse comes down on my thigh.

He begins to slowly drag it back, pushing up my skirt. The tips of his fingers brush against the sensitive flesh of my inner thigh and I have to bite my lip to keep myself from spreading my legs wider.

On the screen, I'm tipping my head back, letting the water soak me.

"I've watched this particular video so many times, I can reenact it in my sleep," he breathes into my ear.

My core clenches at the thought of him watching this over and over.

"Did you touch yourself?" I ask, partly because I'm curious, and partly because I'm still hoping I can turn things back on him.

"Yes," he answers without hesitation and rocks his hips up.

The arm that is locked over my chest suddenly shifts. On the screen, just as I reach up and grab my breast, Simon grabs my breast. He squeezes in perfect timing with the video. He even times it perfectly when he suddenly pinches my nipple through my bra.

He tugs and rolls it between his fingers, and I whimper because he's doing it exactly how I like it. Exactly how I always do it.

"Remember," he reminds me as his other hand suddenly pushes between my thighs. "If you move, I stop."

He grabs my panties and yanks them to the side. My clit throbs with anticipation. I know exactly what's coming next.

On screen, I reach between my legs.

"This is my favorite part," he remarks as fingers slide through my folds, working up and down before settling on my clit.

Fuck, I'm so wet. And I want to rock my hips so bad.

Leaning my head back, my eyes begin to flutter closed as his fingers push down, applying pressure on my throbbing bundle of nerves.

Suddenly he nips my ear. "Eyes on the monitor, princess."

My eyes snap open and I try to focus on watching myself get myself off. But it's so hard when Simon is moving his fingers in tandem with my fingers. He mimics every little push, every little stroke.

This is how, I suddenly realize, he knew exactly how to touch me last night. And how to drive me so quickly to that orgasm after he spanked me. He's truly fucking memorized every way I touch myself to reach a release.

"Fuck," he groans as the me on the screen throws her head back and starts to moan. "You don't know how badly I wished I could reach through the screen and touch you..."

His fingers begin to move faster and faster and he tugs almost viciously on my nipple.

"How badly I wanted to drive my cock into you."

The need to grind down on his erection is so strong I can't stop myself. The pressure building inside me has reached the point that it's almost unbearable.

"Bad girl," he growls as I rock my hips.

I experience one moment of sweet relief.

Then I cry out as his fingers suddenly leave me. Once again, I was so close... so damn close.

He pushes me off of his lap and I stumble into the desk. I slap a hand down on top of it to get my balance.

Behind me, I sense Simon standing, looming over me, then his heat is pushing against my ass.

I try to reach between my thighs and finish the job he started, but he grabs my hand and pins it to the desk with his.

"No, princess. That's my pussy now, only I get to touch it."

I groan and my fingers curl into a fist. The urge to defy him and do it anyway roars through my blood.

"If you touch yourself, I'm going to take your ass," he threatens.

Fuck. I know he'll do it too. The sick fuck.

Just the thought of him violating me there is so damn frightening, so damn exciting, I relax my fingers.

He releases his grip and I swallow back a sigh of relief.

I'm seriously not ready to go down that road yet.

Searching for a distraction from my aching clit, my eyes lock once more on the screen. Honestly, there's just something about watching myself get myself off that brings out the narcissist in me.

While I watch myself reach my release, my face contorting in ecstasy, he grabs me by the ass and tips it up.

He shoves my skirt up and yanks my soaked panties down my thighs.

"You've had years to get yourself off. From now on, if you want to come, you'll come on my cock."

Behind me, I hear the unmistakable zip of his zipper then I feel the warm, silky crown of his cock pushing against my pussy.

Grabbing me by the hips, his fingers dig into my skin as he suddenly drives himself into me without warning.

My body rocks forward and I cry out as the thickness of his cock spreads me open. Despite how turned on I am, despite how fucking soaked I am, I was so not ready to take his girth.

Pulling on my hips, he forces my ass higher into the air as he slowly pulls out.

Suddenly, he surges forward again, the entire length of his cock stroking against my g-spot as he drives himself deep.

"Oh god," I groan as an intense spike of pleasure cuts through me, pulsing through my core.

His next thrust slams into my ass so hard, my hands slide forward, bumping into the mouse.

"Look at that," he growls.

He grabs me by the hair and wraps it around his fist.

Yanking on my scalp, he forces my head up. My

eyes land on the screen and the picture I see steals all my breath.

Somehow the picture on the screen has switched from the video to a live feed of this room.

"Yes, I think this will be my new favorite video," he grunts as he uses my hair to bow my spine back as his hips collide with my ass.

His thrusts come so hard now, so fast, the sound of our skin slapping together fills my ears as I watch us fucking.

Thanks to the live feed, I have a bird's-eye view of everything he's doing to me.

My body bent, completely at his mercy. My skirt hiked all the way up my ass. My panties around my ankles.

His cock glistening with my wetness as he pulls back and drives it into me over and over again.

Pants dropped to the floor, I can catch brief, fleeting glimpses of his tight ass peeking out from beneath his shirt.

Fuck, it's hot, but what's even hotter is watching him lose that cool he projects to the rest of the world.

I've been craving this again, I realize. After witnessing it last night, I need to see him unravel before I can completely let go.

The last of his carefully constructed mask is gone and in its place is the face of a man I don't know. Eyes filled with passion, sweat on his brow, and jaw set with determination, I've never seen him look more *alive*.

And it's fucking beautiful.

Just knowing that I did that, that I forced the real him out of his shell again, sends me spiraling out of control.

Nails clawing at the desk, I scream his name and clamp down on his cock just before the first wave of my release crashes into me.

It's so fucking strong, I can't see, can't think, can't even breathe. Only *feel*.

"Fuck, fuck, fuck," I hear him curse and he yanks viciously on my hair.

He drives his cock upwards, fighting through my clench. His hips driving into me with a relentless determination that forces me up onto my toes.

Pleasure, so much hot, liquid pleasure courses through me, my entire body shudders and trembles.

Then I feel him swelling, his cock pulsing and jerking as he pumps me full of warmth.

Through sheer force of will, I peel my eyes open. Drinking in the sight of him as he bends over me, losing the last vestiges of his own control.

His face contorts with a mixture of pleasure and possession until he finally stills with a groan.

"Simon," I gasp as he releases his grip on my hair and I drop back down to my feet.

The movement causes a little aftershock to flutter

through me and my pussy clings desperately to him as he starts to slide out.

Freezing against me, he presses his forehead against my neck and groans as I shamelessly milk his cock for the very last drop.

"Meredith," he breathes against my neck as the last spasm fades away, leaving me feeling as if I've been hung up and wrung out.

"Are you done, angel?" he asks, reaching up and tenderly brushing back my hair out of my eyes for me.

The movement is so tender, the endearment so damn sweet, I'm caught off-guard.

"I think so," I croak, not sure if I want to try and make a run for it or collapse in his arms.

14

SIMON

"Simon..." Meredith says quietly as we slowly slump back into the chair, my arms tightly wound around her waist.

Even now, my tortuous cock is threatening to awake from its half-life. I'm all too aware that right now I'm so far outside of my comfort zone with this level of intimacy...

It's unnerving.

The comfort and security I feel holding her close to me... it's as if she's become some sort of security blanket.

Our bodies fluids don't even bring out my normal revulsion. Is this what I should feel like when I hold the woman I've craved for so long?

"Yes, princess?" I ask as I sink further into the chair. Staring off into the screen of my computer.

There, in living color, are two lovers, melded together as one. I watch, almost hypnotized by the way her breasts rise and fall as she catches her breath. It has a maddening sexuality to it, the way it mesmerizes me.

My tongue aches to claim each little bump on her skin, to taste her sweat.

"Please don't think I've been... well, thinking of other things while you ravished me. But were you looking for Asad at all?" she asks.

Her naked flesh pressed against my legs has too much of a dizzying effect for me to grasp what she's asking immediately.

Asad... Why would I even...

"Why do you ask?" comes out of my mouth before I can fully comprehend the ramifications of her asking about him.

Ahmed was not in favor with his father. He may have had access to some monies, but he was the black sheep of the family. Asad is not like Ahmed in that regard. In fact, he's the exact opposite. He is fully in favor, his devout lifestyle and strict adherence to his father's wishes makes him... deadly.

Deadly in the sense that he has the full capabilities of getting anything he wants from his father, and far more connections than Ahmed could have ever hoped for.

"Because... yesterday when I... We... Well... When I

was alone in the house, I was looking at some of your live feeds..." she says, and I can tell she's scared now, because of what happened yesterday and of the man Asad.

Sitting up straighter, I pull her tight to my chest as I roll us forward in the chair. My arms encase her in my need to get to my keyboard and mouse.

"When did you see him?"

"Right before you looked up at the camera at Matthew's house. But surely..." she says as she feels my body tense up against her.

Going through the feeds, I ask, "Where exactly did you see him? Which screen?"

She points to the one with the airport feeds and I can feel my face grimace in anger. "He's in the country at least. He wouldn't have flown into the city, my connections with the local airport TSA would have had him detained. But..."

Tapping into the feeds, I shift Meredith around a bit. Her bare ass rubbing against my cock feels immeasurably sexual and torturous at the same time.

"No moving, I need to concentrate," I say as I start going through the feeds that ran during that time frame.

Spreading them out on the screens in front of us, I watch as the other security footage disappears.

"But..." Meredith begins to say.

"Please, this is very serious," I say, trying to sound

as nice as I can instead of just gagging her and tying her to the bed.

On a smaller screen on the wall, I pull Asad's face up. A facial recognition program auto-mapping his features.

Speeding through the multiple camera feeds of the surrounding airports, it begins the slow search of matching his face to the thousands that the cameras capture.

"Where was the feed coming from when you saw him?" I ask.

"He was coming through customs, and then he went out to a vehicle he was chauffeured away in. I think it was Garden City, but..." she trails off. "It might have been an advertisement to come to Garden City."

"Why didn't you say something to me?"

My voice comes out tersely. Now it's too damn late for me to do all I could have originally done if I had known right away.

"Well, by the time you got home..." her voice trails off as she pushes hard back into my chest, as if she's trying to protect herself by making me hold her.

"We were already on a different path, I take it," I say, pulling up the security feeds from Garden City and the airports closest to us.

I wait for a hit. This will at least give me an idea of where and when he came in.

Of course, we were on a different path. She had destroyed my kitchen and my computer room.

She had behaved so wantonly that I had no choice but to bring her to task

"Yes." She lays her head back against my chest as she says, "If he's in the city, I need to leave, Simon. I'm not safe here, he's going to come for me."

Pulling my arms tightly around her chest, she goes on, "Ahmed may have been petty and mean, but Asad, he's evil. His father has him taking over for him when it comes to stepping out of the limelight. He's not right in the head, Simon. Even Ahmed was afraid of Asad's wrath."

"Asad... He's of no concern to us, Meredith. No more than a fly on an elephant's back. He's an irritant, nothing more," I say, and perhaps I'm understating things a touch, but there's no need for her to be overly fearful.

Fear is healthy in the right areas of life, but she needs to know she's mine now. I control her future and destiny.

Pushing her forward, I have her first stand then myself. My cock is almost fully hard now, but she needs to eat before we do anything else. It wouldn't do for her to let herself go on account of our baser instincts.

Turning around to face me, her eyes start from where my pants lay on the ground, slowly moving upwards. I can see the smirk on her lips die as she stares at my almost fully engorged thick cock.

"Jesus, Simon, do you ever get enough?" she asks with a small nervous laugh.

"Of you? No," I say as I pull her close to me, smashing my lips down hard against her pink, perfectly plump ones.

She gasps for air when I finally pull away and I grin. "You need to eat, princess, if you want to maintain your strength."

Bending over at the waist, I pull my pants up my legs. Watching as her eyes remain glued to my hard cock. "We must keep our bodies healthy."

Pushing my shirt into my pants, I pull my belt tight around my waist. Taking her arm in my hand, I lead her out of the room and towards the stairs to the first floor.

Time to feed her lunch.

Food, sex, and work.

Our last two days have been filled with fun and the adventures of new passions.

It's strange that this woman has so easily found herself inside of my defenses. She's pushing and ripping down every sense of normalcy I've built around myself in this home.

It's become so bad I haven't cleaned the bathroom in three days. I can feel the bacteria growing by the moment.

Every time I try to though, she finds a reason to distract me. Anything from walking around the office in just her panties, to asking for more of my favorite recordings.

But I can't let her keep me from my searching for the Yakuza or Ahmed's brother. The Yakuza front has been difficult to crack. We've gone through Garden City to look for their resurgence, but I'm not able to find anything worthy of merit. A few small gambling dens that we take a cut from, and protection businesses.

That's it. No gang activity at all.

The initial ID reports on the one I killed came back a blank. Nothing on any criminal registry. If the Yakuza were smart enough to use two Caucasian males for the bombings it shows that they are willing to use outside contractors for hits.

That's almost unheard of.

The Yakuza don't use outsiders. But that doesn't mean they didn't get wise to the fact that we're still on the watch for them in Garden City after the kidnapping of Lucifer's wife Lily.

Well, we're hoping that the Yakuza were the ones behind the bombing...

A small break in the explosive from Cherry's house

points to a Japanese manufacturer, but that could merely be a coincidence.

I've watched the traffic light feeds of the fleeing motorcyclist, and he ghosted our cameras as soon as he hit the city limits.

In my mind, and Lucifer's, they are moving in and out of Garden City from another surrounding city that we don't have a full toe-hold on.

It's not surprising that we can't cover every city in the state. Even if we wished we could. We need more manpower and more presence in every city if we want to be able to do that.

I know the two white males who set the bomb up in Lucky Tails ran from the city as fast as they could. We've searched everywhere, but from all reports they made it to Chicago and took a flight to Riga, Latvia.

From there I was unable to track their movements.

I doubt they were a part of the Latvian Special Tasks Unit. I also doubt that while they're quite close to Russia that they are Russian either.

But if somehow the Yakuza and Russians are working together... they'll both be executed with extreme prejudice.

The initial reports from the arson investigation show that the explosive was a common type used for demolition. But, the explosive had a surrounding of ball bearings and was mixed with a chemical compound agent.

When it exploded, the initial damage was caused by a large amount of C-4. Then the ball bearings combined with the chemical compound is what truly killed everyone in the club.

The total amount of dead are still sketchy to the public's knowledge. Right now, we have the media on a slow drip of false facts.

Thankfully, we haven't had a large outpouring of prayers and 'in people's thoughts'. It was a strip club... I think that alone has been enough of a discouragement. Sad but true. Most people out there think of strip clubs with the same revulsion as I do.

Or at least I like to think they do.

Asad has become a bane to my existence. No man should be able to disappear off my radar as thoroughly as he has. He arrived at McCarran Airport in Las Vegas, and like the damnable Yakuza bikers and the contract bombers, he's fucking ghosted me as well.

Too much disappearing and then suddenly popping up in Garden City.

We never had this problem before. Lucifer and I both worry it will start to become a trend. We control the city too tightly for someone to land here or get away with much. But so far, all it's taken is people from outside cities to drive over and cause mayhem.

Asad has yet to show up though. We haven't seen him yet. But I have no doubt he will become far more of an issue before we're ready for him to be.

"Simon," Meredith say to get my attention.

"Yes?"

"You need to relax. I can tell you're extremely tense from how white your knuckles are."

Her words come out soothingly as she reaches over the center console to lightly rub my hands.

She's right, of course. My brain hasn't truly shut off when it comes to the outside world. Even if I wished it would, it hasn't.

Forcing my hands to relax, I remain passive as her touch ignites my very soul. She should not have this damnable control over me like she does, but I feel helpless to stop her. She tests me to my very core, and I'm positive she does it to get a reaction from me.

She enjoys the game of give and take, pain and pleasure.

Slowing down at the gate of Lucifer's compound, I wait for my security detail to enter in front of us. All the men of the inner circle have a security detail at their disposal now.

Even James has been forced into obey his betters. The damn playboy.

Parking the Tahoe next to Andrew's armored Mercedes, I quickly glance around us to make sure everyone that should be is here.

"You know, Simon, it looks to me like every one of Matthew's men has an expensive, decked out car... Why the Tahoe's and Escalades?" she asks.

Opening the door, I wait until I walk around the vehicle to open her door before answering.

Taking her hand in mine, I help her down from the seat. "I prefer the sheer weight and power of my vehicles. They are tailored to do exactly as I need. The Escalade is set up for me to run two powerful computer systems in case of an emergency. It also has enough raw weight from the upgraded armor to drive through a couple of brick walls."

Pointing to the Mercedes, I say, "Besides, that car belongs to Andrew's wife Amy."

"Oh! It is beautiful though, isn't it?"

Shrugging my shoulders, I say, "I suppose, but it's also like the Escalade in the fact that it's been modified to be a rolling armored vehicle."

She looks around at the cars surrounding us, motioning to the silver Lexus. "That one?"

Growling quietly so that only she can hear, I say, "That was supposed to be mine for when I needed a lower profile, but that mongrel Johnathan took it over. Now I have to wait for the newest model to be finished up and sent. Though it does warm my cold heart to know Beth has all but taken it over from him."

"So you're telling me all the men are buying their wives big fancy cars?" she asks with a raised eyebrow.

"Yes, I think I am," I say, shrugging my shoulders as we walk towards the front of the house.

Inside, the men of the inner circle will be gathered

around, grieving each in their own way. The funeral today was for Peter's relatives. Tonight will be a time for us, his family, to grieve.

"When are you going to buy me a new fancy car?" she asks with a chuckle to her voice.

"If I ever were to let you out of my sight, you would get one. But as it is... there's no need."

"Simon, if you are going to solve the issues with Asad, like you've said you will, then there will be a time when I'll need to be able to go out on my own."

I turn to look at her and grin. "Maybe if you behave I'll buy you something to go with your bracelet."

"Asshole!" she hisses at me right as the front door sweeps open.

Lily stands there, a mixture of confusion and slight annoyance on her face as she looks at Meredith.

"Ah, Simon, it's so good to see you. Even if it's for such a horrendous reason. Peter..." she says, her voice fading off as she steps to the side and motions for me to enter.

With not quite as much cheer in her voice, she adds, "Meredith, thank you for coming too."

Nodding my head at Lily, I say, "Thank you for the welcome. Has Evelyn been informed of the... news?"

Lily's expression saddens as she looks off towards the inner house. "Yes. She's handling it as well as can be expected... but I fear for her. She forms attachments so easily to Matthew's men."

"She'll be okay. I've been told children are resilient," I say.

Meredith pushes her elbow into my side sharply. "What Simon meant to say was, if she needs anything, or you, please let us know."

Looking down to Meredith, I'm tempted to check her forehead for a fever.

"Thank you, Meredith," Lily says with a warming smile. "Let's join the rest of the group. I'm sure they are wondering where you have been Simon."

Fuck.

This is the last thing I need the men to be wondering about. My personal life is just that. Personal. They have no need to know what I do in my personal time. I have no doubt that if they did, there would be no end to their litany of jokes and off-beat humor. They would most likely expect me to join in their womanly commiserations.

Good gods, I would rather give myself a fucking lobotomy.

As we head into the house, I hear loud laughter from Andrew and then Johnathan's loud braying as well. Wonderful, the gang's all here.

As we walk into the large living room, I feel my phone buzzing in my pocket.

Stopping in the doorway, I release Meredith's hand as I pull it out and push connect. This should be interesting.

"Chief Mar—" I start to say before I am rudely cut off.

"You son of a bitch!" he screams into my ear.

Meredith gives me a wide-eyed look before she smirks. She has learned I seem to have this effect on people.

Smiling to myself, I ignore the ranting of the Fire Chief as I watch her walk into the room behind Lily. Meredith, to me, has the body of a lithesome ballerina. Especially when she does her hair up in a high tight bun. It accentuates her long, slender neck, her tan skin showing a radiant glow.

It's surprising to me that instead of remaining by my side or making her way directly to her brother, she chooses to walk straight up to James.

"How dare you..." Chief Martin continues to blare into my ear as I watch my woman speak with that filthy slut.

My blood is boiling, and I can feel the temperature of the room rise as I think of killing the man right here and now. The laugh they both share is almost enough to injure my heart. It's only when I see her point to me and my feet that I feel even the slightest bit of relief.

Perhaps I should only cripple him. And remove his fucking ears. They're too nicely fucking shaped. Then break his legs so he wobbles for the rest of his life.

Shaking my head, I say to the Chief on the phone, "Shut up. Speak to me with a respectful tone or I figure out how many fingers each of your children will still have after I disconnect the line."

There's a long silence in which I watch the interactions of James and Meredith. She isn't flirting with him, and nor is he with her, but from the slight redness of his cheeks I can tell he's speaking about something that embarrasses him.

"How dare you send a man to scare my poor daughter. I told you I would do what you wanted, you pile of shit," Chief Martin says in a quiet tone.

I know he's trying to sound tough, but in reality, he's a big pussy. Crude as that sounds, he is a weak, worthless male. Not even fit to be called a man.

"What man are you speaking of?" I ask as I watch Meredith lean in close to James and say something quietly so that the others won't hear.

It's uncanny how much Meredith has the same powerful presence in the room as her brother. Though I doubt either of them would care for me to mention something like that to them.

Perhaps I should just get her riled up. She's so spunky when she gets riled up.

"The one you sent to meet my daughter. Don't fucking play games, Simon. I know he's there as a threat to me."

"Whatever it is you believe, Chief, you believe. Remember I simply asked you to do your job as in the description of what I fucking said. This isn't the first fucking time I've asked for you to do something, and don't forget I know all of your dirty little secrets," I say with a smile in my voice.

"God damn you, Simon."

"He did that a long time ago. Now don't fucking call me until you have any new information."

Pushing the disconnect button on my phone, I look around the room and see that Lucifer has turned his attention to me. His eyes are staring straight through me as if he's trying to read me from the inside out.

Good luck to him. I'm not even sure I could tell him what's going on inside of myself right now.

15

MEREDITH

I can feel Simon's eyes boring into me the entire time I talk to James. His anger and jealousy is so strong it's practically radiating off of him in waves.

Waves I want to bask in.

Once again, thanks to me, that cool exterior he exudes is showing its cracks, and in public no less.

Who's breaking who now, Simon?

It wasn't my intention to make him jealous. Honest. Out of all the people in this room, James seemed like the safest bet to engage in conversation with. Not only have we spoken before, but I was curious to know if he actually followed through with what he was planning to do the other day.

Simon's reaction is just an added bonus. A bonus I

can't help but relish. It won't be long now until I have him completely wrapped around my little finger.

And when I do... oh, the things I will do to him...

James leans close, a twinkle in his eye as he says, "I don't think Simon likes me talking to you. He looks like he's about to blow a gas—"

James suddenly snaps his jaw shut and stiffens the moment I feel a looming presence at my back.

Expecting Simon, I smirk and start to turn towards him before I realize my mistake.

"Meredith," Matthew's smooth voice washes over me, instantly chilling me.

I freeze in place, the smirk sliding off my lips.

After all these years, I still have a hard time looking at him. While everyone else sees a beautiful, almost angelic exterior, all I see is the monster that lurks within.

It's like a curse. Once seen, it can never be unseen.

Even now, as I peer up at his face, images slice through my mind like cut scenes in a cheap horror movie.

The blood on the basement walls. The floor. All over everything, including him.

The maniacal grin stretching across his face as he cut through a man lying prone on a table with one of those electric carving knives we used to carve the Thanksgiving turkey with.

But it wasn't a fucking horror movie. It was real.

Too fucking real. Something that haunts my nightmares to this day.

Matthew smiles down at me, and it instantly triggers the memory of his face splattered with blood.

I blink and just as quickly the memory fades away.

Before I have a chance to make an excuse and dart off to safety, Matthew's hand clamps down on my elbow. Trapping me. "James, you don't mind if I borrow my sister, do you?"

I try my best to keep my expression neutral and not show the apprehension I'm feeling as James says, "Of course not, boss."

Showing fear now would only give Matthew more power. Fear to him is like blood in the water near a fucking shark.

"Thank you, James," Matthew says, sounding more expectant than grateful.

James nod his head and walks off.

Matthew waits until he's out of an earshot before he asks, "So, how are you enjoying your new accommodations, Meredith?"

Now he's wearing my discarded smirk on his lips. Oh, I bet he knows exactly how much I'm 'enjoying them'.

I shrug my shoulders, hoping I come off as nonchalant. "I've stayed in better. In fact, my accommodations don't feel like accommodations at all. They feel like a prison..."

Matthew lifts a brow, pretending to be interested as he asks, "Oh?" But I'm pretty sure he could give a fuck. "I'm sorry to hear that."

My lips curve into a tight smile. "The host is a jerk. The food sucks. And the curfew is entirely unreasonable."

"Now, now, Meredith," Matthew says with mock disapproval. "Is that any way to talk about Simon after he's so graciously taken you into his care and his home?"

For a moment, I wonder how Matthew would react if I told him the truth. Would he get angry on my behalf or would he give Simon a pat on the back? There's really no telling with him.

"Simon is an overbearing ass." I double-down.

Matthew sighs. "I'm sure everything he's done is for your protection."

And there's that saying again that just pisses me off. "Seriously, Matthew. You need to talk to him and tell him to back off."

While I don't necessarily want to leave Simon now, especially until the new little game I've started has completely worked its way out, I could use more freedom.

Matthew's eyes gleam and his mouth stretches into a grin. "Now why would I do that, Meredith?"

Oh, I can't wait to wipe that smug grin off of his face when I break his second in command. Putting up with Simon's rules and restrictions almost makes it worth it. Almost.

"Because you're his boss? Because I'm your sister? Because it's gone past the point of ridiculousness?"

"I have complete faith and trust in Simon, and everything he's doing to take care of you," he says as if it puts the matter at rest.

There's so many things I could say. So many that would probably shock the hell out of him... but then again, they might not. I have no clue what he already knows. It's impossible to tell. All I can tell is that he is obviously amused by all of this.

"Matthew, please," I plead, switching tactics, though I doubt it will work on him. Long gone are the days when we were close. When I could trust him to have my back. There was a time, though it feels like an eternity ago, when all we had in this world was each other. "He's treating me like a child."

His grin sharpens and his icy eyes stare into mine. I almost expect him to say something cutting and smart, what I don't expect him to say is, "It's out of my hands now, Meredith."

"What the hell does that mean?"

How can it possibly be out of his hands? He's the one with all the power here. If he wants to fix this for me, he can damn well fix it.

"It means, dear sister, that you're in *his* hands now,"

are the words that come out of his smug, smirking mouth.

But I swear it sounds more like *you're pretty much fucked, Meredith.*

Great. That's just great. Matthew is essentially saying he's wiping his hands of me. Normally, that wouldn't necessarily be a bad thing, but right now I fucking need him.

"Coming to this city was the biggest mistake of my life," I say bitterly and try to jerk my elbow out of his hand but his grip tightens.

"Speaking of which," he says smoothly, easily switching the topic of conversation. "You never did tell me what happened to Ahmed..."

Just hearing Ahmed's name causes this strange sort of numbness to buzz through my veins. It's almost as if my body is subconsciously protecting me from facing the emotional consequences of my actions.

"Oh?" I say, feigning surprise then flash a grin to mask my uneasiness. "Has he not popped up yet?"

Yes, that's pretty morbid, even for me. And just picturing Ahmed's body bobbing to the surface of the Mediterranean makes me feel a little sick.

"No," Matthew drawls out and his expression hardens. "Perhaps if you gave me a clue of his whereabouts, I could find him and fix this little mess you've created."

I stare into the icy blue depths of Matthew's eyes and wonder if evil is contagious. It must be because I somehow find myself saying, "Clue? You want a clue? I pushed him off the yacht after he threatened to kill me. He discovered a detail trailing me and believed I was out to get him. You wouldn't know anything about those men, would you, dear brother?"

For once in his life, Matthew looks a little taken aback.

"Or perhaps I should ask Simon? I would hate to think you purposely compromised me... After all, we're still *family*, yes?"

"Meredith, I would never—" he starts to say in his defense but I yank my elbow out of his grip and cut him off.

"Save it. In the past, I would have believed you..."

Matthew stiffens and his face flashes with annoyance at the reminder that I'll never forget, forgive, or understand what I stumbled upon in that basement.

No matter how badly he ever wanted me to.

I know one of the reasons he hates having me around so much is because I've seen his true face. It's not my charming personality that annoys him. Oh no, it's that when I'm around, he can't buy his own bullshit.

"But not now. Never now," I say lifting my chin in the air. Then I sneer out the moniker *I* bestowed upon him. The name that's made him infamous. "Lucifer."

I turn and walk away from him before he can stop me. I don't necessarily want to join the others, in fact I'd prefer to actually go back to Simon's, which just proves how uncomfortable I am. But I can't stand to remain in Matthew's presence for one more second.

Heels clicking against the dark wood floors, I walk towards the center of the room and stop, taking in those who are gathered. Most of the men are lingering near the fireplace with drinks in their hands as they talk and laugh among themselves. While it looks like they're having a good time, there's this somber undercurrent to their laughter.

The women seem to be concentrated at the sofas near the huge floor to ceiling windows. Lily and a dark-haired woman both hold babies in their laps. And I'm pretty sure the young redhead with them is pregnant.

I recognize a few faces, Lily, James, and of course Matthew's son Adam, but the rest are strangers.

I've never felt more out of my element. Not only because everyone is here to remember and mourn a dead man I don't know, but because I don't know who I can trust in this den of vipers.

Lily is pleasant enough, but she's married to Matthew. I find it hard to believe she's never seen the true him... and yet she's still with him. She subjects her children to him. And she's even had his child.

The baby she's holding in her lap, David, might as well be a clone of Matthew. Blonde hair, blue eyes, excessively beautiful.

Honestly, I'm surprised she's still alive after the birth.

After all, they say Matthew's mother, Anna, died shortly after bringing him into this world because he poisoned her womb.

Then there's my nephew Adam. I know he's not Matthew's by blood, but the resemblance is beyond uncanny. When I look at Adam, I see Matthew when he was the same age, and it gives me the fucking creeps.

Matthew is raising Adam in his image. The boy can't be older than nine, yet the way he holds himself, his entire demeanor, and the sharp intelligence in his eyes, bespeaks of a boy much older.

I wonder if history will end up repeating itself.

Will Adam one day assume the mantle of this fucked up little family by eliminating his father?

While I have no concrete proof, I heavily suspect that Matthew murdered my stepfather, Joseph.

Joseph was getting up there in the years, yes, but he was in decent health. To suddenly pass in his sleep after he and Matthew had a disagreement about running the business...

Shaking my head, I go over my options again. Perhaps I'm being too harsh on Lily. There's a strong possibility she's isn't aware of Matthew's true nature. After all, he fooled me for years...

Simon intercepts me before I can make it to Lily. His hand wraps around my arm and it takes everything

I have in me to keep from jerking away. I'm tired, so tired of being grabbed and restrained.

But I need at least one ally if I'm going to make it through the rest of the night.

"Yes, Simon?" I look up at his face expectantly.

When I note his angry expression though all I can think is fuck this. "I need a drink."

Simon's grip on my arm tightens and he pulls me a little closer. I sigh. Here we go again.

"I don't want you speaking to James again, Meredith," he says calmly, but I think that tic is in his eye is making a reappearance.

"What? Why?" I blink up at him.

"Because he's a shameless playboy."

I roll my eyes and yank my arm out of his grip. Dammit, my arm is probably going to be bruised tomorrow. "He's a baby, Simon. He's harmless."

"That's beside the point," he scowls.

"What is the point again? That you're needlessly jealous?"

Simon steps closer and bends down to speak quietly in my ear. "The point is that you're *mine*, Meredith." He pauses and I hear him take in a breath of my hair before he goes on. "And James is not worthy of your attention."

Two different emotions war inside of me. Two emotions that seem to go hand and hand when dealing with Simon. Annoyance that once again he would try to treat me like a child and dictate who I can and cannot speak to. And arousal. With his body looming over mine, and his heat and scent hitting me, I close my eyes in an attempt to fight off my reaction to him.

My skin tingles and my damn nipples tighten.

I still don't understand this... this weakness I have for him. Like Matthew, he's a killer. A murderer. I watched him shove a knife in Cherry's chest. Yet I can't seem to dredge up the same hate for him that I have for Matthew.

It makes me a complete and utter hypocrite, but I can't seem to change it.

"I'll talk to who I want to, when I want to, Simon." I open my eyes and politely tell him for the sake of not making a scene.

With how much I've already had to keep my tongue in check tonight, I deserve a medal or something.

Simon smiles and his eyes gleam as he leans back just enough to look at me. "Then whatever happens to him will be on your head."

He can't be serious. It has to be an empty threat...

"Don't you dare use me as an excuse to off him," I warn.

"Don't give me a reason to, Meredith. I've already been more than gracious and shared you with the rest of the world for the past five years..." Simon's leans close to speak in my ear again. "I'm done sharing."

And this is where his obsession goes beyond mere

inconvenience. It's absolutely insane. If I had any sense, I'd run away from him, screaming. Yet, once again, the sheer depths of his crazy possession sends thrills through me.

The danger alone that he represents is a lure I can't resist.

Dealing with Simon is like playing a game of Russian Roulette. I keep pulling the trigger, never knowing which pull is going to be my last.

Leaning into him, into the warmth and strong cage of his body, my lips find his ear. "So, if I want you to kill someone for me, all I have to do is talk to them?" I ask, hoping to show him the fallacy in his demand.

"No," he answers firmly. "If you want me to kill someone for you, all you have to do is ask."

I jerk back in surprise and my eyes search his face. He stares back at me with an intensity that shows he's utterly serious.

I frown at him and he smiles. "Within reason, of course."

"Of course," I shake my head and take a step back.

He takes a step forward, putting himself right back into my personal space.

"You can't expect me to talk to you and only you, Simon. I'll go mad," I point out.

The man is so... anal about taking care of me and seeing that all my physical needs are met, you'd think he'd take into consideration my mental health.

"I don't expect you to speak only to me," Simon says and my shoulders start to relax. "You may also speak to those I deem worthy of your sweet breath."

God help me. I'm not sure how I'm going to make it through the rest of this game without strangling him.

"You're purposely trying to piss me off," I accuse him. And it's working.

"Am I?" Simon asks as he reaches out and tucks a strand of hair that's fallen out of my bun behind my ear. "Try me, angel, and see what happens."

Never one to back down from a challenge, I start to turn away from him, meaning to make my way straight to James, when a little body suddenly slams into me.

"Aunt Meredith!" Evelyn cries out with true joy as her little arms wrap around me.

Once I get over my initial surprise, I smile down at her golden head and wrap my arms around her, giving her a tight squeeze back.

She's probably the only person in this world who truly loves me. And I love her right back.

"Evelyn. How are you, darling? I was hoping to see you tonight."

With her arms still wrapped tightly around me, she tips her head back to answer me, but her nanny cuts in.

"Evelyn," Mary, my old nursemaid, says in a chiding tone as she walks quickly over to us as if she's trying to catch up. "What have I told you about throwing yourself into adults?"

Evelyn sighs and rolls her eyes. "That it's rude and I might hurt someone."

"That's correct," Mary says with a stern nod of her head. "Now apologize to Meredith."

"I'm sorry, aunt Meredith," Evelyn says. And though her voice sounds properly chastised, the glint in her eyes is anything but.

Thankfully, Mary can't see it. I love Mary, I truly do. She pretty much raised me after my mother married Joseph, but she can be rather strict about propriety.

Matthew never had any issues with her, he was always her darling little angel. But me, I can't even count how many hours I spent in the corner or writing sentences because I misbehaved.

I give Evelyn one more tight hug and lean down to whisper into her ear. "You can run into me and hug me anytime."

Evelyn flashes me the brightest grin as I straighten and glance to Mary.

"How are you, Mary?" I ask, taking in all the changes to her that have occurred over the years.

"I've been very well, thank you for asking, Meredith," she smiles at me.

Yes, I've probably warmed her old heart by showing some of her lessons stuck.

"Oh!" Evelyn says as she pulls away from me a little

bit and places her hand on my stomach. With a look of wonder on her face, she rubs her hand against me. "There's a baby in your belly, aunt Meredith."

"What?" I gasp in surprise then laugh. That's just... not possible.

Evelyn pulls away and gives me a hurt look.

Hating that look, I immediately try to explain, "I had a very big lunch, Evelyn. That's all."

Evelyn nods her head slowly, but she doesn't seem convinced.

Sighing, I glance towards Simon, hoping he'll back me up, but his face has gone white.

What the hell does he have to be worried about?

"Evelyn, I believe your mother is calling for you," Mary says.

With a nod of her head, Evelyn says cheerfully, "I'll see you later, aunt Meredith."

Then she darts off in a swirl of pink skirts and blonde curls.

Mary smiles with affection, the wrinkles around her eyes crinkling, as she watches Evelyn skip her way to her waiting mother.

Then she turns to me.

"I wouldn't be so quick to dismiss what Evelyn said, Meredith" she says with a twinkle in her eyes. "Young children can be more perceptive than we give them credit for."

16

SIMON

By the time we pull into the garage, my blood is boiling with rage, hormones, and a passion akin to something like burning alive in my own soul.

I know Meredith was pushing her limits on purpose, but the flames of the raging jealous beast inside of me threaten to steal my sanity.

Would I actually end James's life because he pushed too close to Meredith?

Yes, without a second thought.

Lucifer's rules and laws be damned.

The garage door fully shuts behind us and I prevent Meredith from unlocking the doors. Shutting off the engine, I allow my emotions to fully engulf me for five full seconds.

We sit in the pitch black garage, waiting.

"Simon?" Meredith whispers as her hand reaches out to touch my shoulder.

I can feel her delicate fingers resting on my shoulder even through the material of my suit jacket and dress shirt. A fire erupts inside my chest, roaring through my blood due to my hyper-sensitivity to this creature.

I can't call her a woman, she's so much more than that.

She's my salvation, damnation, and my very essence.

She has so unhinged me from my world of laws and placement... everything about her destroys me completely.

Pushing open the door of my car, I slam it shut behind me and move with all the purpose I can in long strides around the car. She's still waiting inside, more than likely unable to grasp just how fucking serious the moment is for me right now.

Sliding my hand into my jacket pocket, the black, cold grip of the stiletto nearly freezes my hand to it.

She's going to be the end of me, I know it now.

One way or the other, my life will end with her.

I've lived far too long in this self-imposed hell. I've lived too long on my own accord, giving nothing of myself to the world. Part of my analytical mind rebels against the change she has brought to me.

From order she has wrought chaos. Chaos I simply

can't understand. In my life there are laws, as in nature. To violate these laws is to invite uncertainty in.

Yanking open the SUV's door, I look into her shocked eyes.

The bright light coming from the overhead light in the car is all that illuminates the enclosed space. My chest is heaving in breath, each one pulled deeply through my nose as I stare at her.

She will only bring my ruin if I don't end this now.

James was the catalyst to this. Just seeing her with him has brought me to this moment. I'm no longer sure if I'm an animal or some savage.

Reaching in past her lap, I push the seatbelt release then look back into her eyes.

She's kept her eyes warily trained on me this entire time, and I have no doubt that she tried to watch me out in the darkness before I opened her door.

Grabbing her by the wrist, I pull her from the seat, but I feel her dig her feet into the cement as she asks, "What in the world is wrong with you Simon?"

"If you want to live through the next five seconds, move your ass," I growl out without looking back.

Tugging her wrist hard, I move us forward, pulling her as much as pushing myself through the darkened garage. When I finally reach the door, it seems as if the lock takes an eternity to get the tumbler inside to open.

Then the keypad for the security alarm inside the

door gives me a failed number entry before I slam my fingers into the pads, finally hitting the correct code.

Too much time has passed for me. I simply can't control what my body wants any further. My mind is falling into a dim awareness. It's somewhere between mindless lust and murderous rage.

What is happening to me? How has she driven me to this point?

Pulling her through the mudroom, I get to the kitchen island before my feet can no longer push me any further.

Spinning around to face her, I rip the stiletto from my pocket.

Pushing the button, it comes up between us.

Her eyes widen in fright and she tries to step back away from me.

"Don't fucking move," I growl as I advance on her.

Bending down, I grab the hem of her dress in my hand, pulling it tight as I begin to slice through the wispy fabric.

The loud hiss of metal slicing through cloth fills the dead air of the kitchen.

"Simon, seriously, what the fuck is wrong with you?" she shrieks as I near her stomach.

"Be silent, Meredith. I would not be happy if we marred your perfection."

My words have the desired effect because she stiffens and stills.

She must sense that I can barely keep control of the razor sharp knife.

The blade slowly, but shakily, travels up the dress, coming to a stop at the right side of her left breast.

Just above the heart, almost at the exact place I pushed a similar instrument of death between Cherry's ribs.

I could end this once and for all right now.

Remove her from my life.

No more headaches, no more uncontrollable urges.

Nothing but silence.

I even have approval to do with her as I wish.

What I wish for though is something entirely different...

Giving the blade a final jerk upwards, the dress falls open. I push the split front apart to expose the tanned flesh of her heavy breasts.

They heave up and down in a hypnotizing rhythm.

I have no doubt if I look up into her eyes, I'll scare her with the intensity of my look.

Pushing the button to close the stiletto, I drop it back into my jacket pocket.

My hands shake as I remove my jacket and drop it to the kitchen floor.

Then slowly I lift the ragged edges of the dress where I split it open.

Pushing them aside, I watch as it slides down her

sculpted shoulders. It falls to the floor in a slow, fluttering sigh, and pools around her feet.

Taking a step back, I look at my perfect ballerina. That's what she reminds me of so fiercely right now. So fiercely that I can't suppress the memory that's springs forth from my childhood.

Siting in the opera box as I watched the ballerinas lift high on their tiptoes, their arms arched above their heads. Their perfect hair pulled tight, their pristine faces made up to be beautiful beyond compare.

Meredith has no idea of how very powerful of a drug her body is for me. It's as if my body craves hers more than it needs air to exist.

Standing before me she wears nothing but heels and a matching white lacy bra and thong. I have no doubt if I were to her turn around, I would see the taut muscles of her shoulders pulled back proudly.

Her ass would stick out, begging for my hand to strike it red.

Punish her for her impudence or ravish her for her being unable to control her own sexuality?

Stalking towards her, I push up into her personal space.

I can see the fear inside of her eyes but I also see the arousal.

She gets off on being forced into uncomfortable situations. She needs the feeling of having no control, to know she is not in any way, shape, or form able to resist.

Taking her by the shoulders, gently I push her back until her ass comes to rest against the ledge of the island kitchen.

Moving my hands from her shoulders to her armpits, I lift her up in one swift move.

Sitting her down on the counter, I push my way between her legs.

"Simon, you just cut up a one-thousand-dollar dress," she states simply.

Shrugging my shoulders, I say, "I'll buy you five new ones, just tell me where you got it."

Shaking her head, she tries to push at my chest, but I don't budge.

My cock is scant inches away from her hot pussy. There's no chance I'll let her control where my body goes right now.

"That's not the point! I got that..." she snaps at me, but her words soon falter as I lean forward.

My mouth falls to her throat.

Scraping my teeth lightly across her jugular, I let my tongue slip out as I kiss and taste the flesh there.

Pulling back from her neck, I peer into her eyes. "Shut up, Meredith."

Nipping at her clavicle, I move around the front of her chest. Nipping gently in spots then kissing in others.

I want to rush, I want to bite hard down on her flesh, marking her like she marked me.

But I can't do that yet.

I must control my urges if I want to continue through with my plan.

Plans are all I have left now. Plans that are easily broken.

She's broken something deep inside of me.

I don't know what it is yet, but I know that it's slowly unleashing something I've never seen or felt before.

Further down, I rest my mouth on the top of her heavy, succulent breast.

Her pale pink nipples are covered by the cups of her lacy bra.

I want to rip it apart with my teeth. To unleash this savage desire to maul her body like a beast in heat.

She must sense this feeling I have to destroy her as much as I want to keep her.

Grasping the back of my head, she digs her fingers into my hair, pulling me hard to her breast.

My hand slides slowly up her stomach, moving up to the rim holding her breasts.

There, I pull hard on the material, and her nipple finally comes within reach of my aching tongue. I spend what feels like an eternity kissing around her tightened bud. I try not give in too fast to my desire, but even I am only so strong.

My mouth covers her nipple with relish, sucking at it hard then softly.

I can't even begin to guess why I can't settle into a rhythm. I'm craving too much of her body. I want to taste too many things.

Moving down past her breast, she shudders as I trail my mouth straight down.

My tongue stops to slowly circle around her small belly button. She knows where my mouth is headed. There is no chance of her being unsure.

Putting my hands in the bands of her panties, I pull both sides until I hear the fabric rip.

My tongue can practically taste her scent as I hover so close to her femininity.

Pulling her ass closer to the edge of the counter, I kneel down in front of her long legs and gently spread her thighs as I push each leg over my shoulders.

Kissing her inner thigh, her quiet gasps turn into low moans of arousal.

"Bear in mind, princess, this will be the first time I've done this. But..." I say as I trail small kisses closer and closer to her pussy.

"Simon!" she giggles so merrily. "Truly, you've never..."

Looking up into her eyes, I frown. "As if I would ever put my mouth on any part of another's body. You alone, my princess. Always you alone."

Not waiting for a response, I push my tongue hard

against her folds as I lick straight up to where her needy clit is.

My tongue swirls around as she locks her legs around my head.

"Holy shit!" she shouts out, her hands grabbing onto the back of my head.

She tastes exactly as I imagined she would. A mixture of ambrosia with a hint of darkness to her. It's like I've found the nectar of the gods, begging to be sucked and licked until I'm drunk with passion.

I continue to swirl my tongue around her clit, not giving her a moment of peace.

There will be no subtle build up right now. I want her to know for a fact I can give her all she'll ever need in so many ways.

I slip two fingers past her folds, the wet skin already giving me enough lubrication to push them deep inside of her.

I crook the fingers into a come-hither motion as I explore, searching for that perfect spot.

Arching her back, I manage to look up enough and catch one of her hands freeing itself from my head.

She grasps at the breast I kissed so recently. She nearly rips the bra free of her chest as she mashes her fingers across it.

Her nipple becomes trapped in a small pinch as she bucks her hips at me.

"Fuck!" she groans out long and loudly as I start to increase the pressure of my fingers on her g-spot.

My tongue is relentless against her clit. Never stopping. If anything, I put more pressure on her as her stomach muscles clench faster and faster.

"Simon, wait…I… wait."

No chance.

I have no clue what she wants me to wait for, but this woman is mine and she is going to fucking come for me whether she wants to or not.

"Simon, I'm going to…"

Yes, you fucking are, I think to myself.

Pressing my tongue hard on her clit, I lick up and down.

No relief is given.

Her walls squeeze hard around my fingers as her body locks up tightly around me. Every muscle of her body is in complete shock.

My eyes have enough view of her to see her mouth open in a silent scream.

I lick her through the peak and then slow the pace of my thrusting fingers and relentless tongue.

Aftershocks rock her body mightily as she moans over and over again my name.

Pulling my mouth from her pussy, I growl, "Know this, princess. I'm in control of your body now. I give you the pleasure and pain you so badly need."

"God, you're a monster," she says with a small laugh as I stand up from her quaking thighs.

It seems she can't get them to quit shaking as she rests her hands on top of them.

Even her fingers are quivering.

"Yes, I am," I say simply.

My hands fall to my belt and I quickly undo the buckle.

Her eyes widen. "You just about killed me, I need a minute to recover."

"No. Not happening."

My cock is so fucking hard right now that it feels as if I somehow hurt it. My balls feel swollen with seed.

I quickly unfasten my pants.

Yanking the zipper down, I finally feel some relief from how damn sore I am. My boxers fall down next.

Looking at my cock with almost greedy eyes, she winces as her eyes slice up to my face.

"Simon, I know what we want to do... But what Evelyn said... We need to protect ourselves here."

"No... we really don't," I growl as I advance on her again, my thick cock leading the way.

It was only last night that we were intimate with each other, but this ache, it fills my entire body. It craves her warmth.

Pushing myself between her legs again, I soak up the look of trepidation on her face. She wants to be with me as badly as I do her. Her whole body is ready for me.

Her pupils dilate as her breath comes in increasingly rapid pants.

"Simon, we really shouldn't," she says.

Her words lie though.

Her spreading thighs... the way her ankles begin to lock behind my waist... prove that.

Rubbing my thick head against her silken lips, I push just enough of my cock in to enter her.

"Simon, we..." she hisses out when I stop.

"We what, Meredith?" I ask her.

Using my hand, I rub the tip of my cock up and down between her folds.

"Simon, this is such a dangerous game you play," she says in what I can only describe as a moment of clarity.

"So the fuck what? You've already destroyed me. What's another nail to the coffin?" I ask.

"I've what?" she asks with her eyes widening.

No words come from me though, too much has been said already.

Shoving forward, I push my long length deep into her body. Eyes closing, I don't wait for her to make some wrong decision about what our future holds.

No, now it's my choosing and she's along for the ride. I am firm in that one belief that I know what's best for her.

Nothing else matters in this world but her, and by that extension *us*.

"Jesus, Simon!" she growls as I finally bottom out inside of her.

Wrapping my arms around her chest, I push my mouth against her sweet lips to silence her words.

I want the sounds and actions of our bodies. Words are a fucking waste.

Her ankles lock in completely now that I'm pushed in to the hilt. My tongue swirls around inside of her mouth.

Pulling my hips back far enough to barely be inside of her, I slam myself back in. Over and over, I thrust into her.

The tight walls of her pussy hold me hostage as much as the arms and legs she has tightly wrapped around me.

Throwing my head back, I roar out my pure rapturous joy. I'm in the moment now. There's no time outside of now.

The thrust of my hips. The warmth and cold of my cock as I pump in deep. In and out.

She's moaning and growling out words to match my own groans.

"Simon... I'm so close..." she says as she puts her mouth to my ear.

Her warm breath pushes me to further heights.

"Don't hold back, Meredith," I grunt as I speed up my thrusts.

I want us to peak together, I need her to peak with me.

Using the heels of her feet, she digs them into my lower back as she pulls me into her. Trying to fuck me as much as I'm fucking her.

There's no sensuality right now, this is about claiming one another. Making our declaration of ownership.

Leaning my head down, I begin to kiss on the soft flesh of her shoulder. Then I work my way towards her breast.

Removing my hand from her back, I slide it around to her chest. I cup her breast hard in my hand as I lift it up to my mouth.

Sucking hard on her nipple, I crush the tightened bud against my tongue.

My balls are aching so badly now, but I must wait though. It is paramount that we peak together... it has the best chance of success.

Control comes in many forms. Mentally, spiritually, and even through the bonds we create together.

"Fuck!" Her simple declaration erupts from her mouth as her pussy clamps down on my cock so hard that I can barely move through the sensations ripping through my own body.

Lifting my head from her nipple, I place my mouth at the same exact spot she bit me.

Latching my teeth on her skin, I bite down hard.

She screeches out so loudly I'm surprised the glass in the kitchen doesn't shatter.

Her legs don't stop moving though. If anything, they slam me into her body harder and harder.

My cock begins to spend long bursts of my cum deep into her womb. Each time I thrust forward, I feel as if I'm dying over and over.

So much pressure has built up over the past day that I think the release is going to kill me.

Our bodies finally come down from the mountain we crested and we sag against each other.

Her head comes to rest on my chest.

Pulling back from her after I catch my breath, I look down at the place I marked on her shoulder.

There, the edges of my teeth have broken the skin. Nothing like she did to me, no stitches will be needed. But she will have the scar for the rest of her life.

Just like I will.

"Your mouth has blood…" she starts to say before it must dawn on her why I have blood on my lips.

Looking down to her shoulder, she gasps, "You… you… you just fucking—"

"Better than any wedding band will ever be, princess. I've marked you for the world to know you belong to fucking *me*."

She doesn't move me or even push me away from her body. I'm slowly deflating inside of her and the squeeze of her silken walls is slowly easing me out. The exquisite, almost painful, sensitivity of my cock is driving me mad.

Looking up into my eyes, she declares, "You're mad, Simon! You're not sane!"

"No, I'm truly not around you."

Pulling back from her, I watch as my thick cock finally falls out.

She hasn't let go of me with her legs though. Whether she is conscious of that fact I'm not sure.

"Have I..." she starts to say but stops to lick her lips.

Trying again, she quietly asks, "Have I truly destroyed you?"

"Utterly," I say just as quietly back to her.

17

MEREDITH

It's official. I've broken Simon.

Unfortunately, I haven't broken him in the way I intended. Instead of bringing the man to his knees and wrapping him around my finger, I've unleashed a beast.

A beast full of lust and fire.

Since that night at Matthew's compound, he's become insatiable. I can't walk within five feet of him without him grabbing me and pushing me up against something.

The walls, the counters, the furniture.

It's all fair game when Simon gets his hands on me.

There isn't a room in this house he hasn't fucked me in. He takes full advantage of my penchant for wearing dresses. Tossing my skirts up and ripping my panties to the side before he thrusts himself deep inside my pussy.

And the way he fucks me... *god*, the way he fucks me.

He fucks me like he can't get enough of me. He fucks me like he's trying to make up for the past five fucking years.

It's like a drug. To be so wanted, to be so desired it's driving him past the brink of madness... It's is the greatest fucking high I've ever experienced.

And I only want more of it.

The only problem is that I'm pretty sure the bastard is purposely trying to get me pregnant.

After he's had his way with me, fucking me so hard I feel the ghost of his cock deep inside me for hours afterwards, he won't let me shower.

Yes, Simon, the germaphobic clean-freak from hell, wants to keep me dirty. He won't let me wash his cum off.

I've tried. I managed to sneak in the shower once while he was distracted with work. Just as I was rinsing the conditioner from my hair though, he ripped the shower curtain open and dragged me out.

He pushed me right up against the bathroom counter, grabbed me by my hair, and fucked me again in punishment.

Watching him furiously drive himself inside me through the bathroom mirror was the hottest thing

I've ever seen. Even hotter than those videos we watch.

His body ruthlessly claiming my body. His cock driving me to orgasmic heights I've never reached before.

But it was the expression on his face that really did me in.

An unholy expression full of possession, lust, and dominance. An expression that roared as he roared that I was *his*.

And he's never ever fucking letting me go.

I should be fucking terrified. I should be plotting and planning, trying to find a way out.

But just as I've managed to claw my way under his skin and unravel him, he's managed to work his way inside me so deep I fear he's dangerously close to reaching my soul.

I crave his attention. I crave his sick desire. So much so that I'll willingly seek him out. Interrupting whatever work he's trying to accomplish with my need for him to make me *feel*.

And he gives me what I want, what I need. Every time. Without question. Without protest.

Whenever his hands touch me, or his eyes burn into me, he makes me feel alive in a way I've never felt before.

It's ludicrous. Logically, it makes no freakin' sense. I had purpose before I met him. I had direction, and what in my mind was a divine, holy calling. He trapped me. He ripped me away from it.

Yet I don't want to run away from him.

I want to see how deep this dark hole we're digging ourselves into truly goes.

Where does this insanity end? When one of us dies? When I do get pregnant?

When the world fucking burns?

I don't fucking know.

All I know is that I've finally managed to break Simon and yet I feel like I'm the one who's cracking. I've lost my goddamn mind.

But at least I'm not alone in this madness.

"I have to leave the house for a few hours today," Simon says, stroking my hair back out of my eyes.

We're lying together, naked bodies and limbs entangled, in bed. He just took me twice in a row after waking and then refused to let me get up to pee.

"You're leaving me alone?" I ask, careful to keep any hint of what I'm feeling out of my voice as I slide my hand slowly up his naked chest.

"Yes," he answers, his eyes dropping to regard me. "But only for a few hours. You'll be safe with the security team I have in place."

I nod my head and snuggle closer to him, hiding my face against his chest. He seems to truly enjoy these small acts of affection I show him. As evident by his arms squeezing around me and the pleased sound he makes.

Simon's leaving. He's leaving. Perhaps I could figure out some way to sneak out...

"And of course I'll be watching," he adds.

For once, I'm not sure if he's saying it because he's purposely warning me or he thinks I somehow feel unsafe without him.

Of course he'll be watching me, I groan inside. If I want to get out of this house, I'm going to have to actually have his damn permission.

I lean back just enough to say, "Do you think..." before I start stamping a trail of kisses up his chest. "I could leave for a few hours too?"

I'm trying to distract him, to earn favor with him, but I'm becoming engrossed in the sweet and salty taste of his skin.

Simon lets me get all the way up to his lips before he grabs me by the back of the head and kisses me hard.

His tongue thrusts into my mouth, overtaking mine. Stroking and caressing until I'm melting against him.

Pulling away, his eyes are so soft when I finally open mine that at first I think I misheard him when he tells me, "No."

"No?" I frown up at him. As soon as the word

settles in, I try to pull away. "No? Are you serious, Simon?"

The soft look in his eyes immediately hardens, and his arms tighten, not allowing me to escape.

"It's not safe—" he starts to say.

"Don't you dare give me that bullshit," I snap at him. "Just a minute ago, you said I would be perfectly safe with your security team."

"Yes, but—"

"No *buts*. Either I'm safe with your security team or I'm not. Which is it?"

Simon's jaw tightens and I swear that eye of his twitches.

"You're safe," he grits out reluctantly.

I smile at him. "Then there's no reason I can't leave the house for a bit."

A variety of emotions flashes across his face. Anger, annoyance, and even worry, then finally acceptance.

"What exactly is it that you want to do, Meredith?"

His hands slide down my back, fingers tracing the curve of my spine, before he grabs my ass and pulls me closer to him.

Pleased that I seem to finally be getting my way, I push my hips into him to get more comfortable.

His cock stiffens against me, growing in the space between us.

"I need a spa day. I'm falling apart. It's been months since I've had my hair or nails done…"

"I'd hardly say you're falling apart," he groans, fingers digging into the flesh of my ass as I once again stamp little kisses along his chest. "You're fucking beautiful."

"That's besides the point," I laugh and brush my lips across his nipple.

His cock jerks, twitching upwards, and leaves a trail of wetness along my thigh.

"What is the point?" he asks, his voice growing growly and husky.

I kiss my way across his chest to his other nipple. "That I need to get out for a bit. I need to air my head out, Simon. I'm starting to go a little crazy."

I lightly nip his nipple to prove my point.

His entire body jerks and a hiss escapes his teeth. Then he reaches up, grabs me by the back of the hair ,and forces me to look at him.

"Very well, princess. You can have your spa day."

"But?" I ask, sensing the word hanging in the air.

"But," he grins, either pleased I guessed there would be more to it, or pleased about whatever he's about to say. "You have to wear your bracelet, and you have to sign something first."

"Sign what? A contract promising I won't try to escape or something?"

Using his grip to drag my head up, his grin grows even wider. "Something like that."

That grin tells me I should be worried, but freedom is so close I can fucking taste it.

"Fine. Whatever," I agree, throwing caution to the wind. "I'll sign your silly paper."

Simon pushes me onto my back and comes down on top of me. With one hard thrust of his hips, he drives himself deep inside me.

"If you try to run..." he starts to warn as he pumps his thick length in and out of my body.

I thrust my hips up suddenly and lock my thighs around him.

"I won't run," I groan. "Just shut up and fuck me, Simon."

18

MEREDITH

Thankfully Simon let me shower when we finally made it out of bed. Unfortunately, he made me shower with him. After insisting on washing my body for me, somehow he found the stamina to go again.

The man is truly insatiable. Who knew there was such a ravenous animal lurking under his skin?

Once clean and dressed, Simon produced a stack of papers. A stack of papers he refused to let me read. I tried, I really did, but he had a blank white paper clipped to the top, hiding the contents. He flipped through each paper quickly, only showing me the bottom part requiring my signature.

He insisted I sign them, all ten of them, before he would even consider making the spa appointment.

Begrudgingly, I did. I may have very well just sold my soul to the devil...

But as my stylist works her hands through my hair, massaging my scalp, it feels worth it. Very worth it.

"So, are you like a celebrity or something?" my stylist, Tiffany, asks after she finishes rinsing my hair and helps me sit up.

She glances nervously towards the three beefy men in black from my security detail blocking off the front door. Four more guys stand outside, one guy in front of the door and the other three keeping watch over our cars.

I laugh. "Or something."

Tiffany nods her head and her hands shake, her fingers trembling as she gently rubs my hair down and then wraps it up in a warm towel.

I'm pretty sure Simon put the fear of god in her and the other employees when he dropped me off. His list of demands was extensive, and in my opinion, unnecessary. Especially when he kicked all the male employees out.

Obviously, his jealousy knows no bounds.

The entire spa has been closed for the day. I'm currently the only customer. I have the entire place and every employee left to myself.

Tiffany is unusually quiet as she works on me, but I don't really mind. Honestly, chatter for the sake of chatter often bores me. I'd rather relax in my own mind.

It takes her over three hours to 'fix' my hair. She touches up my roots, applies highlights and lowlights, tones all the brass out, and finishes with a deep conditioning treatment.

Once she's done with me, she eagerly hands me off to a technician who offers me some champagne before waxing me from head to toe.

By the time all my nails are polished and painted, I feel like a new woman.

Or at least, the woman I was before...

After paying and leaving a generous tip, I step out into the street and turn my face up to the sun. I enjoy the spring rays warming my cheeks for a few seconds before the three beefy guys surround me, shrouding me in shadow.

"Ma'am, it's best not to linger," the head of my detail, Logan, says, reminding me of the danger I'm still in.

I let out a long sigh and nod my head. I'm getting sick and tired of constantly looking over my shoulder and having my freedom restricted because I'm in danger.

But Asad is still out there, somewhere... And even though Simon hasn't seen a blimp on the radar or heard a peep of him being in Garden City, it's best not to take any chances.

The security guys usher me quickly to a black SUV parked between two other SUVs directly in front of the spa. They form a wall of muscle, blocking me from the street as I slide into the back.

Before I even have a chance to get my seatbelt on, they shut my door, climb into the car, and we start rolling.

One guy sits in the back beside me, directly behind the driver's seat, while the other two climbed in the front.

Leaning against the seats and consoles are what I'm assuming are automatic rifles of some type, but I'm not familiar with guns so I can't be entirely sure.

"Precious cargo is secured. We're on the move," Logan says. He's sitting in the passenger seat beside the driver.

I can't help but smirk at that term. Precious cargo? Me? I wonder who came up with that one...

The car I'm riding in is in the middle, wedged between the other two cars.

Honestly, three cars might be a little overkill. But given how overprotective Simon is, I should probably be glad there aren't more.

The drive through Garden City is beyond boring. Without a phone, or anything to read, and with the guys acting all tight-lipped and professional, I'm left with nothing to do but to stare out the window.

Or pick at my freshly painted nails.

I'm really going to need to talk Simon into giving me a device of sort. I need something, anything, to connect me to the outside world.

Tall, looming buildings give way to thick, plush greenery. We're halfway home... Shit, when did I start thinking of Simon's house as home?

Logan suddenly speaks rapidly and my ears perk up. "What's that, sir? Please repeat and confirm?"

The air inside the car grows tense. The guy sitting beside me grabs his gun and starts checking it.

Logan barks out, "Shit! Got it, sir!" He glances toward the driver and orders, "Route A is compromised. I repeat, Route A is compromised. Proceed immediately to Route B."

The car comes to a screeching halt and I'm jerked forward, the seatbelt digging painfully into my chest and stomach. Only to be thrown to the side when we make a sudden and complete u-turn.

"What the fuck is going on?!" I screech as the driver slams on the gas, nearly rear-ending the car in front of us.

Pushing away from the door, I look first to the guy sitting beside me. He completely ignores me, engrossed in the workings of his gun.

Shaking my head, I turn my ire on Logan through the rear-view mirror. "Logan?!"

Grabbing his own rifle, Logan spares me only a flick of his eyes as he goes through the process of checking it. "There's a blockade along our previous route." The car fills with the sounds of clicks and clacks. "We're re-routing and rendezvousing at a safe location."

I gape at him, only understanding half of what he said. "What does that mean?"

"It means you have nothing to worry about. Everything is under—"

"We've got company up ahead!" the driver calls out.

"Don't stop! Don't fucking stop! That's an order!" Logan roars. "Drive right through the bastards."

I lean to the side and peer through the windshield. I can't see anything over the big SUV in front of us though.

"Ma'am, you need to get down," the guy beside me says, finally noticing me.

"How do you want me to get down?" I ask.

Do they want me on the floor? That seems a little dangerous.

He opens his mouth to reply but all I hear is a thunderous crack followed by a high, ear-splitting screech of metal.

My head jerks to the front but our car swerves sharply to the left.

"Get down!" the guy beside me yells and grabs me.

Yanking me out of the corner that gravity pushed me into, he rips my shoulder-belt to the side and shoves me down until I'm bent in half.

"Alpha car has been hit! Beta car is taking fire!" I hear Logan yell.

My nose is jammed so hard into my knees I try to sit up, but a big, heavy hand immediately shoves me back down.

"We've got more company up ahead!" the driver bellows.

"Fuck! They have us pinned in!" the guy beside me curses.

"What the fuck is that? Is that a fucking RPG?!" Logan yells in dismay.

A second later there's a loud whoosh then our car is rocking and shuddering violently as something behind us explodes.

"Stay down! Stay down!" the man beside me yells repeatedly.

"Omega car has been destroyed! We have to engage, sir!" Logan says, sounding more and more agitated by the second.

Our car screeches to a stop and I rock forward so hard against my seat belt I want to puke.

"Get down!" the man beside me yells again and I scream back, "I am down, asshole!"

Someone, I'm assuming him, fumbles with the buckle at my waist then releases it. Untangling me from the belt, he pushes me down to the floor.

I tumble to my knees and glance up.

He immediately shoves my head back down.

Fucker!

"Stay there," he orders. "Don't move!"

Panting heavily, I stare down at the black carpet of the floorboards and my ears strain as I try to figure out what the hell is going on around me.

Doors pop open. The smell of burnt rubber and smoke drifts in.

"Targets at twelve o'clock, three o'clock, and nine o'clock," the asshole who shoved me down barks.

"Don't forget six o'clock! We're completely surrounded!" Logan roars and the doors slam shut.

Gunfire immediately erupts. To my untrained ears it sounds as if hundreds of shots are being fired off.

Screams pierce the air, and multiple pings ring off the body of the car.

I press my cheek hard against the floor and start to pray that no bullets pierce through the armor. I'm not a devout woman, and I've committed many sins over the duration of my life, but I'm not ready to die yet...

God, please, I'm not ready to die yet.

Not when I just found Simon.

The door behind me is ripped open and a pair of strong hands grab me by the waist, dragging me kicking and screaming out of the car.

I claw at the carpet, at the seat, at the door. My nails catching and bending. But I'm no match for the strength behind my attacker's arms.

I'm twisted around and the world spins as I

struggle to free myself from the tight band wrapped around my waist.

"Let me go, you stupid fuck!" I screech, half in anger, half in terror.

Throwing my head back in an act of pure desperation, pain explodes behind my eyes as the back of my skull connects with my attacker's nose.

The man holding me curses angrily and drops me to the ground.

My knees hit the pavement first and the pain that lances up my legs is so strong I'm stunned for a moment.

Then I remember if I want to live I have to fucking *move*.

Pushing myself up with my hands, I jerk my head back and squint up into the harsh sunlight to see a dark figure looming over me.

A rough, unfamiliar voice yells, "I've got the whore!"

Then something cracks against my head and the world goes dark.

19

SIMON

A small stronghold in a town an hour outside of Garden City has caused me to lose Meredith. How the fuck does a small fucking rolling army lose out to these Saudi Arabian fucking bastards?

I knew I shouldn't have left her alone. I knew I should have left her in the house where there was a chance the house's security could've slowed down the attack until some of the inner circle could get there.

Pushing the disconnect button on the phone, I want to slam it into the console until it's broken into a million pieces. But I restrain myself. It's not Logan's fault that all the men are dead, including him.

All I can do now is to keep us moving.

I push the button for the CEO's number of Twin Star Security.

Marcus comes on the phone line quickly, but doesn't even let me speak.

"What the fuck's going on, Simon... We've lost contact with all our point leads... Shit, hold on," Marcus shouts into the phone.

"How fucking dare he put me on hold!" I scream as I slam the pistol in my other hand against the center console.

"See what's going on first, brother," Johnathan says in a calming voice. "We can castrate him later. We need his help right now."

He called me brother, is that what I am now to him? A brother in arms? Does he know the ache that slams into my heart thinking of what losing Meredith would do to me?

Looking over at the bearded man, I want to slam a bullet through his neanderthal fucking skull, but he's fucking right. "Fucking go faster. They are headed for the airstrip, I know it in my gut."

"You got it," he says as he pushes the gas pedal down hard to the floor.

To lose her now, it's unthinkable. Unconscionable.

I simply must get her back.

This is my woman, my world. A world that will cease to exist for me if anything were to happen to her.

The rolling convoy we're riding in is pushing it hard. Three fully armored cars. The Saudi's are heading out of Garden city and thank fuck we are heading in the direction they are leaving.

Directly between us is a small airstrip that has enough landing strip length to accommodate a private jet. That will be Asad's escape route.

I don't know what the fuck to do beyond hope to hell we can gain the advantage in speed. But I doubt it. We simply can't get there fucking fast enough due to us being so god damn heavy from the armor the vehicles carry.

"Simon, vehicle feed shows a bobtailed semi-truck ramming the lead vehicle into a building. Second vehicle had an RPG—" Marcus comes back on the line to say.

"I could have told you that, Marcus!" I shout into the phone. "If you wouldn't have put me on fucking hold!"

"I—" he starts to say, but I quickly cut him off again.

"Get all the men you can to Landow Airstrip. It's off of 87. I do not want you to fucking delay, get them mobile now. You won't get there in time, but we'll need the backup if this becomes a drawn-out firefight."

"Simon..." he says hesitantly, "this is what negotiators are for at this point. Insurance will not cover her kidnapping if we engage with them at this point."

"Marcus, you will be on the helicopter out there with your men or I will personally visit your grandchildren's schools and remove them from your life. Do you understand?" I hiss out.

"Simon!" Johnathan shouts at me to get my attention. Wagging his finger, he says, "No kids. You know how Lucifer feels about that now."

The silence on the phone gives me the bargaining chip I need though. Taking a long breath, I say into the phone, "Marcus, scratch that about your grandchildren. Just get you and your men to the landing strip now. We'll cover any costs."

Pushing the disconnect button on the phone, I look over to Johnathan. "Never fucking correct me again."

"Fuck off, Spider. You know the rules of the game. I'm all for killing the fucker's whole family, I ain't got a qualm against it. I'll do it because you're a brother, but you know the kids rule. They're sacred."

"Brother..." I say quietly.

"Yeah, man, you're one of us now. You got yourself hitched. Nothing left to do but drink beer and gush about soccer practice if you have daughters. Or cheer the boy on in football practice," he says with a laugh.

Even now he considers himself a fucking family man. The fucking uncouth, disgusting bastard who's killed almost as many men as I have killed, thinks of himself as a family man.

How interesting.

Am I one now? I'm positive with the lack of protection, Meredith has been impregnated. I felt it happen the first time we were intimate. A father. Me...

Fuck.

"I will not allow a child of mine to take part in something as lowly and dirty as football," I say simply.

"Dude, you won't stand a chance. Charlie is already begging me to let him play in the peewee football league. Beth is on me to let him since I got to play when I was a kid. Dirt does kids good, Simon. It helps their immune system or some shit."

Whipping the Tahoe to the right, we speed past a minivan full of kids and one tired looking father. The convoy behind us pulls the same move as we race towards the airport.

One child, only one fucking child. There is no way I won't eat my young if I have more than one.

Being a father... What would that entail? Love and commitment to the child, of course. A proper guidance and support system.

Do I have those qualities in me for a child of my own? I think I would. But do I want them? Do I want a lifetime of shit, drool, headaches, and other baggage?

I want Meredith and all that comes with her.

Dammit, we're still moving too fucking slowly.

Pushing the button on my phone for Lucifer, I listen to the phone ring one time before it's picked up.

"Simon, I'm pulling the rest of the men off their details. I have a helicopter lifting off in five minutes."

"Good. I'll update my men. Make sure to bring extra mags of ammunition. We're not low, but refills are going to be needed. James is in the tailing car, but does not have a sniper rifle with him."

"Got it, I'll bring his baby," Lucifer says before disconnecting.

Was it just me or did Lucifer sound almost giddy speaking about coming out to help us?

Probably is. He hasn't been out much when it comes to these operations since Lily. Family life has slowed him. Johnathan and Andrew are the same way... They both fell into the roles Lucifer has been handing out to them.

Damn. Damn all this shit to hell. We need more men and a much larger network. Shit like this should have never happened.

Why do we always seem to be unable to keep our women safe?

"Lucifer's coming in with the helicopter, but I doubt he'll be able to catch them," I say to Johnathan.

Pushing the button on his neck, he breaks the radio silence. "All teams, Alpha will be heading in on the chopper, bringing the baby for our playboy."

"Shit, yeah! I need my sexy little filly to play with," James says over the comms.

"Christ on a hotdog bun, James. Couldn't you act serious?" Johnathan responds with a laugh.

"Let's be professional for this. The Saudi's will be

packing heavily. Possible RPG's, as well as full auto weapons," I say as I glance down to my hands.

I have a pistol and a phone. This isn't going to be enough.

"Fuck RPG's, or well I would say that if I had my girl," James says over the comm. "But I got enough distance with the HK416 I'm using now. I should be able to get some cover if Andrew can drop me on the other end."

"Roger that. Simon send over the map of the landing strip if you can," Andrew says.

Pulling my pad out of a backpack, I flip through multiple maps and eventually have to use a Google Earth map.

Sending it to them, I say, "Best I have right now."

My proximity alarm on my phone starts beeping, telling me that we are now within a fifteen-mile range of the Saudi's convoy.

They have three fast moving BMW's right now heading to the airstrip. I can't tell any more than that because we've gone past the traffic cameras I had control over.

Fifteen miles until I see her.

"The Saudi's have entered the fifteen-mile radius of my tracker on Meredith," I say to the men. "They should arrive at the airport two minutes ahead of us."

Fuck, that is a lot time for things to happen that I

have no control over. This is a small-time airport, no security except some old man with a dog.

"Clear. I'm looking at the map. Give me one minute to see if I can get up high enough to shoot downwards," James says.

"Johnathan, let me pull up in front of you," Thad says over the comms, "I'll try to take lead in front of the plane if possible. Me and the Harrison boys can cover you guys that way."

"We have two oncoming cars. Thirty seconds, then pull ahead," Johnathan says over the radio.

"Simon, I've got a high spot. It looks good, but I can't be positive. Andrew will pull into the rear. He's going to be a bit late to the party, but he can drop me at the radio tower there. I won't go too high, but enough to get some height," James says.

"Roger," I say over the comms.

"Let's get the bosses sister before they get a chance to get funny any ideas," Andrew says in a gruff voice.

"Nah, that's Simon's girl, man," James says over the comms with a laugh.

"What? Are you fucking getting hitched, Simon?" Andrew asks.

"Die in a fire, all of you," I say with annoyance.

I don't need all these assholes knowing my personal business. If they knew the depths of the soul-crushing ache that I feel when she's not near me, I would never live it down.

"That's a negative for me, Simon. I got rid of the clap a couple of months ago. No more burning pee-pee for me," James snickers.

I swear if that fucker was in the car with me right now I would slit his fucking wrists and piss all over his skull before I detached it from his fucking idiotic neck.

"Gentlemen... and James..." Lucifer's voice comes through the comms and instantly the chatter ends. "Let's get this wrapped up as cleanly as possible."

Everything goes quiet for us. We're close to death. I can feel it in my heart. We're going to fight for our lives right now. The bloodshed will be significant.

I rarely wear tactical gear like I am right now, and the damnable bulletproof vest on my chest is constricting me in a way that keeps me from breathing normally. I'm not completely out of my element, but it's close enough.

Is the constricting of breath though from the vest like I want it to be? Or is it Meredith being in harm's way?

Today started out quite pleasantly. I made passionate... is it love... to Meredith. I don't know if that word fits.

It's not all consuming enough.

Love to me is a pitiful metaphor for the feelings I have for this woman. It's all-consuming, soul-crushing, and mind breaking. Is that love? I have no clue.

I trusted the men of Twin Star to keep her safe while I went out to take care of the Yakuza.

Both failed.

We investigated a small laundry shop the Yakuza were supposed to be operating out of. The only thing we found were five men who put up a very large fight. No information was gathered. Everything on the computer hard drives we found was destroyed.

Pouring a jug of sulfuric acid on a hard drive tends to corrupt all the stored data.

We took out three men. One of them had a shoulder wound, and I'm betting it was my shot from when the rider got away on the bike. The other two took their own lives.

Took their own damn lives.

Leaving us with yet another cold fucking trail.

Information on the Yakuza who are hitting us is too fucking small at best. They're using ambush tactics. Hit us and run. I've tried pulling out information on which family it is that links these guys, but so far, I'm grasping at straws.

We need an equalizer. Something to get us back on an even playing field.

Lucifer was right to say we needed more men, we do. We're like a rubber band stretched too thin. You can see something's about to snap if we don't remove some of our burdens.

And right now, as much as I would rather skull-fuck my own eye, bringing in his dog... would be our best bet.

Damn.

✝

"One minute out. Fence on the left is the landing strip's property," I say over our radios.

"Roger that," Andrew says.

"Roger," Thad says shortly after.

"How far is she away, Simon?" James asks.

Checking my phone, I say, "Quarter mile. It shows she's on the landing strip. They are getting ready to move into takeoff position."

"Got it. I'm going to have Andrew stop soon. I need to get a visual of the plane's tires. I want to shoot them out. What's the chance they will hurt Meredith if their plane is disabled?" he asks.

"Eighty-twenty," I say after pushing the talk button. "Asad wants revenge too much, and his father wouldn't be happy with a corpse coming back. They have too much honor at stake."

"Got it. I'll try to hit the pilot first. I'm taking out a wheel... then the engine if it comes down to it. She ain't going anywhere."

"Copy that. If you get the pilot, take out anyone that comes in view through the cockpit window," I say.

The entrance comes up rapidly upon us. Thankfully Johnathan is proficient enough in driving this large vehicle that he doesn't tip us on our side as he takes the turn.

Slamming the pedal back down, I get thrown back into my seat as he guns it towards the already ripped off gate hole.

"Get ready with your gun," he growls to me.

"Pull as close to the plane as you can," I say. "But we need to be careful in case they have another RPG they can use against us."

Pulling up my HK417, I eject the full clip to check it one more time. Never hurts to be thoroughly prepared. Popping it back into the slot, I make sure the safety is turned off.

"Check mine too if you can. I don't want a cartridge breach out there."

Pulling Johnathan's assault rifle up, I quickly go through ejecting his fresh mag and pulling back the hammer. Everything looking good, I set it back up.

"Clean and ready. Excellent looking rifle... I'm surprised it's so well taken care of," I say as I put it down beside mine.

Up ahead, I see a black luxury plane idling on the runway. Johnathan spots it too as he slams the accelerator of the Escalade towards the left side of the plane.

"Halfway to top. I got a shot of the front wheel of the plane. I don't want to wait until it moves," James says.

"Can you spot the pilot?" I ask.

"Yeah, he's looking frantic. Some other asshole is yelling at him. Maybe a gun being waved around," he says. "Fuck, he's pointing out to Thad's Tahoe."

"Yeah, I'm going to park it right in front. They'll have to pull back to get around us," Thad says.

"Wheel shot now blocked by Thad. Going for the pilot."

"Take the shot," I say.

There's a loud cracking noise from our left as we come screeching to a halt next to the plane.

"One of the pilots is down. Will take out the second when he pops up," James says.

"I'm five minutes out, Simon. Can it hold?" Lucifer comes over the radio.

"We'll have to see—" I start to say before the cockpit door opens up.

"Shit! RPG!" Thad screams over the radio.

I watch as he and the two guys he's been training start running from the vehicle.

A white trail of smoke and then a huge red explosion comes from the Tahoe that was blocking the airplane. Chucks of metal go flying out as the guy pulls back into the plane.

"Shit!" Johnathan growls as he grabs his assault rifle from me.

Both of us exit the Escalade at the same time. He

stops in front of the engine and lines up a shot at the back door of the plane.

"Status report. Thad, you and the trainees good?" Andrew asks.

Andrew's vehicle swings wide of where we're parked.

"Bryant's dead. Mark and I are mobile, but we're in the fucking open," Thad answers.

I watch as Andrew's car heads towards the two men before slamming on the breaks not too far from them.

"We'll pick up an angled position from the front of the plane. They won't be shooting out again without having to pop a window," Andrew says.

"Affirmative," I say into the mic.

I can feel cold sweat running down my back as I position myself next to Johnathan. Both of us waiting for something more to happen.

Is it my mortality I worry about or Meredith's?

"Going to take out a wheel, then put shots into the tail wing. I don't trust that engine not to blow in a bad way if I hit it," James says.

"Roger," I confirm.

Watching the plane drop to the front, I turn toward the tail and lift my rifle. "I'm going to help with the tail wing. Let's ensure they know they can't move from here."

Pulling the trigger in five rapid bursts, I put holes

throughout the tail wing and then watch as more appear from James and Johnathan.

"Shit. Fast moving BMW from the rear," Andrew says over the radios.

Turning to my right, I see that it's one of Asad's men. Damn.

"They're going to be desperate. If they can take out enough of us, they'll try to make a run for it."

"Door opening in the back," Johnathan calls, pulling my attention from the rapidly approaching BMW.

"They're going to make a break for it!" I shout before a lone arm comes out of the open doorway of the plane and with it a grenade comes tumbling towards our way.

"Grenade!" Johnathan shouts. He sends three rapid shots into the open doorway then follows behind me as we run away from the explosive.

The grenade stops just on the other side of the SUV we were taking cover behind. And it must be one hell of a good one because both of us are lifted off our feet as the explosion lifts the Escalade onto the tips of its wheels.

Thankfully it slams back down on all four wheels.

Landing not too far away, I thank myself for being intelligent enough to make sure we always buy the best when it comes to armored vehicles.

Moving back towards the Escalade, we're almost

there when the BMW comes screeching up on us. Thank the gods there's only two men inside it.

The passenger leans out of the vehicle and aims a small semi-automatic rifle at us.

Grabbing my collar, Johnathan shoves me out of the fucking way as bullets tear up the ground around us.

"Going for the driver," I shout out as I aim at the driver. My bullets find their way home, slamming through the window and hitting the man.

"Passenger—" Johnathan grunts out as he stumbles against me, his weight almost knocking me off my feet.

"What the fuck?" I yell at him as I lift the rifle again and fire at the passenger.

Almost all my shots go wide as Johnathan falls into my legs. But as I fall down in a heap with him, I see my last shot go through the window and hit the man through the neck.

"Johnathan, where are you hit?" I ask as I can think of only one reason for him falling into me like he did.

Grabbing him by the collar, I pull us to the safety of the vehicle's large body as bullets from the open door of the plane start flying all around us.

"Two minutes out," Lucifer says over the radio.

"Get here quicker," I shout into mic. "Andrew move here. Johnathan's wounded."

"Fuck, on my way. This is gonna suck."

"Embrace it, bitch," I snap into the mic.

Fucking whiney assholes. We need to hurry, this is turning into the bloodbath I foresaw, and it won't end well if we don't finish this quickly.

I look down at Johnathan and assess the situation. The blood leaking from his leg is coming out slow enough, I suppose. But the wound on his left side is starting to flow.

Shit, they're using hollow-points. They're probably Teflon coated to go through our vests.

Dirty fucking bastards.

Kneeling down beside Johnathan, I grab my switchblade from my pocket. Time to make some decisions.

"Fuck... I'm bleeding out," Johnathan grunts as he pulls his rifle close to him.

Leg or stomach... Fuck.

Reaching over, I start cutting off the long shoulder strap on his rifle. "Going to need to tourniquet the leg wound first. Then we'll get some compression on your wound up there."

Pulling out my flashlight, I first wrap the strap around his leg then grab the flashlight and use it to turn it tight.

"Ah, fuck!" he shouts as I cinch it tight.

"Hold it shut," I say then pull his hand from the rifle.

I place his hand on the flashlight to keep the twisted material of the strap tight on his leg.

"Coming in. I'm behind the building on your left, do not shoot," James shouts into the mic.

More bullets come streaming out of the plane door but thankfully I don't hear any metal hitting cement that sounds like a grenade.

Andrew's vehicle comes screeching to a stop behind my own with barely two inches to spare between the bumpers.

Hopping out of the SUV, he yanks a black backpack down with him as he charges over to Johnathan and me.

"Let me in there, Simon. You get with James," Andrew says.

"Tourniquet on leg, serious wound on lower left abdomen," I say

"Got it," Andrew replies. "Let me see what you got going on under the vest."

James comes skidding to a halt on his knees as he sidles up next to me just as two men lay down long bursts out the door of the plane.

"Motherfucker!" I hiss as I lift myself up and shoot over the engine hood of the SUV.

I hit one of the men in the thigh, and James doesn't let me down as he fills the man full of holes as he tumbles down the stairs.

"How many do they have in there?" James asks.

"Should be four more. Four guards, Asad, and Meredith. Not counting pilots," I say in a rush.

"Both pilots are dead, and I got a headshot on a guard. That makes three guards," James adds.

"Any kills from you, Thad?" I ask through the radio

"One. Through the side window. I saw Meredith pulled back towards cockpit," he replies.

Two guards, Asad, and Meredith.

"They're going to be desperate. I wouldn't be surprised if Asad doesn't have some kind of reinforcements coming though," James says.

"Agreed, we need to go in," Thad says quickly, "But I'll need space and time to move around."

"Lucifer, we're heading in," I say into my mic.

"Be careful. We're getting permissions to land now. The air tower is having issues. They are calling the local law enforcement," Lucifer says over the radio.

"Damn, we'll hurry," I say.

"We need to airlift Johnathan, guys," Andrew says from my side.

Looking down to the two men, I frown. Johnathan's eyes are closed and he's growing pale. At least he's breathing though.

"Get him out of here on the helicopter," I say to him.

Moving to the rear of the Escalade, I motion for James to follow me. "Let's get a move on. They've been quiet too long."

Nodding his head, he moves with me towards the

back of the plane. Slowly we inch our way forward. I eject the half spent clip and put in my last one.

This better be a quick fight.

Reaching the stairs, we stand just below them as we look up into the open hatch.

James says, "I've got a flashbang."

"Good, toss it then we head in," I say.

Nodding his head, he pulls it out of a pocket on his tactical vest. Tugging the pin out, he squeezes the handle so it doesn't go off yet.

He lifts his hand and says, "On three."

Nodding my head, I watch as he counts down on his fingers.

Three... two... and he stops with one finger still up.

He cocks his head to the side like he's trying to think of something.

"What is it?" I ask quietly.

"Did I really hear you tell Andrew to 'embrace it, bitch'?" he asks just as quietly.

Oh, for the devil's sake... of all the fucking things...

Rolling my eyes, I nod my head with a grin. "Yes, James."

"Sweet!" he shouts with a laugh just as he tosses the flashbang grenade into the plane.

Ducking our heads down, we both slap our hands over our ears to muffle the sound.

When I drop my hands I hear a man shouting in

anger and then Meredith emits a high-pitched scream of pain.

Enough is enough.

Charging up the stairs, I rush through the opened hatch as quickly as I can.

To my left, towards the cockpit, is a black-haired man holding a pistol out towards me as he tries to control Meredith and blink his eyes at the same time.

Lifting my rifle, I watch Meredith go dead still. She doesn't want me to hit her.

Just as James enters the plane a shot rings out from the back aimed at him. I hear a loud thud next to my head.

The man holding Meredith pulls the trigger of his pistol three times before I'm able to make my one shot.

I feel the bullets slamming into my chest three times.

Each one feels like a fucking elephant just kicked me.

The man starts to drop to the ground with Meredith getting tugged to her knees in the process.

Shit.

I feel more kicks and something else.

I'm fucking hit too.

How many of us will die here on this fucking shitty tarmac?

Meredith is screaming over the gunfire raging

behind me. James begins to shout Asad's name out as Thad charges into the plane's hatch.

I stand up and stumble towards the body of the man holding Meredith down.

His pistol hand is moving slowly towards me, and for some reason I can't figure out, I've seem to have dropped my rifle behind me.

Pulling my switchblade from my pocket, I lurch towards him.

Glancing over, I see Meredith staring at me with wide eyes.

My beautiful ballerina looks at me in horror right before I feel another bullet slam into my right pec.

Thankfully, I think the vest stopped it like the other ones. The hot feeling of blood spilling down my arm tells me he got me at least once though.

"No!" I hear my princess's voice scream.

She scrambles over to the asshole who shot me. Pulling the pistol from his hand, she kneels on top of his chest.

Shoving the gun into his forehead, she doesn't hesitate to pull the trigger twice.

Blood explodes from the head and splatters both the floor and her face.

She's made a mess of herself for me.

I'm not sure why, but if I wasn't hurting so bad I think my dick would be so hard I'd walk with a limp.

My woman. She's my pregnant woman.

Dropping the gun, she crawls over to me. Her eyes tight with worry. "Simon! Oh my god, you're bleeding!"

"It's... take... help me get... vest," I grunt.

Slipping my fingers into the side of my vest, I try to start unfastening the Velcro holding it tight to me.

Too damn tight.

"Clear!" James shouts from the back of the plane.

"Do you have Asad?" I hear Lucifer's voice from outside of the plane.

Meredith pulls my face back to face hers. "Look at me, Simon!"

"Vest. Can't. Breathe," I grunt.

Finally grabbing a strap, I start to pull it off but stop because the pain in my other shoulder lances through me.

Looking to my left shoulder, I see a lot of blood, but it looks like I've been winged more than hit.

That doesn't stop the tears flowing down Meredith's face as she tries to help me with the vest.

"It's okay," I gasp when the vest is finally loosened.

"It's not a bad one, I've had worse. Princess, look at me," I say, pulling her close to me with my good arm.

"Then why did you have to take that vest off?" she asks with worry, still staring at my shoulder.

"Look at me, Meredith!" I command.

Looking up with fear-filled eyes, she stares into my face, "Yes, Simon?"

"I'm so very proud of you." I reach up and wipe at some of the blood covering her face.

"Thank you for coming for me," she sobs as she leans forward, putting her forehead to mine.

A lot of commotion comes from the back of the plane as Lucifer boards. I can distinctly hear Asad screaming his head off about his father.

"Help me stand, princess. We're going to need to get out of here," I say to her.

Nodding her head, she says "Simon... I... I... thank you."

I don't think that's what she was going to say, but right now I don't think she can cope with having put a bullet through a man's head.

"Don't worry, princess, I will always come for you. You've done so well today, I might just spank you as a reward," I say with a painful chuckle

"Jesus, Simon, your incorrigible," she says with a shaky laugh.

I do notice that she didn't say she didn't want one though.

Suddenly my phone begins to buzz in my pocket as we start shuffling towards the plane's open hatch.

Pulling it from my pocket with my good hand, I allow Meredith to keep my bad arm cradled to my side.

On the cracked screen I see it's Marcus.

Pushing the connect button, I say, "What is it?"

"We're ten minutes out, Simon. Can you hold till we get there?"

"Go fuck yourself," I say into the phone before disconnecting it.

Asshole didn't rush to get here and he knows it. He should have been here shortly after us. There is no way that bag of human flesh rushed his way here. Especially since I know for a fact they have access to a helicopter just like Lucifer does.

Lucifer comes out of the back of the plane with a gagged Asad being marched behind him. "Simon, is it serious?"

"No, fucker winged me, and cracked ribs at the most," I say breathily.

Definitely cracked ribs.

"Good. And thank you for rescuing my sister," he says as he gives a smile to Meredith.

Nodding my head, I motion for them to go first. "Let's get him to the warehouse."

"No, you need to go to a hospital," Meredith says from my side in a voice I've not heard before.

This one isn't defiant, pleading, or demanding. She's speaking like her fucking brother.

Full of surety.

Chuckling quietly, I wince as I say, "I'll have Andrew meet us there. He can patch me up. A hospital is not in the cards for me. Not with how bad Johnathan is. We need to keep this as low profile as we can right now."

"Agreed," Lucifer says. "Thad, you head straight to the hospital. Get a guard rotation with our men on the floor. I want Johnathan watched over. Send Andrew to the warehouse for Simon. Make sure he brings a full kit with him."

"Got it, sir," Thad says and rushes out of the plane.

From behind Lucifer, where he is still holding on to Asad by his scruff, James says, "Can we go? I got a bag of dicks in my hand and you know how I am. If it ain't my dick I don't wanna be holding it."

Snickering, Lucifer nods his head. "Let's get off of this plane and get out of here. It looks like we have Andrew's car and one of Asad's men's BMWs."

"Thad!" Lucifer shouts out to the man. "Go get another one of their BMW's and take that to the hospital. We'll be using the last of the armored cars."

Stumbling as much as walking down the steps, I finally feel the cement beneath my feet and stare up into the bright blue sky.

It's fucking beautiful, and for once I don't fucking hate it.

I look back down to Meredith and pull her tight to my chest. Kissing her hard as I can, I push my tongue past her lips. This isn't a claiming kiss. No, this is one that brings too much joy for that.

This is a declaration of life.

"Holy fuck, the Spider really isn't gay?" Thad chortles.

I'd turn around and shoot the bastard then fuck the wound if Meredith wasn't holding me so tightly to her. Her kiss as deep and full as my own.

20

MEREDITH

"I didn't know you could drive a car," I say, catching Matthew's eyes in the rearview mirror as he takes the driver's seat of the armored car we'll be traveling in.

"There's a lot you don't know about me, Meredith," he says with a smirk and starts the engine.

I incline my head, giving him that point, and turn my attention back to Simon. He's leaning heavily into me, with his good arm wrapped around my waist.

"But I hope we can change that," Matthew adds, surprising me.

My head jerks to him, meeting his gaze again in the rearview mirror. Intense icy-blue orbs stare back at me.

As far as I can tell, he's being completely serious. And at this point, I have no clue how I feel about it.

Too much shit has happened today. I almost died

too many times for my liking. But even worse, Simon and Matthew's men were hurt trying to rescue me. At least one has died, and another is so badly injured he might die too.

Simon hisses as he shifts in his seat and his arm tightens around me. I look worriedly to the oozing wound on his left shoulder.

Watching him get hit by so many bullets was the most terrifying experience of my life, hands down. Even now, ice floods my chest as I remember how close I was to losing him. In that moment, I realized how much I want him.

How much I fucking need his craziness.

"Don't cry for me, princess," Simon says, and I reach up to wipe at my cheeks, surprised to find tears there. "I'll be fine. It's only a scratch."

I shake my head and take a deep breath, trying to get my shit together. I can't crack yet. That will have to come later, much later...

"You should have just let me go," I say quietly in admonishment.

He could have died. He almost died. And I had to kill yet another man to stop it from happening.

Even now that man's blood stains my face, and I'm not sure but I think there are chunks of his brain in my hair.

I squeeze my eyes shut, trying to push out the flash of his head exploding as I slammed two bullets into it.

"Never," he says so vehemently I can tell it pains him as my eyes flash open. "I'm never fucking letting you go."

"But—"

His good arm jerks me into him and his jaw clenches as he grits out, "Meredith, I would walk through the fires of hell and fight the devil himself to get you back."

His declaration fills me warmth, but also sends tingling sensations down my spine. Is he implying what I think he's implying?

Glancing towards the front of the car, I see Matthew's hard eyes staring right back at us. Fuck, this is more drama then my poor heart can take right now.

Simon's arm relaxes around me and he winces as he shifts in his seat.

"Simon, you need to go to the hospital," I say, pulling away from him as carefully as I can without hurting him.

The corners of his lips curl up. Oh, how I hate that my concern for him seems to amuse him. "It would draw too much attention, princess."

"I don't care," and I don't. I could give a flying fuck about how much attention we draw. He needs to be treated. I can't stand to see him wincing and shifting around in pain. A pain he's suffering because of me. "You need to be treated by a professional."

All kinds of yucky things could happen if his

wound isn't treated properly and quickly. It only takes a few hours for an infection to set in...

Fuck, he of all people should know this!

Simon's eyes glimmer with amusement. "Trust me, Andrew is a professional. Besides, we still have unfinished business to see to."

"Unfinished business?" I repeat.

What could there possibly be left to do?

All traces of amusement fade from Simon's face and it feels as if all the warmth is sucked out of the car as his expression grows cold. "A message must be sent."

Just hearing those words come out of his mouth thrusts me back into that bloody scene in the basement with Matthew all those years ago.

No. *No.* I'm not going through that again.

"Pull over the car, Matthew," I order, jerking away from Simon.

Matthew shakes his head and I swear he hits the gas. "We're in the middle of nowhere, Meredith."

"I don't care," I find myself saying again. "You can get one of your men to take me back to Simon's."

"All the men are currently occupied with other, more important, matters," Matthew smirks.

"Then I'll fucking hitch a ride," I hiss.

Matthew's eyes meet mine in the mirror and his smirk sharpens. "Even if I were inclined to put you in such a dangerous position, do you think anyone would pick you up looking like that?"

I glance down at myself. My blue dress is absolutely ruined. My stockings are ripped to hell and back. One of the heels on my shoes is cracked and could snap off at any second. I'm covered in blood and other things... Things I rather not know the origin of.

My head throbs, pulsing behind my eyes, and I'm pretty sure I have a huge knot on my forehead from where that asshole cracked me with the butt of his rifle.

He's not wrong but he doesn't have to be so fucking smug about it.

Whipping my head towards Simon, I resort to pleading. "Simon, please. Drop me off at the house first, then take care of whatever business you have to see to."

Simon stares at me for a long moment and I think he's about to give me exactly what I'm asking for, but then his eyes fill with fire. A fire that scorches my heart.

"No. At this time, I don't think I could bear to be separated from you, princess."

Fuck. He's really going to do this to me... He's really going to make me relive my worst nightmare.

Reaching out with his good arm, he grabs me by the wrist and yanks me closer until I'm tucked against his side.

I feel his lips brushing across the top of my head

before he murmurs quietly. "It will be a long time before I let you out of my sight again."

No matter how hard I beg and plead, Simon stands firm in his decision to keep me beside him.

The car ride to wherever they're taking me is long and torturous. Not only is all the shit that just went down replaying in my head, but I'm also having flashbacks of the past.

I hate Asad, hate him with every fucking fiber of my being, but I don't want to watch him get tortured.

By the time Matthew pulls the car up in front of what looks like an abandoned warehouse, I'm ready to puke.

"We're here," Simon says quietly as Matthew shuts the engine off. "Open the door, princess?"

Shaking the tendrils of the past from my head, I look at him. Really look at him. If I forgive him for what he's about to do, wouldn't that make me a huge fucking hypocrite? Wouldn't I have to forgive Matthew too?

"The longer we linger, the longer until I'm treated," Simon reminds me.

"Fuck," I curse out loud and shove the door open.

I slide out and then offer Simon my hand. He

accepts it gratefully, and only grunts half a dozen times as he exits.

As Simon steps into me, leaning his weight into me, Matthew comes up and shuts the door for us.

"This is going to fucking suck," Simon says, eyeing the distance between the car and the warehouse.

I laugh. I fucking laugh. Yeah, I'm losing it.

"We can always turn back," I suggest. If only I could be so lucky...

Simon's jaw tenses with determination. "It's too late for that."

He takes a step forward and I have no choice but to move with him. Slowly, but surely we make it up to the door of the warehouse. Matthew moves ahead and holds the door open.

I can't even look him in the face as we step past him. After all, this is all his doing...

Inside the warehouse is exactly what I imagined. Old, forgotten machine equipment. Years of dust and dirt that floats up into the air as soon as our footsteps disturb it.

What I didn't expect though was how much the concrete floors and walls remind me of the basement.

Oh god, he's pretty much recreated it, hasn't he? Except bigger and scarier.

"Andrew has arrived," Matthew says suddenly behind me and I nearly jump out of my skin.

"Thank fuck," Simon mutters.

We weave through the old equipment, making our way to a room in the back that must have once been an office. I stop in the doorway, every hair on my body standing on end.

I do not want to go in there...

"Meredith, come," Matthew says, giving me a little nudge. "Simon needs to rest."

I shoot him a dirty look but move forward.

Inside the room is a table, a few chairs, and a desk pushed up against the wall. There once must have been carpet, but it's been ripped up, baring the concrete floor. The red fibers lining the edges of the room the only clue it was ever there.

The smell of disinfectant is heavy in the air, and maybe it's just my own sick imagination, but I'm certain I can smell blood beneath it.

I help Simon to the closest chair. He slumps down into it with a hiss. Sweat glistens on his brow and his skin looks a little ashen.

I try to take a step back, fully intent on finding some excuse to go outside, but Simon's hand whips out, his fingers latching onto my hand.

"No," he says firmly and his pain-filled eyes turn up to me. "I... need you here with me, princess."

I hesitate and stare into his face.

Fuck. I want to run far, far away from here.

But how can I deny him when he needs me? When

the only reason he's suffering right now is because of me?

Even though every instinct inside of me is screaming for me to flee, to put as much distance as possible between me and this warehouse, I nod my head.

Simon's shoulders relax, the tension flowing out of him as I move closer to stand beside his chair.

He keeps ahold of my hand, squeezing it sporadically and stroking his thumb along my skin.

I try to focus on his touch, on how amazing the simple act of his skin rubbing against my skin feels, when Andrew and James appear in the doorway.

"Look who I found outside," Andrew says, walking into the room carrying a big black backpack draped over his shoulder.

"Where do you want this asshole?" James asks, shoving a bound and gagged Asad in front of him.

Asad stumbles forward and turns his head, shouting muffled curses at James.

"Save your breath for later, asshole. You're going to need it," James laughs and gives him another shove.

"The table, Simon?" Matthew asks, looking to Simon for confirmation.

Out of everyone, Matthew looks the most calm and collected. In fact, he looks like he's mildly amused by all of this.

Simon's eyes blaze and his skin flushes with color

as he glares angrily at Asad. "Yes, the table will work perfectly for what I have planned for him."

Asad jerks his head towards Simon, glaring back just as angrily at him, then his attention turns to me.

The glare turns downright murderous as he shouts something that's muffled but sounds a lot like 'filthy whore'.

James cracks him upside the head with the pistol he's holding in his right hand and Asad drops down to one knee, nearly collapsing.

"That's no way to talk to a lady. You're going to regret that, motherfucker," James says, his own anger showing now as he grabs Asad roughly by the arm and drags him over to the table.

"So tell me where it hurts, Spider," Andrew smirks and drops his big backpack down to the floor with a loud thump. He squats down in front of Simon's chair.

Simon's angry glare swings to Andrew. "You need to check out Meredith first."

I blink in surprise. Besides the headache, I haven't sustained any other injuries. The cavalry showed up just in time to spare me from whatever Asad had planned.

"I'm fine, Simon," I assure him. "Your injuries should be tended to first.

Simon squeezes my hand. "You need to be checked, Meredith."

"But you're—"

"The longer you stall, the longer until I'm tended to," Simon growls, putting the matter to rest.

I sigh with resignation. Will I ever get my fucking way with this man?

Andrew looks between us then nods his head. He unzips the front part of his backpack, spreading it open.

After snapping some gloves on his hands, he grabs a small flashlight and straightens.

"How many times were you hit?" he asks as he approaches me.

"Only once, I believe..." I answer as he steps close.

"Where were you hit? Here?" he asks, reaching for the top of my head. He probes lightly at the huge tender knot that is forming and I flinch.

Simon growls low in his throat.

Andrew smirks at Simon. "I'll only touch her as much as I have to."

Then he returns his attention to me as he leans back. "Any other injuries I should know of?"

His gaze roams over me critically from head to toe.

Yeah, with all the stuff I have on me, it's probably hard to tell.

"No," I answer and feel Simon squeeze my hand.

Andrew nods and places his gloved hand on my cheek. He shines the beam of the flashlight in my eyes and I immediately squeeze them shut.

"Try to keep your eyes open," Andrew says gently.

Well, as gently as a man with his deep of a voice can.

Forcing my eyes open, they water and burn as I stare ahead.

Andrew clicks the flashlight off and drops his hand from my cheek.

"Well?" Simon asks impatiently as Andrew drops back down to his backpack.

"She's sustained a mild concussion. She'll need some pain relievers and rest."

I shoot Simon an 'I told you so' look.

He frowns as Andrew rises again with a small bottle of water and a bottle of pills.

"Are those safe for the baby?" Simon asks Andrew.

Shock slices through me and Andrew seems to freeze in place.

"I'm not pregnant," I insist, and shoot Simon a pointed glare.

"You are," he says with such surety I have the sudden urge to punch him.

"You don't know that!"

"I do," he grins, his thumb stroking along my hand.

God, help me. If there's a baby growing inside me... his baby...

Andrew chuckles at our little exchange and shakes his head.

He holds the bottle of water and pills out to me and I just stare at them. "It's safe. It's only Tylenol."

But is Tylenol truly safe for my baby?

Fuck!

Am I accepting this? God, I think I am…

I accept the bottle of water, but wave off the pills. "I'll be fine, thank you."

Andrew nods and bends down to shove the pills back into his backpack.

"Alright, let's have a look at you now, Simon," he says as he straightens. "What the fuck happened to you?"

Simon stares at me as he answers Andrew, and there's the strangest look on his face. It takes me a moment to recognize it, but fuck, I think it's pride and affection.

Why would he be looking at me with pride and affection?

"I got winged on the left shoulder and I think I cracked a couple of ribs."

Andrew nods his head. "Remove your shirt and let's have a look."

Releasing my hand, Simon reaches for the buttons of his shirt but I stop him. "Here, let me do it," I offer, knowing that it would probably be excruciating for him to do it himself.

Hand freezing on his button, Simon's face goes slack. I shove my bottle into his hand and bend down to reach his shirt front.

He watches me warily as my fingers work quickly

down his line of buttons. Almost like he's afraid I'm going to suddenly bite him or something.

Good, he should still have a healthy fear of me. Especially since the fucker got me pregnant…

When I reach the bottom, I gently spread the fabric open.

"Thank you, princess," he says quietly, so quietly I barely hear it over my gasp.

Large, angry red welts are peppered across his chest. I knew I almost lost him, but seeing is believing. Fuck. If he wasn't wearing his vest…

Andrew whistles between his teeth. "Looks like someone really wanted to kill you."

"Stop fucking fighting!" James suddenly growls and then there's a loud crack.

"Don't you dare fucking kill him!" Simon roars and then winces.

I flinch back, my ears buzzing, then glance towards the table to see what the hell is going on.

"Here, let me give you a hand," Matthew says, shrugging off his suit jacket and draping it over a chair before he eagerly approaches the table to help restrain a flailing Asad.

For a moment, I somehow forgot where we are and why we're here. But suddenly all the panic I was feeling earlier comes rushing back in.

Matthew helping James seems to pacify Simon

because he slumps down in his chair as I turn back to him.

He gives me a look full of remorse. "Sorry, princess."

I take a deep breath, trying to settle my nerves, but I doubt all the oxygen in the world would help me right now. Not when I know what's about to happen...

Devoting my full attention back on Simon, I try to ignore Asad's struggles in the corners of my eyes and focus on getting Simon's shirt off his shoulders while hurting him as little as possible.

Some of the blood has started to dry though, so I quite literally have to peel the shirt away from his skin.

Once I have his shirt off and bunched at his waist, I take a step back, giving Andrew room to work.

Andrew bends over Simon and closely examines his wound on his shoulder. Gloved fingers poking and prodding at it. "Yeah, you were only winged. A few stitches and you'll be good to go."

Knowing that should flood me with relief, but I'm overwhelmed with a sense of doom.

My eyes wander back over to the table of their own accord. Matthew is grinning as he holds Asad's feet down so James can secure them...

And in my eyes Matthew is no longer Matthew.

With that grin of sick joy on his face and that dark gleam in his eyes, once again he's transformed into that monster that's haunted my nightmares.

Lucifer.

"Let's have a look at those ribs," I hear Andrew say.

Asad thrashes his head back and forth, and I bet beneath his gag he's foaming at the mouth.

"Ah! Fuck!" Simon grunts and Andrew chuckles.

"Yeah, they're cracked alright. Nothing I can do about that though. It will heal on its own."

"Fine," Simon hisses. "Just stitch me up. I have things to do."

"You got it, Spider," Andrew says.

I glance back at Simon. His eyes meet mine then they slide towards the table. A look of eager anticipation passes over his face and I know there's no talking any sense into him. He's hell-bent on doing whatever he wants to do.

But maybe, just maybe, I can still talk some sense into Lucifer.

Reach in and somehow connect with Matthew.

21

MEREDITH

Squaring my shoulders, I lift my chin into the air, turn my back on Simon, and slowly approach the torture table.

"Meredith?" I hear Simon ask behind me, but I ignore him. He's in no place to stop me right now, but he will be in a couple of minutes.

Sensing my approach, Lucifer turns from Asad and regards me warily. I can't help but remember there was once a time when he would welcome me with open arms...

I ignore his look and stop beside him.

I afford Asad one glance and then hold my hand out to Lucifer.

"If you give me a gun, I can end this all right now."

And I will. I'll put two bullets in Asad's ugly head if

it means I can walk out of this room. I've already killed two men, what's one more?

Lucifer looks down at my hand and chuckles. "Now why would I do that, Meredith?"

I arch my brow. "So we can all go home?"

Lucifer shakes his head and his lips spread into a smile as if what I just said amuses him.

I'm not giving up though.

"Look, Matthew," I say, trying to talk some reason into him. "Simon is injured. One of your men is dead, and another is in the hospital... Surely, we all have better things to do?"

Lucifer inclines his head. "We do."

A sense of relief fills me and I almost smile.

Then he says, "But first, this little unpleasantness needs to be seen to."

That's not what I wanted to hear.

"Why?" I demand, dropping my hand. My lips curl up into a sneer as I look to Asad. He's stopped his thrashing to stare up at us. "He's not worth our fucking time."

"I agree," Lucifer nods. "But a message still needs to be sent."

I roll my eyes with disdain. "What the fuck is up with you and messages? I never had to resort to such... such..." I want to say *monstrous shit*, but settle on, "brutal tactics," instead.

Lucifer's icy blue eyes light up with amusement

and I don't understand what's he's getting at when he asks, "Didn't you?"

I scowl and shake my head slowly. "No... No, I never did. Unlike you, I'm not a fucking monster."

All the amusement fades from Lucifer's face and his expression grows cold. So very cold. "Even after all these years, you still think the worst of me?"

I take a small step back instinctually and remind him. "Yes. You didn't have to cut that poor man to pieces."

Lucifer's icy eyes are as cold and hard as a glacier as he says, "I did it to protect you."

Well, that's a new one. But he must be lying. There was no reason for him to torture that fucking stranger to protect me...

"Oh no, don't you dare try to put that on me!" I snap back. "You did it because you wanted to. You did it because you got off on it."

"Oh yes," Lucifer says with relish and takes a step towards me. "I fucking enjoyed it."

I take a hasty step back, needing to put some more distance between us, when that damn cracked heel of mine snaps.

Lucifer's arm whips out and he grabs me to steady me. He pulls me up so I don't fall on my ass. "I enjoyed every one of his fucking screams after he admitted what he planned to do to you."

I shake my head and try to rip my arm out of his

hand but his grip tightens. "Do you know where I found him, Meredith? What I found him doing in our house? I found him sniffing through your panties after he raided all your jewelry."

I stop fighting him and struggle to balance myself on one heel. Yeah, that revelation is extremely unpleasant, and I certainly don't enjoy the visual, but it still doesn't justify what he did.

"So? He was a fucking creep? That didn't mean you had to torture him to death," I argue.

Yet even to my own ears the argument is sounder weaker and weaker.

"You only say that because you don't know what he planned to do. He was going to come back, Meredith, and I put an end to that."

I suck in a deep breath, letting that sink into my head. If the man was truly out to hurt me... Fuck.

But, "Still..."

"You think he was the first fucker to come sniffing after you? He wasn't, but he was the fucking last. You have to admit, dear sister, you have a tendency to attract psychos."

His eyes slide over my head and I have no doubt that he's looking to Simon.

Oh that's rich, coming from him.

I jerk my arm hard out of his grip and curse my unsteady balance on my one heel.

Before I can say another word, Lucifer orders, "James, get my sister a chair."

James shakes his head as if he's snapping out of something and is quick to jump to Lucifer's bidding. Coming around the table, he grabs one of the last two unused chairs and carries it over to me.

"Thank you, James." I smile gratefully at him and sit down.

James smiles back and nods his head. Then Lucifer squats down.

Before I can stop him, he grabs the foot that's wearing my one good heel. He snaps the heel off and then tosses it to the side.

"There," he smirks and rises. "Now I won't have to worry about you twisting your ankle."

I shake my head, drop my foot to the floor, and frown up at him. How can one man be so considerate yet still be such a fucking monster? I've never been able to understand it.

He's always been a bit protective of me, especially after my mother passed when we were children. And I've only seen him treat his own family, Lily, Evelyn, Adam, and little David, with fondness.

Yet he fucking kills people. Not only kills them but tortures them for thrills...

But maybe he's not irredeemable. Maybe I can show him a better way. Maybe I can save him and still put an end to this madness.

"You know, Matthew," I say quietly for only him to hear. "I never had to kill or torture my marks when I was done with them. I destroyed their lives in other ways. Destroyed them so thoroughly they never came after me."

Lucifer tips his head back and laughs as if I just said something funny and I squirm in my seat uncomfortably.

What the fuck about that is so funny?

"Oh, they came after you, Meredith," he says, his chin dropping back down and his eyes gleaming.

What?

I scowl and start to correct him. Surely, he's not calling my integrity into question? "No, I—"

Lucifer stares me hard in the eyes as he cuts me off and says, "They came after you."

I snap my jaw shut and glare at him. Now he's just being ridiculous. Does he really think I'm going to fall for...

"The ones who weren't already dead from suicide or locked up in prison, that is."

No.

No, that's not true. Yet a little tendril of doubt wiggles its way into my mind. What does Lucifer know that I don't know?

"Honestly, Meredith, you're smarter than that," Lucifer smirks. "Do you think the type of men you picked for your marks were the type to let what you did go?"

Yes, I did, in fact. But when he says it like that...

"What are you saying, Matthew?"

"I'm saying you're correct. You didn't have to kill your marks. But you didn't have to kill them because I did it for you."

"No," I say and jump up from my chair.

Lucifer places one hand on my shoulder and gently but firmly pushes me back down. "Sit down, Meredith."

"You're lying. You're trying to twist everything," I accuse him.

And it's completely outlandish. There's no way he killed...

Matthew starts ticking off his fingers. "Russel Clay. Daniel Smith. Edward Watson. Sebastian Martìnez. Lorenzo De Luca. Alastair Walker the third."

Each name he speaks is like a sucker-punch straight to the chest.

He inclines his head as all the blood drains from my face. "Shall I go on?"

"You didn't," I gasp, my lungs suddenly struggling to bring in air.

"Of course I did. They came after you so I fucking killed them. What did you think happened? Did you honestly believe they just disappeared?" he ends with a sneer.

I shake my head and blink my eyes. The fucking room is spinning as I try to wrap my mind around this. If he's not lying then everything I've believed about myself, about my life for the last five years isn't true.

"Now, granted, I didn't make examples out of them because I wanted to continue to indulge you. But I see that was a mistake now."

Oh my god, they're all dead. He really fucking killed them...

"How could you?" I ask him as the first tear rolls down my cheek.

The confidence I've found over the past few years, my goals, my purpose, my fucking reason for breathing, it was all a lie.

A fucking lie.

And recognizing it breaks something deep inside me. Shatters it to pieces.

"How could I what? How could I fucking protect you?"

"You let me believe..." I trail off, laugh bitterly, and shake my head.

He let me believe I was making a mark on the world. Oh, I've made a mark alright. I've painted a large swath of blood across it.

"Yes, I let you believe that a beautiful woman like you can live and prosper in this world without a man to protect her, and I regret that. I regret that my indulgence has brought us to this moment. But it's time to put an end to this, Meredith."

Thank god he didn't give me a gun, because I think at this moment I could fucking kill him.

"Why?" I reach out and grab his hand as he starts to turn away from me. "Why did you do it? Why did you fucking indulge me?" I ask, my tear-blurred eyes searching his face as I continue to struggle with the destruction of my existence.

Matthew looks me hard and deep in the eyes and something flickers inside them. A warmth I haven't seen in what feels like forever. A warmth he hasn't shown me since I ran out of that basement screaming.

He squeezes my hand as he answers, "Because you're my sister."

God help me, when he says it like that, I want to forgive him. I want to put everything in the past behind us and start over fresh again.

But I can't sit here and be a part of a man being tortured. I just can't.

"Matthew, please," I plead, squeezing his hand back. If he cares about me, truly cares about me as he claims, he won't put me through this. "We don't have to do it like this. We don't have to torture him. We can kill him and we can all go home."

He closes his eyes for a moment and takes a deep breath. I know I'm trying his patience, but I'm still hoping logic and reason will win out. That it will spare me the nightmare that's about to happen.

"We could," he says, his eyes flashing open. "We could put a couple of bullets in his head and mail him back to his father and hope that that's the end of it. But then, seeing his beloved son with only two holes in his head might only further anger the father."

"It would be a risk, yes," I admit, and the small bubble of hope I was nursing inside me deflates as I start to realize his reasoning behind this.

Matthew nods his head sharply. "Yes, it would be quite the risk. His father might become confused and not realize that we mean fucking business. That no one fucks with our *family* and gets away with it."

I drop Matthew's hand.

"Today it was Bryant, Johnathan, and Simon," he says, his face flushing red with anger. "Tomorrow it could be Lily, my children, you, or my unborn niece or nephew."

His eyes flick down to my stomach and unconsciously I place my hand over it.

My baby. If I truly am pregnant like Simon says, I'll do anything... *anything* to protect my child.

Fuck. Now I understand why Matthew did what he did.

"Is that a risk you're willing to take, Meredith? Are you willing to put that burden on your head?"

Oh god. Could I ever forgive myself if something

happened to them? Could I live with myself knowing I didn't do everything in my power to prevent it?

There's already so much blood on my hands... so much...

I shake my head, the tears streaming down my face in earnest now. "No..."

"Then you agree with what we're about to do?"

As much as I hate it, as much as it turns my fucking stomach, I find myself nodding my head.

"Good," Matthew says and turns away from me. "Are you about done, Andrew?"

I glance over to see Andrew nod his head and squat back down to rummage in his backpack. "Yeah, just finished putting in the last stitch."

Simon's eyes meet mine over Andrew's head and there's so much intensity in them it steals my breath.

"You want something for the pain?" Andrew asks and Simon's attention drops down to him.

"Yes, I want something for the fucking pain," he snarls.

Andrew nods his head and pops up holding a syringe.

As Andrew gives the syringe a tap, Simon asks, "Why didn't you offer earlier?"

Andrew shrugs and smirks. "You didn't ask, Spider."

I wipe at my eyes with the back of my hand as

Andrew finds a suitable vein on Simon's arm and administers the painkiller.

"You're ready to go," Andrew says, withdrawing the needle and taking a step back.

Simon closes his eyes and leans his head back, moving his neck around. When his head snaps back up and his eyes flash open, once again they're on me.

Rising from the chair, shirtless and covered in wounds, he looks downright savage. He looks like a scarier version of the beast that comes out when he takes me.

He stalks over to me, his long legs easily eating up the distance.

I shrink back in my chair, the look on his face giving my heart palpitations. I know he, and everyone else in this room, overheard every word Matthew and I spoke.

Is he angry? Is he going to shatter my world even more? Stomp all over the fucking pieces and grind them into the floor?

Simon stops in front of me and locks eyes with Matthew.

Something unspoken passes between them as they stand eye to eye. Two behemoths that make me feel so fucking small at this moment...

Matthew steps to the side with a smirk and a nod.

Whatever painkiller Andrew administered must be strong as fuck because Simon bends over, grabs me by the face, and gives me a kiss that's so deep, so fucking hard, I moan into his mouth.

Pulling back, he stares deep into my eyes. "I'm going to make him pay for all of this, princess," he promises. "I'm going to make him bleed for every fucking tear."

I start to open my mouth to speak but he claims it again. With his tongue, teeth, and lips, he speaks to me, showing me what words could never adequately tell.

By the time he pulls away, I'm flushed and panting. No longer chilled by the sense of doom lingering in the air.

His thumbs stroke against my cheek and then he slowly lowers one hand down. His palm covers my belly and his eyes lower.

An expression of pure devotion passes over his features.

"Remember my promise? I protect what's mine," he growls.

Fuck. It's sick, so sick, to be feeling this at this moment, but I can't help it. He just totally turned me on.

Pulling away like it's the last thing he wants to do, he straightens. Then he glances at Matthew.

"I'll stay with her," Matthew smirks.

Simon nods.

Casting one last possessive glance back at me, Simon stalks towards the table.

"Well, as much as I'd like to stay for the party," Andrew says, rising with a grunt and sliding his backpack over his shoulder. "I'm going to head over to the hospital and check on Johnathan."

"Do let us know how's he doing," Matthew says with a look of concern passing over his features.

Andrew nods his head. "I'll be in touch."

I watch his back as he walks out of the room, wishing with all my heart that I was going with him.

I understand this, I do. But I still wish I didn't have to be a part of it.

"I should probably head out too," James says, inching towards the door.

"No," Simon says and then grins. "Stick around. I'm going to need your assistance with this."

James glances towards Asad then Simon.

"Fuck," he mutters.

Simon's grin stretches wider as he moves to the tool box. He glances towards Asad with a critical eye and then yanks the top drawer open.

I find myself leaning forward in my chair. My attention and every one of my senses riveted to him as my pulse pounds through my veins.

I wonder if this is what the prey feels like when it's watching the predator in the wild.

Withdrawing a set of latex gloves, Simon snaps them over his hands. "Normally, this procedure requires the skin to be warmed first, preferably with boiling water. But alas, I fear we don't have any on hand…"

I have to bite my tongue to keep from blurting out 'thank god'.

Eyes wide with fear, Asad starts to struggle against his bonds. Does he know what's to come? Or is he just afraid in general?

Simon rummages around in the drawer and withdraws a knife with a long straight blade.

"Cut his clothes off, James," he orders, extending the knife out.

James grumbles as he walks around the table. Grabbing the knife from Simon, I hear him mutter something about always getting the shit jobs.

Simon bends down and yanks the doors on the tool box open as James starts to slice through Asad's clothing.

"What are you looking for, Simon?" Matthew asks with mild interest.

"The blow torch," Simon answers coolly and my heart drops to the floor.

Matthew makes a face. It would be hilarious if this situation wasn't so horrific. "Please, spare us the blow torch. It took us months to air the smell of Marshall out."

Marshall? Who the fuck is Marshall? No, scratch that. I don't want to know.

Simon sighs and shuts the doors on the tool box. "Very well."

Straightening, he reaches into the top drawer again and withdraws a knife with a curved blade.

With a wicked gleam in his eyes, Simon lifts the blade in the air and turns towards Asad. "Without heat, this is going to hurt a hell of a lot more."

It feels like it takes James an eternity to cut Asad's clothing off and I find myself praying that he'll both never finish and hurry up. I can't decide if I want to continue to prolong this or just get it over with.

Once the last bit of fabric falls away, James steps back and Simon's eyes roam over Asad's naked body.

If I didn't hate his fucking guts, I'd probably feel some pity for Asad. Without his clothing, all his small, shriveled dangling bits are exposed to the world.

Some men look stronger, more beastly when they're naked, like Simon. While others look softer and weaker.

Looming over Asad, Simon looks like a fucking lion about to devour a pale hippo.

"James, I'm going to need you to hold his head still for me."

With some more muttering and grumbling, James moves to the head of the table and grabs Asad by the sides of his head.

Asad bucks and thrashes again, and James's jaw clenches as he uses the brute strength in his arms to hold him still.

Simon bends over Asad's body and my view is obstructed, but I can see his arm moving in short, sharp motions.

Asad starts to groan and cry out behind his gag.

When Simon finally pulls away, there's so much blood pouring down Asad's face I can't tell what the hell he did to him.

"Okay, James, you can let go now," Simon says and lowers the blade.

"Thank fuck," James says and leans back. Reaching up, he wipes the sweat off his brow with the back of his arm.

Simon turns away, sets his bloody knife on top of the tool box and turns back just in time to catch James taking a step back.

"I'm not done with you yet, James," Simon sneers.

"Fuck. What do you want me to do now?"

Simon grabs Asad by the cheeks and says, "I want you to very carefully slide your fingers under the incisions I created around his hairline and pull."

"What?" James asks as if he doesn't understand.

"Slide your fingers carefully under the fucking incisions and pull," Simon snaps.

"I don't have any fucking gloves on," James protests.

"Well, you should have fucking thought of that,"

Simon says, his smirk curving into a malicious grin. "And it's too late to stop now."

James shakes his head in disbelief and glances towards Matthew.

Matthew makes a motion with his hand. "Go on, James. Do as Simon says."

"This is punishment, isn't it?" James asks as he looks back to Simon and reluctantly leans over Asad's head. "You're fucking punishing me for talking to your woman."

"Perhaps," Simon says, flashing his teeth.

"Fuck," James curses then that curse turns into a groan. My stomach flips as James works his fingers under a long cut on Asad's forehead. "I can feel his fucking brains."

"That's his skull, you idiot," Simon hisses.

James wiggles his fingers under Asad's skin and the visual has me jumping up from my chair.

"Meredith," Matthew says in a chiding tone as he turns towards me. "Sit back down."

"Whatever," James huffs. "Now what do you want me to do?"

"Fucking pull," Simon growls.

I watch in horror, unable to look away for precious seconds, as James begins to pull on Asad's skin, peeling it back from his face and revealing a bloody skull.

Slapping my hand over my mouth, I try to rush

past Matthew but he grabs me by the arm and spins me around.

"Too much?" he asks with a grin tugging at the corners of his lips.

I swallow back the bile burning in my throat and somehow manage to choke out, "Too much."

"Princess?" I hear Simon say, his voice worried, but I don't dare glance toward him.

"She'll be fine," Matthew says to him. "Continue."

"I can't, Matthew... Please..." I groan as he guides me back to the chair.

"You can," Matthew assures me. Using his foot, he nudges the chair around until it faces the wall then helps me sit back down.

"Please," I beg, reaching out and grabbing the front of his shirt. Clinging to him as he squats down beside me.

"You can do this, Meredith," he repeats, looking into my eyes. He reaches up and strokes my hair back. "Next to my wife, you're the strongest woman I know."

That little compliment makes me feel better. I always enjoy a little stroke to my ego now and then.

Taking a few deep breaths, I try to get the churning in my stomach to die down.

Then I hear Simon snap, "Be careful."

"Fuck," James snaps back. "He won't stop squirming, give me a break."

Asad's muffled screams grow louder and louder, and I can only imagine what they're doing to him.

My stomach lurches again.

"Fine, I can do it," I groan, my fists tightening in Matthew's shirt. "But I don't *want* to do it. I'm pregnant, have a mild concussion, and I'm going to get fucking sick."

If he doesn't do something about this, I'm going to aim my fucking puke at him.

Matthew lets out a long, drawn out sigh. He glances over my head and then back to me again.

"You want me to put a stop to this?" he asks.

"Yes," I immediately hiss back.

"Are you sure?"

"Yes," I repeat impatiently. Isn't that what I've been asking all along?

His hand lowers to his waist and his fingers brush across the top of his gun. "Okay. I'll deal with Simon…"

Wait. What?

My fingers tighten in his shirt as he tries to rise. "What are you going to do?"

"I'm going to put a bullet in Asad's head," Matthew says with annoyance.

I start to relax and my fingers begin to let go.

"Then I'm going to put one in Simon's."

"No," I gasp, yanking on his shirt. "Don't you fucking dare…"

I don't even have to think twice about it. I swear, if he lays one hand on my man I'll rip him apart.

"Don't I dare what?" Matthew asks, one brow arching while a smirk threatens to spread across his lips. "The only way to put an end to this, to stop Simon from protecting his family, is by killing him. Isn't that what you want, Meredith?"

"No," I growl at him.

"Good," Matthew says and he begins to relax, allowing the smirk to finally takeover his mouth.

God, is there no end to this craziness? How much more can I endure?

"I would hate to have to kill my best friend..."

I narrow my eyes and shoot him a dirty look. Knowing what I know now, I honestly think he's being serious.

"You'd do it, too, wouldn't you?" I accuse.

Matthew looks me dead in the eyes as he answers seriously. "Yes, Meredith, I would."

Fuck. I don't know if I want to hate him for threatening Simon or love him because he'd kill his best friend for me.

I settle on accepting a little of both.

Shaking my head, I take a deep breath and lean back in my chair. Trying to reconcile all the shit that's in my head while I tune all the stuff going on behind me out.

"How are you holding up, princess?" Simon calls out to me suddenly, pulling me out of my thoughts.

How am I holding up?

"I've been better," I answer back.

"Not much longer, I promise," he says.

I sigh wearily. How fucking long does it take to torture a man to death? Shit. Did I really just think that?

"Does he treat you well?" Matthew asks quietly.

I glance up at him in surprise. Does Simon treat me well? What a tricky question. It was rough in the beginning, yes, but now that's he completely enamored with me things have been going rather well.

"Yes," I answer tentatively. "The only complaint I have is that I'd like to get out more...

Once again, Matthew's brow quirks up, and there's something about that brow that makes me feel like I need to add, just in case he gets any ideas, "I'm sure once this... message is sent though, it won't be a problem."

Matthew nods his head and says, "I'll speak with him. Tell him to bring you around the compound more."

I smile at him. "Thank you."

"Evelyn has been asking about you. And I'm sure you'd like to get to know your nephews better."

My heart swells a little at the thought of spending more time with my family.

My family... I have a family. Well, I've always had a family. I guess it's only real now that I've forgiven Matthew.

I answer him honestly, "I would."

Matthew nods his head and we fall back into a comfortable silence again.

A couple of minutes later there's a loud squelching noise and James starts to gag. "Fuck, I didn't know a cock could do that."

"Stop fucking whining and put it in the box," Simon sighs.

Despite Simon's promise that it will be over soon, it feels like I stare at the wall for eternity. Thinking of everything we've gone through. Thinking of what he's doing right now to protect me...

Then I blink my eyes and he's suddenly there, grabbing my hand and pulling me up.

"Is it done?" I ask.

Relief floods through me now that he's standing in front of me.

Simon nods his head. "It's done. Fucker is going back to his father in pieces to show no one fucks with the woman I love."

Love.

That word slams into me so hard I nearly fall on my ass.

Did he mean to say it? Searching his face, I don't think he did.

But now that he has, I'm not going to let him take it back. No, I'm never going to let him forget he said it.

Fuck. To be loved by this man.... To be the beginning and end of his craziness... To drive him to do such dark, twisted things for me... for us... for our *baby*...

It fills me with a purpose no game in my past ever has.

After everything I've been through today. After having my world broken, my sense of identity shattered over and over again. Reliving the nightmare...

I just want to drown and sink and choke on this emotion.

I want to die. To let the old Meredith go.

And be reborn again.

"I love you," I say and press my body up against his body.

He welcomes me despite the pain he must be experiencing. He can never resist me. He'd probably hold me and kiss me even if he was in the cold arms of death.

"I fucking love you," I repeat and smash my lips against his lips.

And I do. I love this crazy man. I've killed for him and he's killed for me. Now that we've come this far, there's nothing I wouldn't do for him.

"After what I've learned today, Simon, I do hope you're planning on making an honest woman out of my sister," Matthew says as I finally pull back.

Simon grins at him. "I already have."

I gasp at his lie, especially because it's such an obvious one. "You have not."

His eyes gleam at me. "What do you think all those papers you signed were, princess?"

Matthew laughs. "Taking a page out of my book, Simon? Well done."

The realization of what Simon did sinks in. He tricked me into marrying him? Seriously?

I take back everything I said earlier.

I'm going to kill him.

EPILOGUE

Simon

It's been two weeks since the firefight at Landow Airstrip and my ribs still ache every fucking time I move.

Everything is painful.

Driving down these shitty roads, my two fucking cracked ribs make my life a living hell.

Every single bump in the road hurts. Stop lights offer no relief.

If I wasn't such a stubborn ass of a man, I would have had Andrew or Johnathan come and do this job for me. In truth, I should have made Lucifer come wait outside of a supermax prison in the cold.

Should have made him stand here, on the side of

the road, like some reprobate as he waits for his hellhound to get out of its cage.

No, I'm the stubborn jackass who left the woman of his life behind at Lucifer's compound. It's the only place I feel that she will be safe, besides at my side. But even I know better than to bring her here with me for this job.

This job. It's a job, isn't it? It's a choice we're all making to bring hell back into the world. Opening a gate that, in my opinion, should have been left shut.

Shifting on my feet, I lean against the vehicle. Not that it gives me much comfort. *Comfort*. I haven't known comfort for some time now. I'm unable to find a position to stand, sit, or lie down in that isn't miserable.

The only time I feel any sense of normalcy right now is when I have my cock locked tightly inside of Meredith.

Meredith, let me count the minutes until I am back home with you. You safely nestled away in our house where it is sterile and clean. Not filthy like the sides of my Escalade.

Rolling my left shoulder for the third time in as many minutes, my stomach grumbles for food. I haven't been eating as well as I should have this past week.

Too much work to be done and not enough time to do it.

The Yakuza haven't made any more brazen attacks

and the message we sent back to the Saudi's has been received.

Or at least I hope it has been received.

Because if they even dare try to stick their noses back into my personal life again and come near Meredith, there won't be a rock in the whole damn country they will be able to hide under.

I'll fucking have the President of the United fucking States nuke the country back to the fucking stone age.

Without fanfare or warning, I watch as the gate to the prison slowly opens itself. A man wearing khaki pants and a khaki button down work shirt appears in front of the entrance, walking next to a prison guard.

The man in tan clothing looks to me then back to the guard. There's a shake of hands and then the free man is walking towards me down the entrance road to the prison.

He's my size except he's put on weight since I last saw him. All muscle, from what I can tell. His hair and beard are in a serious need of grooming. Right now he looks like a copy of Johnathan that has been stretched out with muscles and tattoos.

Disgusting.

I can only guess how many bacterial infections he has crawling around on him. I'm going to have to thoroughly sanitize my SUV after I drop him off at the compound.

Sanitizing might not be enough though... I might just set it on fire.

Turning away from him before he even gets across the road, I open my door and slowly pull myself into the warm leather seats. Making sure the seat warmer for the car is turned all the way up, I lean back and let out a huge breath.

Thankfully the heat gives me some comfort. Not much, especially while the vehicle is moving, but it's better than nothing.

Looking out my window, I watch as the hellhound smirks at me through the windshield.

Cocky asshole.

Up closer now, I can definitely tell he's gained muscle mass, and probably a pound of new tattoo ink in his skin. None on the face though. I guess that's saying something.

The door to the car swings open and then slams shut as he crams his large frame into the seat. I probably should have adjusted it for him from when Meredith was in that seat. She prefers to sit a little further up and closer to the dashboard.

It's a petty thing to enjoy, but I do. One must find joys where one can.

Reaching down to the side of the seat, I watch as the big blonde-haired, blue-eyed man grumbles as the seat slowly slides back.

"Simon," he grunts out at me.

"Gabriel," I say as I turn from him.

I noticed tattoos crawling up past the collar of his prison release clothing. He's wearing a white thermal undershirt under his tan top, and I have no doubt it's covering up tattoos from his shoulders to his wrists. Sleeved, as Johnathan calls it.

Not saying anything else, I put the SUV in drive and pull onto the road, heading downstate back towards Garden city.

Glancing over briefly, I watch as he stares out the window. It's the first time he's seen the world like this in over ten years. A lot has changed in that time—the family, the politics, the internet even.

He's a relic that should have stayed in the damn past.

Fifteen miles down the road in the middle of nowhere, I pull onto the side of the road again.

Now's as good as time as any.

Putting the SUV in park, I reach into my suit and pull the .45 pistol from my under-the-arm holster.

Pointing the gun at his chest, I say, "Get out."

Yet again he smirks at me from behind that thick beard of his. "You gonna make me do that right now? In the cold fucking wasteland out here?"

"Last chance, Gabriel," I say quietly.

"Fuck you," he says, but reaches for the door handle. "Let's get this shit over with."

I keep ahold of my pistol as I step out of the vehicle

myself. Walking around the front of the car. I come up to him. "Strip fully."

"Fuck you," he growls.

"I don't give two shits about Lucifer's directives," I say without emotion. "I only care if you're a liability."

"Again, fuck you," he snarls.

"Gabriel, it's going to be dark in half an hour. Do you want to be left out here in the dark, dying from a couple of gut shots?" I ask.

Pulling his two shirts over his head, he shrugs at me when he drops them to the hard ground. "Not like it will change much. I've been dead long enough now. I probably won't notice the difference."

Like I thought, he's full of tattoos. Each, I have no doubt, has a meaning to him and him alone.

When he finally gets down to his bare feet, I motion with my gun. "Turn around slowly. Bend and cough."

"We're going to go a couple of rounds, me and you, Simon. Soon as you're healed up," he says with a laugh.

I suppose we will. It's been fifteen years since we last went against each other in a fight.

We're about due, I suppose.

He must have noticed my slower steps and the way I'm moving. He's always been too perceptive.

When I'm satisfied that I don't see any gang affiliation tattoos or Aryan Nation brandings, I put the pistol back in its holster.

"The black backpack in the back passenger seat is yours. You can get cleaned up at the first trucker's stop we get to," I say, walking back to the car, leaving his naked ass standing on the side of the road.

He grabs the bag from the back and pulls out a pair of underwear, jeans, and a t-shirt.

All packed up by Johnathan.

Johnathan wanted to make sure his best friend was set up for his welcome home party. He even left Gabriel his special custom gun from before he went to prison.

Johnathan, luckily enough for him, is doing better than I expected. The shot to his stomach wasn't as serious as it first looked.

Though, if not taken care of quickly, he would have died.

The hospital stay for him was rushed because we were getting too much heat from local law enforcement, but he pulled through. That was a lot of bullets and explosions to just ignore. We paid off enough of the right people to make ourselves disappear, but it still wasn't easy this time.

There were quite a few dead bodies... not to mention a destroyed plane on an airstrip tarmac.

When he's finally dressed in clothes at last, Gabriel tucks himself back into the SUV. Pulling on his socks and boots as I pull away from the side of the road.

"So, when did you get married, big brother?" he asks as he's lacing the boots up.

He's noticed the wedding band on my left hand, just like everyone else has. I'm surprised he didn't ask earlier, but it's of no concern to me. "Two weeks ago."

"Well, fuck me. My big brother, the fucking asshole he is, got married and didn't bother to invite the only living family he has left to the wedding," he laughs.

We may be related, but there's only so much blood between us. He could give two shits about what I do with my life.

I feel completely the same about him.

"There hasn't been a ceremony yet. And no, you're not invited for when it happens. We have to wait until the baby is born first. Meredith's ruling on that," I say with a frown.

If I had my way, I would have made her marry me in front of everyone the moment we knew she was pregnant.

"I'm just trying to find the angle here, Simon. What leverage did you have on the poor woman?"

I would shoot him if I was allowed to right now. Family or not.

"None at all," I say, and while that isn't exactly true, Meredith will never leave my side now.

We're together in this.

"Alright, whatever," he says as he reaches up to

scratch his thick beard. "I can't wait to shave this shit off; it's been too long since I've had a good razor."

"Then you might actually look like a partial human being for once..." I say.

"Eh, fuck off. So, what's the job?" he asks as he stares out the window.

"What do you mean?" I ask him.

"Why now? I figured I was supposed to rot in that cell for the rest of my life," he says, turning to me.

"If it was up to me, I would have left you there."

"I know. Love you too, big brother," he chuckles.

"Lucifer wants you out, and we're finally in position to call in favors large enough to get you out."

"That's a pretty big favor to call in, Simon. Who the fuck did you get on your payroll? The Governor? Cause that's the... Fuck, you got your hand in the Governor's pocket?" he asks skeptically.

"Around his throat is more like it, but yes."

"So, what does Lucifer want?" he asks.

"Mayhem. Bedlam... The Yakuza have blown up two people. One of them was Peter from the inner circle. The Russians are fucking playing nice at the worst time possible. The Saudis are going to be starting a war soon. We've lost a lot of the inner circle, and we're not replacing them as fast as we're losing them. He wants you to do what you do best."

"Death and destruction."

"Absolute death and destruction. Lucifer wants the state under his control."

Nodding his head, he leans it back into the headrest and closes his eyes. "I can do that."

The End

STALK US

Seriously, stalk us and be our Simon.

Join our Facebook reader group where we talk about our books, give exclusive sneak peeks, offer random fan appreciation giveaways, access to ARCs, and live chats where you can ask us anything.

Facebook reader group: Izzy's Sweeties and Sean's Side Chicks:
https://www.facebook.com/groups/IzzysSweeties

Sean is a member of the Romance and Erotica Author Fraternity. 12 awesome male authors who do giveaways, live chats, and talk about their books. Check them out.
You don't want to miss Sean on his Toga Tuesday!

https://www.facebook.com/groups/REAuthorFraternity/

Never miss our next release.
Follow us on Facebook:
https://www.facebook.com/authorizzysweet/
https://www.facebook.com/authorseanmoriarty/

Follow us on Amazon: amazon.com/author/izzysweet
amazon.com/author/seanmoriarty

Follow us on Bookbub:
https://www.bookbub.com/authors/izzy-sweet

Join our no-spam mailing list. No spam ever, promise. Only get emailed when we have a new release or sale:
https://dl.bookfunnel.com/bbfg23ehl8

Check out our website: www.dirtynothings.com

ABOUT US

Izzy Sweet & Sara Page – The one and same brain.

Sean Moriarty — The real life alpha bad boy that Izzy tamed.

Residing in Cincinnati, Ohio, Izzy and Sean are high school sweethearts that just celebrated their 11th wedding anniversary, though they've been together since they were teenagers – over fifteen years.

Both avid and voracious readers, they share a great love and appreciation for a great story, and attribute their early role-playing days as the fledgling beginnings of their joint writing career.

You can see more of our works at our website - www.dirtynothings.com

PLAYLISTS

Simon's Playlist

Available on Spotify - https://spoti.fi/2JLQPmI

I Can't Help Falling In Love - Perfume Genius
Square Hammer - Ghost
I'm Not Jesus - Apocalyptica, Corey Taylor
Physical (You're So) - Nine Inch Nails
Here - Vast
Closer - Asking Alexandria
Killpop - Slipknot
It's No Good - In Flames
America - Motionless In White
Move It - Down & Dirty
Four Walls - While She Sleeps

Meredith's Playlist

Available on Spotify - https://spoti.fi/2K2c9DF

Sail - Jack Trammell
Look What You Made Me Do - The Animal In Me
Control - Halsey
Run For Your Life - K.Flay
Bad Wolf - In This Moment
Pit Of Fire - 3TEETH
Turn You On - Stitched Up Heart
Stitch In Time - Genitorturers
Comfort You - Letters from the fire
Gangsta - New Years Day
Black Wedding (feat. Rob Halford) - In This Moment

ALSO BY IZZY AND SEAN

Disciples

Keeping Lily (Lucifer & Lily)

Stealing Amy (Andrew & Amy)

Buying Beth (Johnathan & Beth)

The Pounding Hearts Series

Banging Reaper (Chase & Avery)

Slamming Demon (Brett & Mandy)

Bucking Bear (Max & Grace)

Breaking Beast (Alexander and Christy)

By Sean Moriarty

Gettin' Lucky

Gettin' Dirty

Star Joined Series

Craving Maul

Taming Ryock

By Izzy Sweet

Letting Him In

Stepbrother Catfish

PREVIEW: KEEPING LILY (DISCIPLES 1)

My husband traded me away to save his own life...

And now I belong to the devil.

One night and everything in my life changed. Two words and my world turned dark.

"Take her."

Owing the most ruthless crime lord in Garden City five million dollars, my husband chose to trade me and my children away to save himself.

I was on the cusp of freedom, so close to divorcing that scumbag I was married to.

Now I'm enslaved to a man who is obsessed with me. A man so wicked and beautiful they call him Lucifer.

So alluring, he makes the angels weep with envy. He's so powerful, I can't stop myself from bending to his will.

He's determined to master me, and he won't rest until I give him all.

He wants my light, and he wants my dark.

He wants my body, and he wants my heart.

But most of all, he wants the one thing I can't give him. The one thing I can't bear to part with...

My soul.

Chapter One

Lucifer

"Motherfucker!" Comes out of my mouth in a growl as I shake my hand.

The punch to this piece of shit's jaw sent tingling sensations up my arm.

Mickey Dalton sputters gibberish out of his busted lips. "I... I... Swear I will pay... just gotta..."

I'm tempted to keep this up, but fuck it. I have bigger fish to fry than this small time fucking gambler.

Looking over the man's shoulder, I nod to Andrew. "Ensure he fully understands how much he owes. Remove his pinky."

"Yes, sir." Andrew nods.

"Wha... No!" Mickey shouts as Andrew heads to the table where he keeps a black bag stowed.

Turning around, I look at Simon, my right-hand man. "Where are we at with the other three files?"

"Two have been collected on, the last I was waiting on your judgment."

"Marshall Dawson."

"He has flat out refused to cooperate with any of our attempts to collect. He believes his status is untouchable. He will give us no answer on where he was or what has happened to our money."

"Is he finally home?" I ask.

"Arrived earlier tonight."

A metallic snip rings out into the room followed by a high-pitched scream. I turn to see Andrew wiping the blood on the guy's t-shirt.

Andrew raises his voice only slightly as he grabs the man by the throat. "Stop fucking squealing, asshole. Lucifer doesn't like hearing pigs fucking about."

Walking out through the door and into the hall, I look to Simon. "How are the spreadsheets with Bart coming along?"

"Clean, with everything accounted for…"

"Yet, you still have doubts?" I ask him as we walk.

"I do. I just can't explain why."

"Keep an eye on him then."

Simon holds an umbrella over my head as we walk out of the abandoned hotel. The shattered glass door slams shut behind us as he ushers me into the sleek black Mercedes SUV.

Getting comfortable in the backseat, I reach over and pull the file left on the other seat for me. The name Marshall Dawson is neatly typed on the tab.

I let out a quiet sigh to myself. I knew this one was going to come back as a thorn in my side.

Marshall Dawson is a waste of breathable air. The man used the connections he had with my father and another city boss to secure a loan from us. Five million in *cash*.

Five fucking million dollars with nothing to show for it.

Five fucking million dollars down the drain.

I took this on as a favor to Sean O'Riley. A favor to a now dead and buried man.

Shit like that doesn't sit well with me. But when I went to the top to seek retribution, I was stonewalled. I was told the man who killed Sean, and all the surrounding issues, have been dealt with.

Fuck that. I want my pound of flesh.

Shaking my head, I open the file. It's no use going down that train of thought right now. I can pursue it another time if I need to.

I slowly flip through the pages we have on Marshall.

It's funny how we can put a file together on a person where he is reduced to twenty or so pages. I can see every payment he has made on his mortgage to how many times he has been in the overdraft with his bank.

I look at his legal outstanding debts, and I look at the five-million-dollar debt he now owes to me personally. Anger is slowly creeping through my veins.

Flipping through the pages, I look at his family life. Since he borrowed the money I have had one of my men keeping close tabs on his family. He is married to Lilith Merriweather, aged twenty-seven, and has two children, a boy and a girl. Both children under the age of seven.

I look at the picture of Marshall for a long time as we drive through the late-night rain. The man is closer to my father's age than mine. How did he marry a woman so young? Money and his slimy charm must have played a large part of it.

I look through the pictures of his family quickly. The children are pretty in a child way. Blonde hair and blue eyes, they must take after their mother. Marshall must have married way out of his league.

My fingers stop as the picture of his wife comes up. Emerald green eyes, sensuous pink lips, high cheekbones, pale flawless skin and long blonde hair. All of those parts on their own would make her remarkable. Even if her face was overall plain just one of her features would stun a person. But together they make something otherworldly.

She is beauty incarnate.

Fingers tracing the lines of her lips, I frown. How the hell did that man marry a woman like this? I flip further through the pictures of her. There aren't many, but what I do see shows me that she is unlike any other woman I have ever laid eyes on.

She is perfection.

There is a rather candid photo of her putting groceries in the back of her red Volvo station wagon. Her hair is all over the place. Her slender legs are encased in yoga pants, feet in Uggs. Her daughter looks like she is giving her problems as she tries to watch her and still put groceries in the back.

Even this... domesticity calls to me.

There is a glamour shot of some type mixed in and

I can see just how haunting those eyes are. They are calling to me, pulling me in to get forever lost. I can feel my hands curling into themselves. She is pulling me from where I sit in the SUV.

"Take me to Marshall's, James," I say to my driver.

Looking back at me from the front seat, Simon says, "Now? You don't want to wait until tomorrow?"

"No. We're going there *now*."

The car makes a few turns as we pull off the freeway and then back on again.

My eyes drift out the window for a moment to look at the rain that has been pelting down on the city all week.

Looking back to the picture, though, I see something I haven't seen before—a light. Inside I feel an ember flaring to life.

My muscles are going taut with expectation.

I need to see this woman; I need to see if what the pictures show me is true.

Lily

MY HUSBAND, MARSHALL, is sleeping beside me, snoring loudly, and I have the strongest urge to smack him.

I want to scream in his pale, pudgy face. I want to tell him to wake the fuck up. I want to ask him why he's back in my bed.

But I just lay beside him and stare up at the ceiling instead.

It's time to accept reality.

Our marriage is done.

Dead.

Today was the final nail in the coffin.

First thing in the morning, after I get the kids off to school, I'm going to meet with a divorce attorney. I can't go on like this. This is no way to live, this is just...existing.

And I'm sick of it.

After growing up dirt poor, I married Marshall thinking I would finally have financial security. I would always have a roof over my head. I would never go hungry again.

Foolishly, I believed his lust for me would turn to love. That like an arranged marriage, our feelings for each other would grow after time. If we had children, we could make a real go of it.

But this, the lack of love, the lack of care, isn't worth it. I rather starve than stay in this loveless marriage.

Marshall has been gone for weeks, *traveling on business*. He's gone more than he's home. Ever since our first child, Adam, was born six years ago, he's been finding more and more reasons to leave us.

There's always some client on the other coast that needs his help. Or some corporation up north that has to have his expertise or they're going to lose millions on… something…

It's funny, even after almost eight years of marriage I still don't know exactly what his job title or true profession is. Whenever I ask him about it he just brushes me off, doesn't have time to explain it, or says I wouldn't understand.

Like I'm some kind of idiot.

If I was an idiot I wouldn't know about all the women he's been hooking up with. I know that's one of the reasons he's always leaving us. He has a girlfriend in every city.

Yet, he won't even touch me when I throw myself at him.

I sigh, looking down at the red nightie I bought from Victoria's Secret and pull the blanket up to cover my breasts.

He won't even touch me when I've taken great pains to dress up for him.

Suddenly my eyes feel swollen and my nose stings. I have to blink back my tears and take a deep breath. Rolling my eyes back up, I focus on the ceiling.

This shouldn't hurt, dammit. This isn't a bad thing, this is good.

This is… *freedom*.

I no longer have to pretend this is a real marriage. No more keeping up appearances on Facebook. No more making excuses for him with my family and friends.

No more trying to explain to the children that daddy is sorry but he had to miss their birthday—again.

This is a fresh start, a new beginning.

I've been doing everything on my own for years now. Losing him won't make much of a difference.

Marshall suddenly grunts loudly and rolls over.

The air turns sour and I resist the urge to gag.

Gah, he is such a pig.

Chapter Two

Lily

I'm not sure what wakes me up. It could have been the light turning on.

Marshall's loud, "What the fuck?"

Or the soft, menacing voice that says, "Hello, Marshall. I'm not interrupting anything, am I?"

Even under my warm blanket, that voice sends a chill down my spine and I peel my eyes open, shivering.

At first, the light is too harsh on my eyes and I have to blink several times before the strange man standing in our bedroom comes into focus.

This must be a dream, I convince myself and squeeze my eyes shut. I open them again but I still just can't believe it.

There's no way that man is real.

Standing in the center of my bedroom, the man is illuminated by a halo of light coming from the lamp. The light seems to love him, clinging to him. He's glowing and so alluring, he looks almost angelic.

"What the fuck are you doing in my house? You can't just come walking in here..." Marshall sputters. His fat fists grab the blanket, yanking it away from me as he pulls it up his hairy chest.

I gasp as the cool air hits my breasts and the sound draws the attention of the angelic stranger. He turns his icy blue gaze on me and I'm utterly stunned as our eyes meet.

With just a look I feel held by him.

Trapped.

Frozen.

Helpless.

He's so beautiful it *hurts* to look upon him. The kind of beauty that's so strong, so deeply felt, it's like experiencing a piece of music that *moves* you and staring into the sun at the same time.

Tears prick my eyes and my skin tingles as I break out in gooseflesh.

His face is a composition of features so perfect that

now that I've glimpsed them I fear all other men will be forever compared to him.

Chiseled cheeks, full, pink lips. A strong jaw and straight nose. Blonde hair so pale it's nearly snow white and brushed back from his forehead.

It feels like an eternity passes as we stare at each other across my bedroom and then his eyes break away only to slide down, warming as they lock on the pale swells of my breasts.

A flush creeps up my chest. I'm not naked but in this little lacy nightie, I feel like I am.

I grab the blanket and Marshall cries out as I yank it back. He shoots me a dirty look but I give him my coldest glare and practically dare him to try and take it back.

Screw him, no one cares about his hairy man-chest.

The stranger watches our little tug of war, his lips curving with a hint of amusement.

Marshall finally gives up on trying to wrestle the blanket away from me and decides to steal my pillow instead. Covering his chest with my pillow, he hugs it tightly and puffs up as he says, "If you leave now, Lucifer, I'll forget this incident ever happened."

Lucifer? Is that the stranger's name? How strange and morbid. Yet, I swear I've heard that name before, on the news or in the paper...

The stranger's eyes flash and the amusement disappears from his lips. Two dark shadows shimmer behind him and I swallow back a gasp as I realize those two shadows are two other men.

What the hell is going on? Who are these men and why are they in my bedroom? I turn to Marshall and watch him squirm uneasily.

What did Marshall do?

"You'll forget this ever happened?" Lucifer says coolly and his eyes narrow with menace. "Just like you forgot to pay me back the five million dollars you owe me?"

All the color drains instantly from Marshall's face and his eyes dart from side to side as if he's trying to figure out an escape plan. "I already paid that back. You'll have to talk to Sean if you want your money."

"Sean's dead."

I watch Marshall's mouth open then close, then open again. He sputters and gasps like a fish out of water, his face starting to turn blue from the lack of oxygen.

I can't believe Marshall borrowed five million dollars. What would he need with so much money? I know I haven't seen a penny of it.

"I paid Sean the money," Marshall finally gets out, and then rushes on to say, "I don't have five million to pay you..."

Lucifer takes a step towards our bed. "That's too bad."

"Wait!" Marshall cries out in panic, the grip of his

fingers tearing at the pillow he holds to his chest. "Maybe we can work something out? I could—"

"I've had a look at your assets. You have no means to pay me back," Lucifer says dismissively and takes another step toward the bed.

I look between Lucifer and Marshall and now I'm starting to feel panicked. Lucifer has only taken two steps towards our bed but there's clear menace in the way he's moving.

What is he going to do? Are they going to hurt Marshall?

Are they going to hurt me?

Lucifer takes another step and Marshall whimpers. He *whimpers.*

The sound has my hackles rising and I wonder if there's something I could do. I glance towards my phone on my nightstand. The moment I don't think they're looking at me I'm going to make a grab for it.

But it might be too late for Marshall by then…

I could start screaming, but the only good that will probably do is wake the children.

Marshall is pushing back against the headboard like he believes he could escape through the wall if he tries hard enough. Then he shoots a pleading look towards me.

As if I could help him…

Marshall's eyes widen suddenly as if he's had a revelation.

"You want my life as payment?" he squeaks out.

Lucifer lifts an eyebrow and inclines his head. "Yes. That's how these things usually go, isn't it?"

Marshall licks his lips nervously, looks to me then back to Lucifer. "Would you accept another life as payment?"

He's not about to say what I think he is, is he? No, he wouldn't. No decent human being...

Lucifer's upper lip curls with disdain but his voice sounds interested. "What are you proposing?"

Marshall is too cowardly to stop hugging his pillow so he nods his head to me instead. "Take her. Take my wife in my place."

I'm so shocked, so floored, I suck in a sharp breath that never ends.

"You want me to kill your wife?" Lucifer asks and it feels like all the warmth was just sucked out of the room.

"No, of course not..." Marshall recoils at the murderous look on Lucifer's face. "Just hold her as a deposit, an insurance, while I get you the five million."

"You mean a ransom?" Lucifer clarifies.

Marshall nods his head up and down. "Yes, yes, that's it. A ransom."

My lungs full of air, I expel it all in a loud, "How could you!" and make a lunge for Marshall.

I'm not an object he owns. He can't just trade me

away to some creepy, beautiful stranger to save his own neck.

Marshall squeaks and scrambles away from me. I end up chasing him until he falls out of bed, landing on his ass.

I grip the edge of the mattress, panting with anger as I watch him scuttle backward until he bumps into Lucifer's legs.

"As much as I would love to accept your offer," Lucifer says as he pushes Marshall away with the toe of his shoe. "I'm afraid your wife is not worth the five million you owe me."

Damn. I blink up at Lucifer, feeling utterly conflicted. On one hand, I don't want to be given away, but on the other, it stings the ego a bit to hear I'm not worth five million dollars.

I snort though as Marshall goes to his hands and knees, kneeling in front of Lucifer to beg for mercy.

"Please," Marshall begs, reaching out and grabbing Lucifer's leg.

I'd pity him and try to help the poor bastard if he didn't just try to trade me away in his place.

"There has to be something else I can give you..." Marshall sobs.

Lucifer makes a face of disgust and looks down at Marshall like he's a bug he'd like to step on.

"Anything," Marshall wails as Lucifer kicks at him. "Anything."

I sit back on my heels and watch Marshall beg while taking the kick, wondering how all of this happened.

Lucifer's head lifts and his eyes lock on me. His features are still, utterly calm, but there's something dark stirring in the depths of his icy irises.

"Anything?" Lucifer queries.

"Yes, anything!" Marshall nods his head with sudden enthusiasm.

"I'll accept your offer," Lucifer grins at me. "If you give her to me permanently, and throw in your children."

"No, no! You can't!" I scream and I'm off the bed in an instant.

Marshall yelps and scuttles back until he's hiding behind Lucifer's legs.

Lucifer between us, blocking me, my hands clench into fists and I pant, trying to control the rush of rage that has flooded my head. I swear if Marshall offers this... this... inhuman monster my children, I'll strangle him with my bare hands.

Lucifer smirks down at me as if he finds all of this amusing. I bristle under that smirk but suddenly feel self-conscious standing so close to him. He's tall, with at least a foot on me, and I feel puny now standing in front of him.

"Well? Do we have a deal, Marshall?"

Marshall continues to use Lucifer as a shield like

the coward he is. He pokes his head out only long enough to peek at me. "Yes!"

"No!" I screech and lunge forward, reaching around Lucifer to grab Marshall.

Marshall squeaks and stumbles backward, just out of my reach.

Lucifer grabs me by the arms, stopping my forward lunge and hauls me back. Chuckling, he pins my arms to my sides and I screech and struggle, trying to escape his grasp.

"We're done here, Marshall. I suggest you leave now before I change my mind..."

"Leave? Why do I have to leave? This is my house!" Marshall protests.

Head tipping back, I glare up at Lucifer and continue to struggle. Damn, he's stronger than he looks, though it is hard to tell just how built he is under that suit he's wearing.

Once again Lucifer looks me directly in the eyes, staring into me as if he can *see* inside me. "Not tonight."

"But... but..." Marshall starts to sputter.

Lucifer's face hardens, his features as cold and harsh as the blizzard swirling in his irises. "Simon, remove him."

"No. No! I'll go!" Marshall says, panicked, and though I can't see what's going on due to the huge body blocking my view, I can hear a great deal of shuffling going on behind Lucifer.

Marshall grunts loudly and then there's a thump. "Hey! I'm going, I'm going!"

The bedroom door opens and then slams shut.

I jerk in Lucifer's arms in surprise but then feel all the fight go out of me. No matter how much I squirm, no matter how much I try to free myself from his grasp, I can't escape him. If anything, I feel like all my struggles have only tightened the grip he has on me.

Head dropping forward, I quiet my panting so I can listen to Marshall stomping and continue to throw a tantrum about being removed from his own home.

After a minute, Lucifer sighs and I feel his grip loosen a little. "James, assist Simon. If Marshall wakes the children, feel free to make him regret it."

"Yes, boss," the second shadow answers and I don't even hear him as he walks out. I only know he's gone by the sound of the closing door.

A moment later there's some muffled arguing coming from the hallway then all goes quiet.

The seconds tick by. My panting slows as I catch my breath.

All at once I am suddenly aware that I'm alone with this strange man.

The air thickens.

Slowly, I lift my head and peer up at him. He's looking down at me so intensely I gasp.

My gasp seems to amuse him, and a slow smile spreads across his lips.

I stare at him in disbelief, my mind racing a mile a minute, trying to process everything that just happened. My mouth feels dry and my stomach is twisted. I want to believe this is a nightmare, that I'm still sleeping in my bed.

My husband didn't just trade me and our children away to save his own neck. He couldn't... He wouldn't...

Yet the fingers tightening around my arms remind me that he did.

I can't let this happen. I can't accept this. I have to protect my children. He cannot have them! I won't let him hurt them.

Gathering up every ounce of courage I have inside me, I lift my chin and say, "You can't have us. We're not objects you can own or trade away at whim. I am a *person*, a person with rights, and I will not stand for this!"

Lucifer's eyes twinkle at me and it's so condescending I just want to spit in his face.

My anger only seems to amuse him even more. Head tipping back, he chuckles with mirth and just as I start to struggle again, he lifts me up.

It only takes him two long strides and then he throws me.

I go flying through the air and land on my bed with a grunt.

He's not far behind me, and quickly I get to my hands and knees, scooting back as he approaches.

Long, strong fingers going to the bottom of his suit jacket, he begins to unbutton it as he asks me, "Who's going to stop me?"

Buy on Amazon: Keeping Lily (Disciples 1)

Made in the USA
Lexington, KY
30 July 2018